As I entered the hou ... from the kitchen. "No! Let me go!"

"Not a chance, kid."

My initial instinct was to race down the hall, but I froze when Sophie let loose a bloodcurdling shriek. "Oh my god! He's dead! You killed him!"

Acclaim for the Anastasia Pollack Crafting Mysteries
Assault with a Deadly Glue Gun

"Crafty cozies don't get any better than this hilarious confection...Anastasia is as deadpan droll as Tina Fey's Liz Lemon, and readers can't help cheering as she copes with caring for a host of colorful characters." – *Publishers Weekly* (starred review)

"Winston has hit a homerun with this hilarious, laugh-until-your-sides-hurt tale. Oddball characters, uproariously funny situations, and a heroine with a strong sense of irony will delight fans of Janet Evanovich..." – *Booklist* (starred review)

"A comic tour de force." – *ForeWord Magazine* (Book of the Year nominee)

"North Jersey's more mature answer to Stephanie Plum." – *Kirkus Reviews*

"...a delightful romp through the halls of who-done-it." – *The Star-Ledger*

"Make way for Lois Winston's promising new series...I'll be eagerly awaiting the next installment in this thoroughly delightful series." – *Mystery Scene Magazine*

"...once you read the first few pages of Lois Winston's first-in-series whodunit, you're hooked for the duration..." – *Bookpage*

"...madcap but tough-as-nails, no holds barred plot and main character...a step above the usual crafty cozy." – *The Mystery Reader*

"...Anastasia is, above all, a JERSEY girl..., and never, ever mess with one of them. I can't wait 'til the next book in this series..." – *Suspense Magazine*

Death by Killer Mop Doll

"Anastasia is a crafting Stephanie Plum, surrounded by characters sure to bring chuckles..." – *Booklist*

"Several crafts projects, oodles of laughs and an older, more centered version of Stephanie Plum." – *Kirkus Reviews*

"... readers who relish the offbeat will be rewarded." – *Publishers Weekly*

"...a 30 Rock vibe...Winston turns out another lighthearted amateur sleuth investigation." – *Library Journal*
"Winston...plays for plenty of laughs...while letting Anastasia shine as a risk-taking investigator who doesn't always know when to quit." — *Alfred Hitchcock Mystery Magazine*

Revenge of the Crafty Corpse

"Fans of craft mysteries will like this, of course, but so will those who enjoy the smart and snarky humor of Janet Evanovich, Laura Levine, and Laura DeSilverio." – *Booklist*

"...a surprisingly fraught stew of jealousy, greed, and sex..." and a "Sopranos-worthy lineup of eccentric characters..." – *Publishers Weekly*

"...amusing characters, a...good mystery and a series of crafting projects featuring cloth yo-yos." – *Kirkus Reviews*

"A fun addition to a series that keeps getting stronger." – *Romantic Times Magazine*

"Chuckles begin on page one and the steady humor sustains a comedic crafts cozy, the third (after *Death by Killer Mop Doll*)... Recommend for Chris Grabenstein ("John Ceepak" series) and Jess Lourey readers." – *Library Journal*

"You'll be both surprised and entertained by this terrific mystery. I can't wait to see what happens in the Pollack household next." – *Suspense Magazine*

"The book has what a mystery should...It moves along at a good pace...Like all good sleuths, Anastasia pieces together what others don't...The book has a fun twist...and it's clear that Anastasia, the everyday woman who loves crafts and desserts, and has a complete hottie in pursuit, will return to solve another murder and offer more crafts tips..." – *Star-Ledger*

Decoupage Can Be Deadly

"*Decoupage Can Be Deadly* is the fourth in the Anastasia Pollock Crafting Mysteries by Lois Winston. And it's the best one yet. More, please!" – *Suspense Magazine*

"Every single character in these books is awesomely quirky and downright hilarious. This series is a true laugh out loud read!" – Books Are Life–Vita Libri

"This is one of these series that no matter what, I'm going to be laughing my way through a comedy of errors as our reluctant heroine sets a course of action to find a killer while contending with her eccentrically dysfunctional family. This adventure grabs you immediately delivering a fast-paced and action-filled drama that doesn't let up from the first page to the surprising conclusion." – Dru's Book Musings

"Lois Winston's reluctant amateur sleuth Anastasia Pollack is back in another wild romp." – The Book Breeze

A Stitch to Die For

"*A Stitch to Die For* is the fifth in the *Anastasia Pollack Crafting Mysteries* by Lois Winston. If you're a reader who enjoys a well-plotted mystery and loves to laugh, don't miss this one!" – *Suspense Magazine*

Scrapbook of Murder

"This is one of the best books in this delightfully entertaining whodunit and I hope there are more stories in the future." – Dru's Book Musings

"*Scrapbook of Murder* is a perfect example of what mysteries are all about—deft plotting, believable characters, well-written dialogue, and a satisfying, logical ending. I loved it!" – *Suspense Magazine*

Books by Lois Winston

Assault with a Deadly Glue Gun
Death by Killer Mop Doll
Revenge of the Crafty Corpse
Decoupage Can Be Deadly
A Stitch to Die For
Scrapbook of Murder
Drop Dead Ornaments
Crewel Intentions
Mosaic Mayhem
Patchwork Peril
Crafty Crimes
Definitely Dead
Literally Dead
Love, Lies and a Double Shot of Deception
Lost in Manhattan
Someone to Watch Over Me
Talk Gertie to Me
Four Uncles and a Wedding
Hooking Mr. Right
Finding Hope
Elementary, My Dear Gertie
Once Upon a Romance
Finding Mr. Right
The Magic Paintbrush
House Unauthorized
Bake, Love, Write
We'd Rather Be Writing

Drop Dead Ornaments

LOIS WINSTON

Cover design by L. Winston

ISBN-9781940795447

DEDICATION

I sometimes hear from readers who are dealing with difficult personal issues. They thank me for giving them a few hours of laughter to escape their troubles. I treasure those notes. They fill my heart with joy knowing that writing about Anastasia and her problems has enabled others to escape theirs, even if only for a brief time.

As I finished writing *Drop Dead Ornaments*, my world was rocked by news no one ever wants to hear regarding friends and loved ones. Hopefully, there will be happy endings all around— not only for my friends and family, but anyone who is struggling with life's often-cruel challenges.

This book is dedicated to all of them.

ACKNOWLEDGMENTS

Special thanks to Donnell Bell and Irene Peterson for their superb editorial skills.

ONE

I stared at my bandaged wrist before zeroing a sigh-punctuated scowl at my front door. "I can't deal with them right now," I told Zack. A moment ago we had pulled into my driveway and now sat with the engine running. Both my arm and my head throbbed—my arm due to the local anesthesia wearing off, my head undoubtedly from the stress of the last few hours.

Earlier today I'd found myself in a life-or-death struggle with a deranged killer. As we fought for possession of her gun, she'd sunk her teeth deep into my wrist, hitting bone. With any luck, Virginia Owens would spend the remainder of her life in an orange jumpsuit, not only for attempted murder but for several heinous crimes that spanned half a century.

After the police hauled Virginia away, Zack drove me to the hospital where I received a few dozen stitches and a tetanus shot. We had arrived back at my house to find Harriet Kleinhample's VW minibus parked at the curb, which could mean only one thing: Lucille, the Communist mother-in-law from Hades, and her Daughter of the October Revolution sidekick had made bail. Both had spent the last two nights as guests of the county after Harriet was charged with hit-and-run and Lucille with assaulting an officer.

"You don't have to," said Zack. He turned off the engine. "Stay there." He then came around to the passenger door and helped me from the car. With my woozy-from-painkillers body leaning against him, we made our way up the stairs to his apartment above my garage.

When life hands you lemons, you have two choices—either accept the sour turn of events or add sugar. Lucille was my lemon; Zachary Barnes was my sugar.

Zack walked into my life nearly a year ago when he rented the apartment over my garage. At the time I had no idea how instrumental he'd become in preserving my sanity and helping me survive the tsunami that had hit me head-on when Karl Marx Pollack, my duplicitous husband, dropped dead in a Las Vegas casino. In the blink of an eye my kids and I went from firmly entrenched in the middle class to one step away from residing in a cardboard box. To make matters so much worse, I was also now saddled with Karl's mother, a woman who has never uttered a kind word to me, as a permanent houseguest.

My name is Anastasia Pollack, and I've had more than my fill of sour lemons—not to mention murders and near-death experiences—lately. I often ask the universe why it's picking on me. So far, the universe has kept mum.

Although I must admit, the chaos has certainly moved the needle of my life from humdrum to way over-the-top. Personally, I'd settle for moderately interesting, especially if it meant fewer encounters with deadly weapons.

Once inside the apartment, Zack helped remove my coat, then

settled me onto the sofa. I glanced longingly toward the kitchen cabinet that housed the adult beverages. "A glass of wine would definitely hit the spot right now," I said.

He shook his head. "Bad idea."

I sighed. "I know." Along with the pain meds, the doctor had given me an antibiotic to ward off any possible infection. I wouldn't be imbibing in anything stronger than coffee for the next week.

Zack placed a throw pillow behind my head. Then he removed my shoes, swung my legs up onto the sofa, and tossed an afghan over my body. "How about an omelet instead?"

~*~

I must not have answered Zack, let alone sampled even a single morsel of omelet, judging from the rumbling protests emanating from my stomach. With my good arm I leveraged myself into a seated position and glanced around the empty room. Moonlight played peek-a-boo through the clouds, intermittently streaming in from the window above the sink.

I rubbed the sleep from my eyes and yawned, wondering how long I'd slept. My purse sat on the coffee table. By the dim light I dug out my phone and checked the display. No wonder my stomach wouldn't shut up. I hadn't eaten anything since eight o'clock that morning—nearly twelve hours ago!

I blindly swept my feet across the floor in front of the sofa and under the coffee table until I found my shoes. Then I hunted around for my coat, which I found draped over the back of the sofa. After gingerly slipping my injured arm into one sleeve, I contorted my body in such a way as to shove my good arm into the remaining sleeve without the use of my mauled wrist. After a quick pit stop I opened the door and stepped onto the landing.

From my second-story perch I noticed red, white, green, blue, and yellow lights twinkling throughout the neighborhood. Stringing up the Christmas lights had been an item on today's to-do list—before the homicidal maniac bit into my schedule.

With a death grip on the handrail, I carefully made my way down the exterior staircase. The temperature had dipped considerably since Zack and I arrived home, and a light dusting of flakes coated the steps. However, my body no longer wobbled, and I noted my head no longer throbbed. Too bad I couldn't say the same for my wrist. If anything, it hurt more. One thing I knew with certainty—any woman who'd ever swooned over a sexy fictional vampire had never experienced the excruciating pain of a skin-puncturing bite.

When I opened the back door, I was greeted by a cacophony of teenage chatter fighting for dominance over the latest Imagine Dragons album. I followed the noise into the dining room. A half-dozen teens were spread out around my dining room table; another six sat in a sheet-covered circle on my living room floor. A plethora of craft materials and stacks of plastic boxes holding clear glass Christmas balls surrounded each group.

"Hey," I said, slipping out of my coat.

"Mom!" Alex jumped up from his chair and raced around the table to greet me. He clasped my good hand in both of his and stared down at my bandaged wrist. Worry spread across his face. "Are you okay?"

"I will be. Zack told you what happened?"

He nodded. "Does it hurt?"

"Only if I play racquetball."

He leaned over and kissed my cheek. "Good thing you don't play racquetball."

Someone lowered the volume on Imagine Dragons. The other kids had stopped chatting and were now listening in on our conversation. A girl I didn't recognize, who resembled a curly-haired, petite Nicole Kidman, was the first to speak. Her eyes glued to my gauze-wrapped wrist, she asked, "What happened to you, Mrs. Pollack?"

Given the murders that had recently occurred on our street, I thought it best to downplay this morning's events. I squeezed Alex's hand, hoping he understood I didn't want the gory details emerging. "I tripped in the foyer this morning and injured my wrist."

Not a complete lie, although I hadn't tripped as much as I'd launched myself at Virginia Owens, tackling her to the ground in an attempt to pry the gun from her hand. And technically, *she* was responsible for the injury to my wrist, not me.

My gaze darted around the living room and into the foyer. I found no signs of the struggle, not even the bullet holes in the walls. Someone (if I had any money, I'd bet on Zack) had puttied over the telltale evidence, swept up the plaster dust, and removed the shattered remains of a living room lamp felled by a bullet intended for Ralph, my Shakespeare-quoting African Grey parrot. I didn't know if the crime scene unit had needed to dust for prints while we were at the hospital, but if so, Zack had cleaned those up as well.

I turned my attention back to the explosion of craft materials covering my living room and dining room, a perfect opening for changing the subject. "What's going on? I thought you were finished with all the ornaments for your community service project."

The community service project was a high school graduation requirement. This year's committee had decided to volunteer at and raise money for the county food bank. However, the students balked at the traditional fundraisers that placed a huge percentage of the profit from candy, candles, popcorn, or wrapping paper sales into the coffers of professional fundraising companies. Alex, as chairman of the committee, came up with the brilliant idea of enlisting the aid of a magazine crafts editor—otherwise known as his mother.

How could I say no?

I suggested the students make Christmas ornaments and created various projects easy enough for even the non-craftiest kid in the school to execute perfectly, yet elegant enough to hang on a professionally decorated tree. I then tapped my industry contacts to donate the necessary supplies. The kids would net one hundred percent of the profit from the sales.

On a Friday afternoon in late September I left work early to teach Ornaments 101 to a cafeteria filled with four hundred seniors. And because I believe in killing two birds with one craft project, I photographed the session for an article in next December's issue of *American Woman*, thus also avoiding having to take half a vacation day.

The kids were disappointed to learn they'd have to wait a year to see themselves in the pages of the magazine, but production schedules are set months in advance. By late September I was already swimming in Easter chicks and bunnies. Right now I'm working on a Father's Day spread. I did, however, arrange for some local press that should entice shoppers to stop in Westfield over the coming weeks for some of their holiday gifts.

Each of the students was responsible for making three ornaments. They set the price at ten dollars apiece. If all the ornaments sold, the seniors would make twelve thousand dollars, which would go a long way toward stocking the county food bank through the winter.

All the ornaments were completed and boxed up several weeks

ago, some designated for this weekend's Holiday Crafts Fair and Bazaar, others distributed to the various downtown shops and businesses that had agreed to display and sell them without taking a cut of the profits.

Mini-Nicole sidled up next to Alex. "My dad offered to match dollar-for-dollar whatever we raised from the ornament sales."

"So we decided to make as many extra ornaments as we could with the leftover supplies," added Alex. "This is Sophie Lambert, by the way, Mom. She moved here over the summer."

Which explained why I didn't recognize her. And judging from the smitten, puppy dog expression on my son's face, I pegged her as the new girlfriend Alex's younger brother Nick had mentioned the other day. According to Nick, she worked with Alex at Starbucks. Not that I had a clue when Alex found the time for a girlfriend between his studies, sports, and part-time job. I plastered a friendly smile on my face and said, "Nice to meet you, Sophie. That's quite a generous offer."

She shrugged. "Dad's that kind of guy, always stepping up for a good cause."

"We're lucky we had so many glass balls left over," said Alex.

I had requested fifteen hundred clear glass ornaments from the manufacturer, expecting a certain percentage of breakage as the kids handled them. After the committee had collected the finished ornaments, nearly a hundred unused glass balls remained. I scanned the two rooms once again. In various states of completion, the ornaments covered every available flat surface of my dining room and living room.

"How did sales go today?" I asked. The fair was a two-day event held at the National Guard Armory and included outside vendors.

"Great," said Sophie. "We sold nearly all five hundred

ornaments we'd designated for today's sale. We're hoping we'll do even better tomorrow. That's why we wanted to make more ornaments tonight."

"I'd better let you get back to work, then," I said before heading off in search of Zack and Nick. As I made my way toward the den, someone cranked Imagine Dragons back up to ear-piercing volume.

~*~

I found Zack and Nick engrossed in a chess match. Ralph sat perched on Zack's shoulder, his parrot gaze locked on the chessboard, absorbing every move. Given his total recall of all things Shakespeare, I wondered if we'd soon be adding chess Grand Master to his list of talents. After all, if Watson, the IBM computer, can win a million dollars on *Jeopardy*, anything is possible. "Think we should enter Ralph is a few chess matches?"

Zack glanced up from the board. "Didn't you see my note?"

"What note?"

"The one I left on the coffee table, telling you to text me when you woke up."

"I never turned on a light."

"I didn't want you navigating the steps by yourself."

"I'm fine." I lifted my arm and scowled at my wrist. "Except for this."

A loud doggie snore drew my attention to Manifesto—AKA Mephisto, AKA Devil Dog—my mother-in-law's French bulldog, snoozing underneath the coffee table. That's when I realized Casa Pollack was shy one family member. "Where's Lucille?"

"She and her minion stormed out once Alex's friends arrived," said Nick.

"Before or after dinner?" I asked.

"What do you think?" asked Zack. He stood and waved me

toward the sofa. "Sit down. I'll heat up some dinner for you. I set some aside before Lucille and Harriet wolfed down every last crumb."

Zack had had a busy day. He'd saved my life, cleaned up a crime scene, and judging from the telltale aromas of something Italian still lingering in the air, apparently cooked dinner for everyone.

After Karl, I probably would have built an impenetrable fortress around my heart if not for the universe dropping Zachary Barnes into my life at the most opportune moment. The guy was definitely a keeper.

I settled onto the sofa. Zack headed toward the kitchen, Ralph still on his shoulder, probably because he knew he could cajole a treat from his moveable perch once they entered the kitchen.

Nick moved the chessboard out of the way and curled up next to me, his head on my shoulder. "You scared me," he said. "Stop doing that."

I ran the fingers of my good hand through his shock of sandy-colored hair. "I didn't do it on purpose."

"None of this stuff ever happened before Dad died."

"I know."

"This is all his fault."

I sighed. "Your father had nothing to do with what happened this morning."

"He had everything to do with Ricardo trying to kill you."

"True." Ricardo had been Karl's loan shark. When Karl gambled away all our money and left us with debt that rivaled the GNP of most Third World nations, he also left me to deal with Ricardo, who was nowhere near as understanding as the mortgage company or my other legitimate creditors.

"And it just keeps happening," said Nick. "It's like his death whisked us into some weird alternate universe where people are always trying to kill you."

I couldn't refute his observation. Our lives had certainly turned surreal in the aftermath of Karl's death.

"I want our old life back," said Nick.

Did I? My old life hadn't included Zack. I wouldn't mind going back in time to when I had no debt, no communist albatross of a mother-in-law around my neck, and no one trying to kill me, but that life was built on a foundation of lies. The debt was there; I just didn't know it existed until Karl died and all the bricks came crashing down on me.

Along with losing my financial security, I'd lost any love I once had for my husband. I could never forgive him for what he had done to our kids and me, but I tried to keep my resentment and bitterness from Alex and Nick.

"Your father had an addiction he couldn't control, Nick. Addiction is an illness. You can't blame him for that."

"Lots of people are addicts," he said. "The smart ones seek help. I don't blame Dad for his gambling addiction. I blame him for not getting help, for not telling us, for putting his need to gamble above his family and screwing up our lives."

Hard to argue with that, as well. I felt the same way. "We're managing, though, right? Life is better than it was last winter, isn't it?"

"Thanks to Zack."

"Yes. But also to you and your brother for the sacrifices you've made."

"We didn't have much choice, did we?"

"You had a choice of attitude, Nick. I'm extremely proud of how both you and your brother have handled the adverse changes to our lives."

He wiggled out from under my arm and turned to face me. "So

when are you and Zack going to get married?"

TWO

I answered Nick with a pointed *Mom Look*, no words necessary.

Sheepishness spread across his face. "Wrong question?"

"From you? Definitely." As much as I loved Zack, given the outcome of my first marriage, I wasn't sure I was ready to plunge back into matrimonial waters any time soon.

Perhaps, given my trust issues, I'd never be ready. Part of me was convinced Zack was far more than just a photojournalist, no matter how much he protested otherwise. Maybe I'd let my imagination run amok, but I couldn't shake the suspicion that he hid a closely guarded secret. When I added two plus two, the answer I came up with was government operative.

I changed the subject. "So I take it Sophie is Alex's new girlfriend?"

Nick speared me with the classic *Teenager Look*.

"Wrong question?"

"Touché, Mom."

At least his French was improving.

Zack returned with a steaming plate of spaghetti squash topped with mushrooms and turkey meatballs in a marinara sauce. I supped while he and Nick continued their game.

~*~

By the next morning Lucille hadn't returned home. Since the police never called, I assumed she'd camped out overnight at Harriet Kleinhample's apartment. As much as I enjoyed a Lucille-free breakfast—or any meal, for that matter—her absence left the rest of us with Mephisto duty.

"Why doesn't she take her dog with her?" grumbled Nick, who drew the short straw and was in the process of bundling up to take Devil Dog for his morning walk while Zack and I prepared bacon and eggs.

"I don't think Harriet's apartment complex allows pets," I said.

Alex paused from setting the table. "Since when does Grandmother Lucille care about rules and regulations? Heck, she doesn't even obey the law most of the time."

Ralph, perched atop the refrigerator, flapped his wings and squawked. "*The brain may devise laws for the blood, but a hot temper leaps o'er a cold decree. The Merchant of Venice.* Act One, Scene Two."

"Good one, Ralph." Zack broke off a small piece of eggshell, rinsed it clean, and offered it to the bird. He grabbed the shell with a claw and greedily stuffed it into his beak.

"It's more convenient for her to leave us with taking care of her dog," I said, answering Alex. "She doesn't have to lug food and doggie dishes with her." However, part of me would put up with Mephisto permanently if Harriet—or any of the other Daughters of the October Revolution—offered Lucille permanent residence. I think secretly they all agreed their fearless leader was a royal pain in the patootie.

Although politically simpatico, I suspected the other women could only tolerate my abrasive mother-in-law in small doses. Certainly none wanted her as a permanent roomie, even Harriet, who was Lucille's staunchest defender.

Nick clipped a leash onto Mephisto's collar. The moment the back door closed behind him, I heard the front door open. "So much for a Lucille-free breakfast," I muttered.

However, it was Mama, not Lucille, who entered the kitchen. "Good morning, all," she said.

"You're extremely perky for so early in the morning," I said as she eyed the activity at the stove. "I take it you haven't eaten yet?"

"I thought I'd join you this morning." She pointed to one of the frying pans as Zack poured egg batter into it. "Better add a few more eggs, Zachary, dear. I'm famished. What is it about cold weather that makes me so hungry?"

The cold weather didn't stimulate Flora Sudberry Periwinkle Ramirez Scoffield Goldberg O'Keefe Tuttnauer's appetite. It was the prospect of a free meal, but I held my tongue. I knew Mama was lonely since the arrest of her latest husband and her subsequent divorce. Truthfully, I'd rather put up with her unannounced mealtime visits than hear I was about to meet Stepfather Number Six. And for all her annoying habits, I'd take ten Mamas over one Lucille any day.

She stripped off her outerwear and handed her coat, gloves, scarf, and purse to Alex. "Would you mind, dear?"

As he headed for the hall closet, she settled herself at the kitchen table. I poured her a cup of coffee before pulling the bacon from the hot fat and placing the strips on a paper towel-covered plate.

Mama stirred some milk and sugar into her coffee. After taking a sip she said, "I thought we could do some Christmas shopping today, dear. Lord & Taylor is having a big sale."

Mama has single-handedly kept Mr. Lord and Mr. Taylor in business for years. At least it seems that way. The woman will spend hundreds of dollars on a dress she doesn't need, only because it's on sale for twenty-percent off.

Her shopping addiction began when Harold Periwinkle, my father, drowned while scuba diving in the Yucatan on my parents' twenty-fifth wedding anniversary. Retail therapy helped Mama deal with her grief. She immediately invested the modest nest egg Dad left her with the two retail gigolos and continues to spend. And spend. And spend. Which is why ever since Dad's death she's been on the prowl for a man who would provide her with the lifestyle she believes she deserves.

Unfortunately, her husbands' financial shortfalls never come to light until after their untimely deaths. To date Mama has buried four additional husbands and divorced one. Lawrence Tuttnauer was the only husband with money, but the Feds seized every last dime of his ill-gotten gains before hauling his tush off to federal prison.

I placed the platter of bacon on the kitchen table. "The only shopping I'm doing today is at the holiday craft fair."

Mama knit her brows together. "Anastasia, you earn a living designing crafts. Why would you buy items you're quite capable of making yourself?"

"It's for a good cause."

Alex jumped in to explain the senior community service project to his grandmother.

"Well, in that case," said Mama, "I'll come with you and do my part to help. We can go to Lord & Taylor afterwards."

No way Mr. Lord and Mr. Taylor were getting a nickel of my paycheck, but I've learned to choose my battles when it comes to Mama. If she insisted on spending money she didn't have, I couldn't stop her, but I wouldn't be party to her extravagances.

As soon as Nick returned from walking Mephisto, Zack served the eggs. Alex wolfed down his breakfast, finishing before I'd taken two bites. "Gotta run," he said, bolting from the table. "I'm on set-up duty this morning."

"We'll see you there later," I said.

~*~

Westfield's annual Holiday Crafts Fair and Bazaar, sponsored by the Chamber of Commerce, featured more than a hundred local vendors and artisans selling everything from gourmet kettle corn to one-of-a-kind precious metals jewelry.

Because of their charitable project, the high school seniors had scored prime real estate in the center of the massive assembly hall. With the help of several handy parents and two faculty advisers, a group of students had designed and constructed an intricate latticework structure. They'd painted the display with shimmering white latex. Ropes of miniature LED lights wove around the perimeter. Additional lights ran along either side of the faux snow path that meandered through the display. Hundreds of handmade decorative glass ornaments hung from hooks inserted into the structure.

At the far end of the display Alex and several other students handled sales. He waved when he saw us, at the same time continuing to place sold ornaments into boxes.

"They're packing in a huge crowd," said Zack.

I glanced around the Armory. No other booth had anywhere near the number of customers that wandered through the kids' display. "If the crowds continue, I wouldn't be surprised to find

17

them sold out by the end of the day."

While Alex worked his hour-long shift in the booth, Mama, Zack, and I strolled up and down the aisles, checking out the various other vendors. I "window-shopped" while Mama did more than her share to spur on the economy, including purchasing ten of the glass ornaments. "You're not buying anything, Anastasia?" she said as she handed over her credit card to purchase a rhinestone-studded winter white cashmere scarf, her voice more an accusatory statement than a question.

My mother took denial to new heights. She refused to accept that I no longer resided firmly in the realm of the middle class, no matter how much evidence to the contrary smacked her in the face. I'd given up trying to convince her. "I intend to buy some of the students' ornaments as gifts for my co-workers, but I'll wait until we're ready to leave."

I inwardly cringed at the expense. After all, I had designed those ornaments and taught the kids how to make them. I could easily whip up half a dozen without spending a penny. However, instead of wallowing in my financial quagmire, I consoled myself with the knowledge that the money would go to a good cause. Besides, I was managing to scrape by, thanks to a decent-paying job, a little unexpected luck, and the generosity of certain people who had recently entered my life. Other families weren't nearly as lucky. Glass half full, I reminded myself.

With Mama's latest purchase in hand, the three of us circled back toward the school display to meet up with Alex. As we rounded the corner, he approached hand-in-hand with Sophie, a man I didn't recognize walking with them.

"This is Mr. Lambert, Sophie's dad," said Alex as they caught up with us. He proceeded to make introductions.

Mr. Lambert's weathered face suggested he'd spent much of

his adult life outdoors. With his blue-gray eyes, steel gray hair, and matching stubble, he reminded me of a cross between Daniel Craig and Hugh Laurie. When I offered him my hand, I received a firm handshake. "Sophie told us of your generous offer to match whatever the kids raised, Mr. Lambert."

"Shane," he said, releasing my hand. Then he shrugged. "My pleasure. I like to help when I can."

"I love your attitude," said Mama. "And where is Mrs. Lambert? Shopping?"

"I'm not married," said Shane.

"Oh?" Mama's husband-hunting antenna jumped to attention, no matter that she easily had at least fifteen years on Shane Lambert. When she first met Zack, she'd made a play for him as well.

Shane quickly changed the subject. Turning back to me, he said, "Alex tells me you're responsible for much of what the kids have been able to accomplish here."

I shrugged. "I pulled some strings and called in a few favors to get the materials donated."

"And taught us how to make those gorgeous ornaments," added Sophie. "We're raising so much more money than if we'd sold popcorn or wrapping paper. Just look." She waved toward the booth. "We're nearly sold out, and the fair isn't over for another four hours."

Before we could check out the booth, someone called, "Mr. Lambert?"

"Yes?"

A man who looked like he'd stepped out of the pages of *GQ* approached us. He wore charcoal gray designer jeans and a pale gray cashmere pullover sporting a white Ralph Lauren polo pony logo. When he offered his right hand, the diamond encrusted gold Rolex on his wrist peeked out from under his cuff and flashed like a camera strobe. "I'm Trey Krause, board treasurer of the county food bank. I wanted to thank you personally for your extremely generous matching funds offer."

Shane shook his hand. "You're quite welcome."

"You may not be aware of this, given that you're new to the area, but we're completely dependent on community donations. Your generosity means so much to so many struggling to get by."

Smooth operator. I pegged the guy as either a Wall Street broker or a highly successful insurance agent in his day job, occupations that required skill in convincing people to spend large sums of money. Poor Shane. The guy makes a generous charitable donation out of the goodness of his heart, and he's immediately set upon with guilt-trip appeals to donate more.

How many meals would a diamond encrusted Rolex buy?

"You receive no state or federal funding?" asked Shane.

"None. Your contribution will go a long way toward keeping us stocked throughout the winter."

Shane reached into his pocket, pulled out a business card, and handed it to Krause. "We should talk. Give me a call."

Krause palmed the card and smiled. "Thank you. I'll be in touch."

He nodded to the rest of us before taking his leave. "Sorry to interrupt. Enjoy the fair."

"If you're not careful, you'll wind up as their primary benefactor," I told Shane.

"I don't mind."

Mama's ears perked up at that. I swear her pupils transformed into dollar signs. She turned to me. "Anastasia, you'd better grab what you want before all the ornaments are gone."

Ah, Mama. She's so transparent. Her ulterior motive was like a neon sign flashing over her head. "I'll do that, Mama, but you behave yourself while I'm gone."

"Really, dear! I have no idea what you mean."

"I do," muttered Alex under his breath. Luckily, the noise level in the Armory prevented his grandmother from hearing him.

I walked over to the display, quickly chose six ornaments, and got in line to pay. As I inched toward the register, I kept an eye on Mama. Although I couldn't hear the conversation, her body language spoke volumes. She'd entered full-on flirting mode. I had to rely on Zack and Alex to keep the sixty-five-year-old siren in check until I returned.

But I also noticed something else—a platinum blonde hovering near Zack. She wore a crimson fashion model pout as she pretended to examine merchandise on a nearby table, but her eyes kept darting toward Zack. While Mama threw herself at a bemused Shane Lambert, the woman with curves in all the right places and legs that went on forever appeared to have set her sights on my guy.

I sighed. Women were always throwing themselves at Zack and for good reason. The man's DNA had cavorted in the same primordial soup as Pierce Brosnan, George Clooney, Patrick Dempsey, and Antonio Banderas. No one ever saw me, a pear-shaped plain Jane, as competition—if they saw me at all. I watched as the woman sidled closer to Zack, pretending to be otherwise occupied as she eavesdropped on his conversation with Shane.

Finally, I arrived at the register, paid for my ornaments, and headed back to claim my man before the interloper pounced. Not that I needed to worry about Zack. He could take care of himself, but at times like these my insecurities got the better of me.

"Do you recognize that woman?" I whispered as I looped my arm through his and surreptitiously nodded in the direction of the eavesdropper who had stepped several feet away upon my return.

Not surreptitiously enough, though, because Sophie overheard me and immediately gave the woman the once-over. "She looks like a model."

Maybe at one time but Westfield wasn't exactly brimming with fashion models. We did have our share of trophy wives, though, and I pegged her as a member of that class, probably married to a hedge fund manager or investment banker, given her head-to-toe pricey designer duds.

When Zack turned to look at the woman, she quickly shifted her attention to a ceramic candy dish. "Never saw her before," he said. "Why?"

"She seems very interested in you."

He chuckled. "Are you sure? Maybe she's eyeing Shane."

Shane knit his brows together, turned to look at the woman, and shrugged. "Not my type."

"Nor mine," said Zack.

THREE

Something about the way that woman continued sniffing around caused my Spidey Senses to reach maximum tingle mode. Since Mama and I had completed our shopping, I suggested we leave. "We have Christmas lights to string," I reminded Zack.

"We?" He pointed to my wrist.

"I can untangle, at least."

"No need. I'm an expert at untangling."

I raised both eyebrows. To my knowledge, members of the alphabet agencies often engaged in "untangling."

Zack obviously read my mind because he quickly added, "Christmas lights."

"I should leave as well," said Shane. "I've got errands to run."

"Sophie and I are going to hang around to help break down the display and pack up later," said Alex.

Sophie tugged at her father's sleeve. When he cocked his head toward her, she stood on tiptoe to whisper something in his ear. He nodded, then turned to us. "Why don't you all join us at our home for a celebratory dinner later this evening?"

Mama placed her hand possessively on Shane's sleeve, raised her chin, and batted her eyelashes. "How very sweet of you, Shane. We'd love to." She turned to me. "Wouldn't we, dear?"

Alex executed an eye roll. Sophie stifled a giggle. "Are you sure?" I asked Shane.

He responded with a wink. "I'm looking forward to it."

Hopefully this meant he viewed Mama's overt overtures with amusement. "What should we bring?" I asked.

"Just yourselves. I enjoy cooking."

"A man after my own heart," said Mama.

We all stared at her.

"Should be an entertaining evening," said Zack.

If nothing else, Mama infused a certain amount of comic relief into our lives.

As we made our way toward the exit, I noticed the platinum blonde wandering into the kids' display.

~*~

Shane's dinner invitation gave Mama even more reason to take advantage of the sale at Lord & Taylor. "I'll need a new outfit for this evening," she said.

"Why?" I asked.

"Really, Anastasia, I don't understand you sometimes."

And I'd never understand her.

Zack dropped Mama off at the store. "Phone when you're ready to be picked up," he said.

"No need. I'll get an Uber." She stepped from the car and waved to us as she headed into the store.

"Uber?" asked Zack as he pulled back into traffic. "Is Ira paying for that, as well?"

Ira Pollack was my husband's long-lost half-brother, born

several years after Lucille gave Isadore the heave-ho prior to Karl's birth. Ira claims his father never knew about Karl.

Lucille insists Ira is an imposter, but when he walked into our lives last summer, he brought with him undeniable proof. Besides, genes don't lie. Ira is a slightly younger and thinner spitting image of Karl.

Mama's most recent husband was Ira's now former father-in-law. Ira owns a string of car dealerships around the state and lives with his three super-spoiled kids in a home whose kitchen is larger than my entire house. For all his business success, the man is incredibly insecure, not to mention guilt-ridden when it comes to his personal life. He uses his wealth as a way to buy love, respect, and inclusion. Unfortunately, he's too clueless to realize his generosity only makes him an easy mark for his manipulative kids and people like the unscrupulous Lawrence Tuttnauer.

Ira bought Mama and Lawrence a condo in Scotch Plains as a wedding present. Luckily for her, since he hadn't transferred the title prior to Lawrence's arrest, the condo wasn't seized under New Jersey's forfeiture law.

Mama now lives mortgage-free instead of sharing a bedroom with Lucille, which does alleviate a certain amount of tension within the walls of Casa Pollack, given that Mama claims descent from Russian nobility. I suspect Ira also pays most, if not all, of her other living expenses.

"For all I know, Ira may even pay Mama's monthly Lord & Taylor credit bill," I said. "Nothing would surprise me."

Ira introduced Mama to Lawrence and is consumed with guilt over the match that went dead wrong—literally. In addition to orchestrating the recent murders of some of my neighbors, Lawrence put out a hit on his own daughter, Ira's trophy wife Cynthia. He also tried to kill me.

Family is everything to the Mafia—until you cross them.

~*~

Zack and I arrived home to find the exterior of the house ablaze in miniature white twinkling Christmas lights. Strings of lights ran along the roofline, around the perimeters of each window, and the sides and top of the front door. Net lights draped the shrubs in front of the house. Additional lights led from either side of the walkway from the house to the sidewalk. Another string wrapped around the light post at the end of the walkway. Even the garage was festooned in lights.

"I don't own nearly this many strings of Christmas lights," I said.

"Do you think Nick is responsible?" asked Zack.

"Doubtful."

That left only one other person. "Ira," we both said in unison.

I sighed. I'd tried nearly everything to discourage Ira's need to shower us with unwanted gifts. "Short of a restraining order, how do I get him to stop?"

"Find him a new wife?"

"I'm not sure even that would work." Ira held onto an unrealistic dream of the remaining Pollacks coming together as one big, happy family. Given that his kids hated us—me, especially—and Lucille couldn't stand the sight of him, Hades would turn into a massive iceberg before that dream ever came true. Even then, odds were less than fifty/fifty. The more Ira pushed, the more everyone else pushed back.

Nick greeted us as we entered the house. "Uncle Ira strikes again."

"We figured," I said. "Did he do all of this himself?"

"Of course not. He sent over a crew from one of his dealerships."

"I suppose I'll have to call to thank him," I said.

"He phoned earlier," said Nick. "He's stopping over later. Said he had some exciting news to share and wants to take us out to dinner to celebrate."

"Not tonight," I said. "We already have plans. Sophie's father invited all of us to dinner."

"Grandmother Lucille, too?" asked Nick, screwing up his face.

Did Shane even know about Lucille? "I didn't think to ask."

"Why don't you text Alex?" suggested Zack. "He can have Sophie talk to her father."

"Why don't we just not mention it to Grandmother Lucille?" said Nick.

"Sounds like a plan to me," said Zack. "Flora and her never-say-die pheromones will be enough for us to handle this evening."

Nick appeared perplexed. "Huh?"

"Your grandmother is back in full-out husband-hunting mode," I said.

His eyebrows arched toward his hairline. "With Sophie's dad?" He pondered this for a moment. "So if Alex and Sophie got married, Grandma would be both his mother-in-law *and* his grandmother? Yuck!"

My head began to pound at the thought of such a scenario. "No one's getting married," I said. "Not your grandmother and certainly not your seventeen-year-old brother."

"If you say so," said Nick, "but I don't remember Grandma ever asking your permission with any of her other husbands."

Now my wrist began to throb in sync with the crescendo drumbeat gathering steam in my skull. Time to down some Motrin. Then I needed to deal with Ira.

Within a minute I'd accomplished my first task, but that's where my luck ran out. Zack entered the bedroom as I stepped from the bathroom. "Ira's here."

He couldn't have waited until the Motrin worked its magic?

I masked the pain by pasting a phony smile on my face, took a deep breath, and stepped out into the hallway. We found Ira sitting in one of the living room chairs. Zack and I settled onto the sofa. "I was just about to call you, Ira. I wanted to thank you for the Christmas lights—"

"It was my pleasure."

"—but I really wish you'd asked first."

"I wanted to surprise you."

"And you did, but you can't keep showering us with gifts."

"Why not? I have the money; you don't, thanks to my brother."

"Half-brother. A half-brother you never knew. Besides, my finances aren't your problem."

"I don't see it as a problem; I see it as one family member helping another."

Zack placed his hand on my knee, and squeezed gently, his way of silently telling me I should choose my battles. I was never going to win this argument with Ira.

I sighed. "Nick mentioned you had some exciting news and wanted to celebrate by taking us to dinner tonight. Unfortunately, we have previous plans."

Crestfallen, Ira said, "I suppose we can postpone the celebration until tomorrow night."

"Weeknights are always difficult. Besides, won't your kids have homework?"

He nodded. "Of course. How about next Friday night?"

Could I come up with an excuse for Friday night? Short of contracting bubonic plague, I'd eventually run out of excuses, legitimate or otherwise. And even the plague was no guarantee.

Ira would probably suggest we come dressed in hazmat suits.

Since I found myself at a loss for an excuse for next Friday, I punted by saying, "I'll check our calendar and let you know."

"Meanwhile, what would we be celebrating?" asked Zack.

Ira's face brightened. "I decided the kids and I needed a change. The house in Hunterdon County holds too many unpleasant memories for us. We need to move on."

Ira's first wife had died of cancer in that house. His marriage to Cynthia ended in her murder—after she'd run off with the pool boy. But I had a sinking feeling this conversation was about to veer in a direction I wouldn't like—one that led due East.

"Last week I put the house on the market," he continued. "It sold yesterday. Today I put a deposit on a house in Westfield. We're going to be neighbors!"

Sometimes I hate when I'm right.

FOUR

Clichés notwithstanding, my mouth really did literally drop open. Across the room Ira beamed as if he'd just won an Oscar. I, on the other hand, felt like Mr. Oscar had magically sprung to life and delivered a swift gold-plated kick to my stomach.

"Isn't this great news, Anastasia?"

Oh. My. God. Please let me wake up to find this is a bad dream! Ira a forty-five-minute car ride away was Ira forty-five minutes too close, but Ira in the same small town? Which god had I pissed off to deserve this? "Why Westfield?" I finally managed to ask.

"To be closer to all of you, of course."

Of course.

I finally got rid of Ira by using my wrist as an excuse, but that involved an explanation of how I'd sustained the injury. Zack stepped in with a plausible lie. Ira finally left after we assured him numerous times that I didn't need him to assist at chores or run any errands for me.

"He means well," said Zack, closing the front door on Ira's departing back.

"So did Calamity Jane."

~*~

Shane and Sophie Lambert lived in a Craftsman-inspired McMansion on the north side of town. During the latest housing boom, builders vied with one another to buy up the nineteen-fifties cape cods and nineteen-sixties ranchers and split levels that once dominated much of Westfield. After they bulldozed the properties, they erected new homes that sold for five to ten times their initial investment.

Even homes of modest size with one-car garages situated on small lots sold for nearly a million dollars. The larger homes, those with three-car garages on half an acre of land or more, went for as much as three million dollars. Luckily, Karl and I bought into Westfield back when real estate prices were reasonable. Even if Karl hadn't gambled away all our money, an auto parts salesman and his magazine editor wife certainly couldn't afford to buy into the town now.

"What a lovely house," said Mama as Zack pulled up to the curb. We had picked Mama up at her condo before driving to the Lambert home.

As far as McMansions go, the Lambert house was relatively understated, unlike some of the more ornate, ostentatious homes that now dotted the Westfield landscape. Although large for two people, it was more a mini-McMansion than a McMansion, certainly nowhere near the size of Ira's home—now ex-home—in Hunterdon County.

Sophie answered the door and ushered us inside after Zack rang the bell. Alex, who had gone home from the holiday crafts fair with Sophie, stood beside her, his arm around her waist. They looked like a young married couple welcoming guests to their home. Suddenly I realized my firstborn would fly the coop in the not-too-distant future, and I fought to contain the sadness that overwhelmed me.

Where had the years gone?

I swallowed down the lump welling up in my throat and cast my gaze around the foyer as I blinked away a few gathering tears. A gray, tan, and black Navajo area rug partially covered the dark gray hand-scraped hardwoods. White wainscoting wrapped the lower walls with the upper walls papered in a neutral-toned nubby tweed. To the left of the foyer behind a pair of French doors was an office, to the right a formal living room. A hallway to the left of the staircase led to the back of the house. A Mission oak console table set into an alcove under the staircase held a Frederic Remington bronze statue, a cowboy on a bucking bronco.

When we slipped out of our coats, I noticed Mama's new outfit for the first time. A black crepe cocktail sheath with organza sleeves and satin piping, the dress was better suited for a romantic dinner with a lover than a home-cooked meal at the residence of her grandson's girlfriend.

In contrast, I wore a pair of black tweed woolen trousers that I'd topped with a black, gray, and ivory Fair Isle sweater. Zack had dressed in a pair of black jeans with a gray button-down no-wale corduroy shirt, and Nick wore the same jeans and long-sleeve T-shirt he'd donned first thing this morning.

While Alex hung our coats in the foyer closet, Mama got right to work, asking Sophie, "Where is that handsome father of yours?"

"And she's off," Nick stage-whispered, but either Mama didn't hear him, didn't realize he referred to her, or chose to ignore him.

Sophie blushed. "In the kitchen."

I grabbed Mama before she bolted down the hallway in search of her prey and pulled her aside. "Behave yourself," I whispered. "The man is too young for you."

"Age is merely a number, dear."

I played my ace. "If you embarrass Alex in front of Sophie and her father, he'll never forgive you."

"Really, Anastasia!"

"Really, Mama. I mean it. Rein in your hormones."

"Did anyone ever tell you that you suck all the fun out of life?"

"Only you, Mama."

"You should listen to me. Mama knows best."

"Not this time."

"Why don't we all join Dad in the kitchen?" said Sophie. "We've prepared some hors d'oeuvres."

She led the way into a large open-concept great room, a combination of kitchen, dining room, and family room. Shane stood chopping romaine lettuce at one end of the marble-topped island. "Welcome," he said, waving his chef's knife in the direction of the family room. A platter of cheeses, a basket of crusty bread slices and a selection of beverages filled the reclaimed wood coffee table. "Help yourselves. I'll join you momentarily."

Zack placed the bottle of chilled pinot grigio we'd brought and a bottle of sparkling cider for Alex, Nick, and Sophie on the counter. Shane glanced at the wine label and gave a nod of approval. "That will go quite well with dinner. Thank you."

"Our pleasure," said Zack.

Sophie led us over to the overstuffed gray sectional sofa that surrounded the coffee table on three sides. I noted a second Remington on an end table and a third sitting on one of the shelves of the built-in bookcases that flanked the fireplace.

Before taking a seat, Mama looked around, assessing the room and its contents, which were straight out of the Pottery Barn catalogue. "What a lovely home you have, Shane. Did you furnish it yourself or hire a decorator?"

Sophie answered for him. "Dad and I picked out everything."

"You both have excellent taste."

And expensive—a fact not lost on my mother.

Sophie mumbled her thanks, then immediately turned away from Mama to speak to me. "Remember that woman at the crafts fair? The one we all thought looked like a model?"

I nodded. "What about her?"

"After all of you left she came into the display. The way she was skulking about I thought she might be a shoplifter. So Alex and I decided to keep an eye on her."

"Did you see her steal anything?" I asked.

"No," said Alex. "But she started up a weird conversation with Sophie."

"What?" Shane abandoned his salad prep. He hurried across the room. Grasping his daughter by the shoulders, he asked, "What did she say to you?"

"She said I was really pretty and asked if I'd ever thought about modeling." Sophie rolled her eyes. "I told her I wasn't interested and walked away."

"Anything else?" asked Shane. I understood his concern. Too many child predators lurked in plain sight these days.

Sophie nodded. "She asked which ornaments I'd made. When I pointed them out, she wound up buying five."

"That was very nice of her," said Mama.

"I suppose, but she really creeped me out, especially since she didn't buy any of the other students, just mine."

Shane hadn't taken his eyes off his daughter. His initial alarm now settled into a deep-seated frown. "Did she leave after that?"

"I think so. We didn't see her again."

At that point Mama decided it was time to change the subject and began peppering Shane with questions. "And what is it you do for a living, Shane?"

Before he could answer, I turned to him and said, "You don't have to answer that."

He chuckled. "I don't mind. I'm a money manager, Flora."

"How interesting," said Mama, her face lighting up.

I glared at her, but she refused to make eye contact, continuing her interrogation as though she and Shane were the only two people in the room. "Are you from around here originally?"

"No, we're transplants."

"Really? From where?"

"Out west."

"California?"

"No, not that far west." Shane turned to Zack. "Alex tells me you're a photojournalist for *National Geographic*."

"Among other publications," said Zack.

As the two men became engrossed in conversation, Mama tried to pump Sophie for more information. "Where out west?"

Instead of answering, Sophie jumped up and said, "Alex, we never finished setting the dinner table." She grabbed his hand and waved to Nick to join them. The three of them practically ran toward the kitchen cabinets.

"Well, that was rude," said Mama.

"So were your questions," I muttered under my breath.

"I beg your pardon!" Mama spoke loudly enough that Zack and Shane paused their conversation for a moment to glance our way.

I continued through gritted teeth. "Some people don't care to share the details of their lives with strangers."

"We're hardly strangers. We're in their home about to have dinner with them."

I rolled my eyes. "You only met Shane and Sophie several hours ago. That doesn't entitle you to pry into their lives."

"Honestly, Anastasia, I was merely making small talk. What's the big deal about asking what someone does for a living or where they previously lived?"

"You want to make small talk? Try the weather."

Mama huffed out what sounded like a growl. "I blame this on that commie mother-in-law of yours."

"Lucille? She's not even here, Mama." Mama would blame Lucille for global warming if she thought people would believe her.

"That's not the point. You were never like this before she moved in with you."

"But you're always like this when you're on the prowl for a new husband."

Mama jumped to her feet. "I need to powder my nose."

"No snooping, Mama!"

If looks could kill, my mother would now be minus her only child. She stormed off in search of the powder room.

"First door on the left in the foyer," Shane called after her. Then he chuckled.

"You caught all that?" I asked.

"Hard to miss," said Shane. "But no worries. Alex told me earlier all about Flora."

"You need to impress upon her that you're not interested. Otherwise, she won't stop. The woman is relentless."

"So I gather, but I wouldn't want to embarrass her."

"You may have to."

When Mama returned from euphemistically "powdering her

nose" (I'm sure said nose had spent time poking inside the medicine cabinet rather than receiving the attention of a makeup brush), we all moved to the dining room table, where Shane served up a dinner of chicken Parmesan, grilled zucchini, linguini, and Cesar salad. Throughout the meal Mama continued to lob questions at Shane, which he deftly deflected.

Mama's annoyance grew. "Why do you refuse to answer any questions about yourself? Are you in Witness Protection?"

"If I were, I certainly wouldn't be able to tell you."

Mama's eyes widened. "Then you are!"

He laughed. "No, Flora, I'm not. I just don't like to talk about myself."

"Why not?"

"Mama, enough already!"

The conversation came to a halt when the doorbell rang. "I'll get it," said Sophie, obviously relieved to have an excuse to remove herself from the second coming of the Spanish Inquisition. She grabbed her napkin from her lap, tossed it on the table, and pushed back her chair.

A moment later Sophie returned with three very familiar faces—Detective Sam Spader, flanked by Westfield Officers Harley and Fogarty. The three men and I had history, all involving murder and mayhem. From their serious countenance, I knew they weren't soliciting contributions to the Police Benevolent Fund.

Both Shane and Zack stood. Spader approached Shane. "Mr. Lambert?"

"Yes. Is there a problem?"

"We'd like to ask you a few questions, sir."

"About?"

"An investigation."

Shane's brows knit together. "Of what?"

Spader glanced around the table, pausing for a few extra seconds when his gaze fell on Sophie. She quickly looked away, avoiding eye contact with him. Was Spader here because of Sophie? My heart sank. She seemed like such a nice kid. I glanced at Alex. My son knew right from wrong. I trusted him. But I also knew he was head-over-heels for this girl, and that had me worried.

Spader turned back to Shane. "Actually, sir, we'd prefer to have this conversation down at headquarters."

"Why don't we step into my office?" suggested Shane. "I'll be happy to talk with you there, out of earshot of my dinner guests."

Spader nodded to Harley and Fogarty who took up positions on either side of our host. My pulse skyrocketed into the stratosphere. I'd seen people hauled off by the police. Spader wasn't interested in Sophie. He was after her father.

In a voice tight and measured the veteran detective said, "We'd like your cooperation, sir. The officers will escort you to the precinct." Then Spader spoke to Harley and Fogarty. "I'll follow shortly."

Shane turned to us, his expression perplexed. "I'm sorry. I don't know what's going on here."

"Best to go with them to clear things up," said Zack, "but make sure you have an attorney present before you answer any questions."

Shane nodded.

Spader shot Zack a dirty look. If I hadn't already figured out something serious was going down, that look removed any doubt.

As Harley and Fogarty led Shane from the dining room, Sophie jumped up and shouted, "Why are you taking my dad? What's going on?"

Shane pivoted. "Don't worry, Sweetheart. I'll be home shortly." Then he turned to me and asked, "Would you take her home with you? I don't want her here by herself."

"Of course," I said.

The moment the front door closed behind Harley, Fogarty, and Shane, Mama slapped her hand on the table. "I knew that man was hiding something."

FIVE

"Mama, shut up!"

"I'm just saying I'm glad I didn't get involved with him. That's all."

"Enough, Mama! This isn't about you."

Detective Spader focused on Mama, perhaps waiting for her to blurt out something more. When Mama remained silent, he addressed me. "We meet again, Mrs. Pollack."

Sophie's body shook with uncontrollable anger as a stream of tears cascaded down her cheeks. "My father is a good man. He hasn't done anything wrong."

"I never said he did, Miss Lambert. I simply want to ask him some questions."

"Then why can't you do that here?" She balled her fists. "I don't believe you." She then made a beeline toward Spader.

"Don't, Sophie. This won't help." I grabbed her just in time to prevent her from assaulting him. Releasing my grip on her wrists, I cupped her face in my hands. "The police simply want your dad's help with something." I had no idea what that something was, but from Sophie's reaction and the way Spader had zeroed in on her, I suspected she might.

"We'll get everything sorted out," I told her. "But right now you have to allow the police to do their job." I shot Spader a questioning look. "Whatever that is."

Spader had come to Union County by way of years in Homicide as a member of the Essex County Police Force. When I first met him, he looked like he was one cigarette and one beer away from a massive coronary. Working homicides in Union County had proven a healthy move for him. Now it would take at least a pack of cigarettes and a six-pack of beer to land him in ICU, but I lauded his effort.

I handed Sophie over to Alex. "Take Sophie to her room." He wrapped his arms around her and led her away as she continued to sob. I turned to Nick. "Go with them."

Once the kids were out of earshot, Spader asked, "What's your connection to this guy, Mrs. Pollack?"

I first met the detective last summer when my mother-in-law was the prime suspect in the strangulation death of her roommate at the Westfield Assisted Living and Rehabilitation Center. Since then, his initial animosity toward me has grown into a grudging admiration of my ability to solve murders, even if he'd never admit it to my face.

His parents had probably sealed the detective's fate the day they named their bouncing baby boy. One of these days I'd work up the courage to ask him if the senior Spaders were fans of Dashiell Hammett.

"He's Alex's girlfriend's father," I said. "We first met today. What is this about, Detective?"

"Really, Mrs. Pollack, do I need to remind you yet again that I

42

can't divulge information regarding an ongoing investigation?"

"So you think Shane Lambert is either involved in some sort of crime or has information concerning one?"

"I wouldn't be here if I didn't."

"I don't suppose you'd be willing to share any details," said Zack.

"You suppose correctly. Sorry to disturb your dinner, folks." With that he turned and headed for the front door.

As soon as Spader left, Zack, Mama, and I quickly cleaned up the remnants of dinner. Then we gathered our coats and with Sophie clinging to Alex, departed the Lambert residence.

Given Sophie's state of mind, I didn't feel comfortable with Alex driving the two of them back to our house, even though it was only a mile and a half. I wanted my son concentrating on the road, not his distraught girlfriend. So while Zack, accompanied by Nick, drove Mama to her condo, I slid behind the wheel of Alex's Jeep and chauffeured the two older teens back to my house.

Once home, I heated up some warm milk for Sophie and gave her a pair of my pajamas and a bathrobe to wear. The pajamas were at least two sizes too big for her petite frame, but the waist cinched closed with a drawstring, and she could roll the legs up to keep from tripping.

She stared at the pile of clothes. "Dad's coming right back, isn't he?"

"I'm sure he is, Sophie." Although everything about Spader's demeanor led me to doubt my own words. "But given how upset you are, I think you should lie down, and you'll be more comfortable if you change."

I don't think she believed me, but she accepted the pajamas and robe, changing into them in the bathroom before I led her to the spare bed in Lucille's room. Thankfully, the curmudgeonly commie was still AWOL. With any luck she'd stay away until all the drama was over and Sophie was safely back home in her own bed.

Sophie stopped at the entrance to the bedroom and stared at the curtain hanging in place of a door. "Why doesn't this room have a door?"

Alex, hovering protectively beside her, answered before I had a chance. "When both my grandmothers lived here, Grandmother Lucille kept locking Grandma Flora out of the room. Zack came up with the brilliant idea of removing the door and hanging a curtain."

"Why didn't he just remove the lock?"

"Good question." He turned to me. "Why didn't he, Mom?"

I shrugged. "I guess he figured she might try to barricade the door with some of the furniture."

Sophie chuckled. I saw that as a good sign. "Try to get some sleep," I told her.

"I don't think I can. I'm too worried about Dad. I don't understand why the police needed to talk to him at the station. Why couldn't they just ask him their questions at our house?"

"After Zack dropped off Nick, he drove to police headquarters to find out what's going on." I itched to question Sophie because I was certain she knew something about the reason for Spader's visit, but I didn't want to upset her further.

Her lower lip quivered, and she bit down on it as she fought back a fresh onslaught of tears. I wrapped my arm around her shoulders and led her to the bed, sitting down beside her. "I'm sure Zack will return with your dad, and he'll be able to explain everything once he's here."

Sophie curled up into a fetal position. "Can Alex stay with me?"

"We'll both stay until you fall asleep." Not that I didn't trust my son, but why tempt fate?

"I'll be right back," said Alex. A minute later he returned with his desk chair, which he placed alongside the bed. Alex settled into the chair and reached for Sophie's hand. I stood and moved over to Lucille's bed, propping my back against the headboard.

Although Sophie insisted on staying awake, the emotional exhaustion, coupled with the sleep-inducing properties of the warm milk, took effect, and she fell into a restless sleep. I ushered my son from the room.

~*~

Two hours later Zack arrived home with Shane. The man appeared to have aged a decade in the hours since his encounter with the police. He made his way over to the living room sofa and literally collapsed onto the cushions, not even bothering to remove his coat.

"Did he say anything to you?" I whispered to Zack.

He shook his head. "Not a word, but something's got him rattled. I'm going up to the apartment to get him something to drink." Zack headed out the back door, returning shortly with a bottle of Maker's Mark and a tumbler. Shane had remained silent the entire time, the boys and I quietly keeping him company.

Zack poured Shane two fingers of bourbon and handed him the glass. He downed the drink in one gulp. Then, staring into the empty tumbler, he said, "I feel like I fell down a rabbit hole. The idea that I would...I don't understand why the police think..."

"Start from the beginning," said Zack. "Why did the police want to question you?"

"Wait," I said, holding up my hand. I turned to my sons. "Adults only, guys."

45

"They can stay," said Shane.

I shook my head. "Parental prerogative, if you don't mind." I pointed toward the foyer. "Let's go, guys." Alex and Nick reluctantly dragged themselves from the living room.

Zack and I took seats on either side of Shane and waited for him to continue. "When we arrived at the station, I was brought into a room for questioning. The first thing the detective asked was if I knew a Dawn Heathwood."

"Do you?" I asked.

He shook his head. "Never heard of her. The detective pulled out a photograph and slapped it on the table in front of me." Shane reached for the Maker's Mark and poured another two fingers of bourbon, downing half before he continued. "Remember the woman hovering around us at the fair?"

I nodded, a bit puzzled by the change of subject. "What about her?"

"The photo showed me standing outside the Armory talking with her. Her name was Dawn Heathwood."

"*Was?*" When speaking about a person, past tense was never a good sign.

"Someone strangled her."

I inhaled sharply. Until this past year we'd gone for decades without a murder or attempted murder in town. Now they're occurring on a regular basis. If that weren't disturbing enough, I've found myself connected to each one of them. I was terrified to ask the obvious.

Zack beat me to it. "What does her death have to do with you?"

"The detective accused me of killing her."

SIX

"What!"

We all turned at the sound of the loud gasp to find Sophie, still dressed in pajamas and robe, standing at the entrance to the living room. Alex and Nick flanked her.

"Sorry, Mom," said Alex, his arm draped around Sophie's shoulders. "She woke up and heard her dad."

Shane stood, and Sophie ran into his arms. She lifted her chin and peered up at her father. "Why do the police think you killed a total stranger?"

"They did, but they don't anymore." He held his daughter in a tight hug and planted a kiss on the top of her head.

Shane walked Sophie back to the sofa. He lowered the two of them onto the cushions with Sophie squeezing in next to me. She clung to her father.

Zack stood and offered Alex his seat, moving to one of the living room chairs. My son first turned to me, silently begging me to allow him to stay. Since he'd already overheard the worst of

Shane's tale, I reluctantly nodded my agreement.

"What about me?" asked Nick.

I sighed. If I didn't allow them to stay, they'd only learn the details from Sophie afterwards. "I suppose you can stay, too."

"It was all a misunderstanding," Shane continued. "I cleared everything up."

"But you were gone so long. I was really scared."

"I'm sorry, Sweetheart. I spent most of the time waiting for the lawyer to show up."

"I don't understand. If you didn't do anything wrong, why did you need a lawyer?"

"It's always a good idea to have an attorney present when being questioned by the police," said Zack.

"But he's innocent. You heard him. He said it was all a misunderstanding."

"He's right," said Shane. He nodded toward Zack. "I should have taken your advice before answering any questions, but at that point I stopped talking and called the lawyer who handles my business affairs. He arranged for a defense attorney to meet me at the station. I waited until he arrived before I agreed to say anything else."

"Why were you talking to that woman?" asked Sophie.

And why hadn't Shane revealed this earlier in the evening when Sophie mentioned her own encounter with the woman?

"She was speaking to me."

"Why?"

"She was thanking me."

"For what?"

"For keeping her from getting hurt."

"Sophie, why don't you let your father explain from the beginning," I said.

Shane mouthed his thanks over Sophie's head. "Yes, everything will become clear once you hear the entire story."

Sophie heaved a deep sigh. "Okay."

Shane drained his glass, placed it on the coffee table, and spoke directly to his daughter. "After I left the fair, I was halfway across the parking lot when I remembered I forgot to ask if you needed any money. I turned around and headed back into the building."

He leaned his head back and closed his eyes. "Everything happened so fast after that. I'm not quite sure of the timeline. I heard a scream. A woman slammed into me. Or maybe she slammed into me, then screamed."

He shook his head and opened his eyes. "I don't know. I may have wrenched her arm when I broke her fall. She was shaken, but at least she didn't hit her head on the concrete floor. I asked if she was hurt. She said she wasn't, thanked me, and we parted ways. At that point it didn't even register that she was the woman loitering near us. I had only given her a quick glance earlier."

"I'm surprised the Armory has exterior surveillance but no cameras within the building," said Zack.

"I asked about that," said Shane. "Video of her tripping and me breaking her fall would have cleared everything up immediately. The detective said none of the cameras captured the incident. Too many people were milling around, blocking the camera's view."

"Great surveillance system," I muttered.

"Anyway," Shane continued, "she was outside smoking a cigarette when I left the second time. She approached me and thanked me again. I got in my car and drove off."

"I still don't understand why Spader suspected you," I said.

"He suggested we arranged to hook up, that she followed me a short time after I left."

"How did he connect her to the crafts fair?" asked Zack.

"The items she bought were found with her body. That led the detective to check out the security footage at the Armory."

"How did Spader identify you?" asked Zack.

"By combing through all the surveillance footage. One of the cameras captured me speaking with the kids' faculty advisor. She identified me."

"So he believes you now?" asked Sophie.

"Yes." He kissed the top of her head again. "Now he believes me."

I knew Spader well enough to know he never took anyone's word without proof. So what proof did he have to back up Shane's story? Or maybe he had no proof of Shane's innocence and was biding his time until he uncovered proof of his guilt.

"Was there surveillance of this Dawn Heathwood speaking to anyone else?" I asked.

"I don't know. For the most part the detective asked, and I answered. He wasn't in a sharing mood."

"Typical Spader," I said.

"If she did speak with anyone else, I'm sure he's tracking down those people to question them as well."

Outside brakes screeched, followed by a dull thud. Nick jumped up and ran to the window. "The Wandering Commie is back."

Just what I didn't need at the moment.

"My other grandmother," Alex explained when he saw the puzzled expression on Shane's face.

"I see."

"Trust me," I said. "You really don't." To which his expression grew even more puzzled.

"The good news is the tree's still standing," said Nick.

In the war between Harriet Kleinhample's VW minibus and

my oak tree, the minibus had yet to inflict a deadly blow, but it was only a matter of time. Harriet was incapable of parking *at* the curb, always driving *over* the curb and coming to a stop only after making contact with the oak. I don't know how much more abuse the poor tree could endure.

A short time later the front door flew open. Lucille stomped into the house, followed by her Mini-Me minion. Without so much as a nod of greeting, the two women marched down the hall to Lucille's bedroom. I held my breath, awaiting the expected outburst. I didn't have long to wait.

With her minion in tow, Lucille stormed into the living room, her cane pounding out an angry cadence, muffled by the carpet once she transitioned from the tiled foyer. "Who's been in my room?"

"I allowed Sophie to rest on the spare bed," I said.

My mother-in-law glared at Sophie, then turned her wrath on me. "You have no right to allow anyone to invade my privacy."

"That's Lucille's bedroom," said Harriet. The diminutive minion compensated for her lack of stature with a booming voice and a misplaced sense of righteousness.

"Technically, it's my bedroom," said Nick, matching Harriet's hostility attitude-for-attitude. He'd been forced to give up his room and double up with his brother when Lucille moved in with us.

Scarlet rage suffused Lucille's neck, spreading across her cheeks and up toward her steel gray hairline to disappear under her cropped utilitarian cut. She lifted her cane and jabbed it in the air in Nick's direction. "If my son were still alive, you'd never get away with such insolent behavior."

"But he's not," said Nick, raising his voice. "He ruined our lives, then dropped dead. And to top it off, we're now stuck with you."

I knew I should say something mom-like, but I couldn't force the words out of my mouth. My art degree hadn't included courses in psychology, but my gut told me Nick finally unleashing his anger at his grandmother was preferable to keeping it simmering inside. His father's betrayal, coupled with his grandmother's intolerable behavior toward us, had Nick itching for this confrontation for a year now.

I'd fought that same urge, but as the responsible grownup of the family, I'd bitten my tongue each time the urge threatened to overtake me. I just wished Nick hadn't chosen to vent in front of Shane and Sophie, especially given the events of this evening.

"How dare you!" Lucille transformed into an apoplectic purple volcano of rage, the color so perfectly matching her polyester pantsuit that it was hard to determine where fabric ended and skin began.

"Enough!" said Zack, rising from his chair.

Lucille shot him the evil eye, but his menacing stance would have cowered Genghis Khan. She turned her back on us and without another word, pounded her way out of the living room and down the hall. Harriet followed in her wake.

"Good riddance," muttered Nick.

Moments later the den television blared at ear-deafening volume.

For decades my mother-in-law had turned her commie nose up at the television, which she lumped in with religion as the "opiates of the masses." However, recently she'd commandeered the remote with more and more frequency, binge-watching reality TV shows. At first her tastes ran to *Dancing with the Stars* and *The Bachelor*, but she'd recently segued to the most bizarre offerings on cable TV—everything from shows about gypsy weddings to hoarders to polygamists.

I failed to understand Lucille's sudden addiction to reality TV, considering we were stuck in the middle of our own version of reality TV for the past year. Her doctors had said she sustained no permanent brain damage from her stroke last summer, but this new behavior was so out of character that as far as I was concerned, it couldn't be anything but brain damage.

However, Lucille's choice of programming didn't bother me as much as the noise that invaded every corner of the house. Neither she nor Harriet was hard of hearing, so I could only assume she chose the deafening decibel level out of spite to annoy me and the other members of our household, including her own dog and poor Ralph.

Given my new reality, perhaps I should consider inviting a camera crew inside Casa Pollack. Monetizing my life would help pay down my debt. Of course, my kids would probably put out a hit on me if I suggested such a scheme.

I voiced none of these thoughts, though. Instead, I turned to Shane and offered a lame explanation. "My mother-in-law has issues with us. And unfortunately, as Nick so indelicately put it, we're stuck with her."

"No need to apologize," he said, his words in direct contrast to the discomfort evident on his face. "But we should get going. The kids have school tomorrow. Thank you for taking such good care of my little girl."

"*Little?* Dad, I'm seventeen!" Sophie wiggled out from under her father's arm and stood.

"You'll always be my little girl, Soph."

She replied with the universal teen eye roll. "I'll go change."

Alex jumped up. "I'll drive you both home."

"No," I said. "Zack and I will drive Shane and Sophie home." I turned to Nick. "Go walk Mephisto."

"Why me? She's home now. Why can't she walk her own dog?"

"Because you need time to cool off. Besides, Mephisto has taken a shine to you lately."

"He likes you better."

I pointed toward the back door. "Go. Now."

~*~

No one spoke much on the short ride back to Shane's house, but once we'd dropped off our passengers, Zack asked, "Do you believe him?"

"I don't know. I get the feeling we haven't heard the full story."

"That makes two of us."

Not what I wanted to hear. If Zachary Barnes, a man I suspected of being a government spy—no matter how often he denied it—had suspicions regarding Shane Lambert, that upped my worry-meter a hundredfold.

SEVEN

I cashed in some of my comp time to leave work early the following evening. I couldn't afford to get stuck in rush hour traffic and risk arriving home late. We needed to eat an early dinner in order to show up at the high school on time for the winter concert. Both Alex and Nick were scheduled to perform in the Select Choir.

To my amazement, my sons could not only carry a tune, they both possessed perfect pitch—or so I'm told. I've got two tin ears and wouldn't know a C-sharp from an E-flat if my life depended on it. So they certainly didn't inherit their musical gifts from me. I never once remember hearing Karl sing. If he had any musical talent, he took that secret to the grave with him.

When Alex first joined the choir his freshman year, the school music director had presented the students with a long list of foods and beverages they were not allowed to eat prior to a performance. Who knew certain foods were bad for the vocal cords? The list hung prominently on our refrigerator and limited the choir members to a diet consisting only of bland baked or broiled chicken or fish, a selection of veggies and fresh fruits, and room temperature water.

Before leaving for work this morning, I had arranged two cut-up chickens in a large casserole dish, covered it with foil, and placed it in the fridge, ready for whichever boy arrived home first to set it in the oven. I'd also prepared a salad.

On my way out the door I had left a note for Lucille on the kitchen table: Under no circumstances was she to cook the chicken and serve tonight's dinner to her Bolshevik sisterhood, should they pop in, as they often did, for a free lunch.

I picked up Mama, who was attending the concert with us, on my way home. The aroma of baked chicken greeted us as we stepped into the house. I didn't realize until that moment that I'd proverbially held my breath throughout the day in anticipation of arriving home to nothing but chicken bones and an empty salad bowl.

Then again, I had entered a Lucille-free Casa Pollack. As much as I loved the peace and quiet that filled the house whenever she was gone, I couldn't help shake the feeling my mother-in-law was up to something. And when Lucille was up to something, it usually resulted in a confrontation with the police.

"I should warn Harley and Fogarty," I told Zack as we quickly cleaned up the dinner dishes. The boys had already departed, needing to be at the school an hour before the scheduled performance.

"About what?" he asked.

"Lucille. She's plotting something."

"She's always plotting something," said Mama. "They should lock that traitor up and toss away the key."

"Mama!"

"You know you feel the same way, Anastasia."

True, but I wouldn't give my mother the satisfaction of agreeing with her. With Lucille locked up, I'd not only be rid of the communist albatross around my neck, I'd also no longer have to deal with constant invasions of the mooching Daughters of the October Revolution.

A girl can dream, can't she?

~*~

We bumped into Shane Lambert in the high school parking lot. Sophie was also performing in the choir. We invited him to sit with us.

Mama not only didn't flirt with Shane, she even refused to acknowledge his greeting when he said hello to her.

"Does this mean the wedding's off?" he asked Zack.

"Consider yourself lucky."

Once again, Mama either didn't hear the exchange or chose to ignore the two men. After we entered the auditorium, she maneuvered the seating arrangements so that Zack and I were positioned between her and Shane.

"You don't have to be rude to the man," I whispered to her after we had taken our seats.

"Really, Anastasia, I don't know what you're talking about."

"You most certainly do, Mama."

"Fine. One lawbreaking husband was one too many as far as I'm concerned. I have no desire to encourage that man."

When Mama embarks on a husband hunt, she becomes laser focused on snaring her chosen man—whether he wants to be caught or not. "He hasn't broken any laws, Mama. Besides, he was never interested in you."

"A woman always knows when a man is interested, and believe me, that man was interested."

"That man is about fifteen years younger than you."

She lifted an eyebrow. "So? Anyway, it doesn't matter now. I have no desire to strike up a relationship with a jailbird."

At that moment the lights dimmed, thankfully putting an end to the conversation.

~*~

We were standing in the school vestibule waiting for the kids to join us when I noticed Detective Spader, accompanied by Harley and Fogarty, enter the school. The three men scanned the crowded lobby. When Harley and I made eye contact, he tapped Spader on the shoulder and pointed in our direction.

"I knew Lucille was up to something," I whispered to Zack. He followed my gaze, and we both waited for the detective to approach. But Spader bypassed us and stopped directly in front of Shane. "Mr. Lambert," he said.

"Yes?"

"Or should I call you Mr. Arnold?"

"Who?" My head swiveled back and forth as I focused first on Spader, then Shane.

A crowd of parents and students had gathered around our little group, curious to see why the police had entered the school. A few kids pulled out their cell phones and began recording the encounter.

"Lambert is my legal name," said Shane.

"Either way," said Spader. "You're under arrest for the murder of Tammy Arnold."

Mama gasped. She tugged at my sleeve and said, "Now do you believe me?"

"My ex-wife? That's impossible," said Shane. "I haven't seen Tammy since our divorce seventeen years ago."

Spader snorted. "Until yesterday when you strangled her."

Shane's mouth dropped open. "What? You can't be serious! That woman wasn't Tammy, and I had nothing to do with...with..." He sputtered, unable to force the words out. Finally, he said, "I didn't strangle her. I barely exchanged two words with her. I told you that yesterday."

"Now you'll have a chance to tell your story to a jury and see if they believe you," said Spader. He nodded to Harley and Fogarty. "Cuff him, read him his rights, and get him out of here."

Shane cast pleading eyes toward Zack and me. "I don't understand what's going on. I didn't kill that woman. You have to believe me."

I didn't know what to believe. Zack and I had both sensed Shane hadn't been completely truthful with us, but I never expected a bombshell like this.

"Please," he continued, "can I impose on you again to take Sophie?"

I nodded. "Of course."

Sophie, Alex, and Nick arrived as Harley and Fogarty led a handcuffed Shane toward the exit.

"No!" Sophie screamed and rushed toward her father.

Spader intercepted her. For a guy carrying an excess of a hundred pounds, he was surprisingly agile. "Don't," he said, holding her firmly as she tried to wiggle out of his grasp.

Shane twisted his head to look over his shoulder as the police continued to march him to the door. He called to her. "Everything will be okay, Sophie. I promise. Go with Mrs. Pollack."

Harley and Fogarty had reached the school doors and pushed them open. A blast of frigid December air rushed into the lobby as Shane was led out into the cold night.

When the doors closed behind them, Sophie let out a bloodcurdling scream. "No! You can't do this!" She kicked wildly at Spader as he held her with her arms pinned to her body. "You're making a big mistake."

Spader had dealt with some of the most hardened criminals in the state during his tenure as a Newark detective, but he looked completely out of his element here. His eyes beseeched me to intervene. "I don't want to have to arrest her for assault," he said.

In my opinion, no child should ever have to witness her father being dragged away in handcuffs, no matter how egregious the crime. Spader could have handled the situation better—not to mention in a more private setting than a crowded high school lobby.

I had to bite my tongue to keep from giving him a piece of my mind, but that tongue wouldn't remain trapped between my teeth forever. At some point I'd let loose and tell him exactly what I thought of his tactics. Now was not the time, though.

I stepped over to him, placed my hands on Sophie's shoulders, and leaned my head against hers. "Sophie, this isn't going to help. You need to come with me now."

Her body went limp, and she began to whimper. I drew her away from Spader and wrapped her in my arms. "I promise we'll do whatever we can to help your father."

For the second time in two days I drove Sophie and Alex back to the house in Alex's Jeep while Zack first drove Mama home, then dropped Nick off before heading over to the police station.

Sophie was in a state of shock. She silently accepted another pair of pajamas and without any urging on my part, climbed into the spare bed in Lucille's room. However, this time she didn't want anyone to stay with her, not even Alex.

"What's going to happen to her dad?" asked Alex after we returned to the living room.

I shook my head. "Hopefully we'll know more after Zack returns."

"Do you think he killed that woman, Mom?"

I didn't know what to think, but I couldn't bring myself to say that to my son, not with his girlfriend curled up in a fetal position on one of our beds. "I don't know why the police would think he killed a total stranger."

Or was she a total stranger? Spader insisted the woman he'd called Dawn Heathwood yesterday was actually Tammy Arnold, Shane's ex-wife.

Even after a period of seventeen years, I thought it strange that Shane wouldn't recognize the woman he'd married. But I also knew that Spader wouldn't make such a rookie error. He'd been at this for decades, for most of his career as a homicide cop, dealing with murders on an almost daily basis. If Spader insisted the woman was Tammy Arnold, he must have some rock-solid proof to back up that assertion.

And why were Shane and Sophie living under assumed surnames, even if, as Shane had insisted, their new names were legal? Maybe Mama wasn't entirely off base when she suggested Shane and Sophie were in Witness Protection.

Or perhaps Shane had an Order of Protection against his ex-wife, and that's why he had changed his and Sophie's name. Had his ex harmed Sophie in some way?

However, Shane had denied having seen Tammy Arnold since their divorce. Had he lied to Spader when he said he hadn't seen her in seventeen years or did he lie about not recognizing her yesterday? Maybe he had recognized her and killed her to protect Sophie. I hoped that wasn't the case, but something definitely wasn't adding up. Either way, the situation didn't look good for Shane.

EIGHT

Zack didn't return from the police station until after midnight, and when he finally walked into the house, he entered alone.

"Are they charging him?" I asked.

He nodded. "They'll arraign him first thing tomorrow morning. I convinced the D.A. to request bail."

I wondered what sort of pull my photojournalist boyfriend, a man with no deep ties to Union County, had over our district attorney. I knew that sometimes murder defendants were allowed to post bail, but Shane Lambert had no strong ties to the community and as such, would probably be considered a flight risk. "How did you manage that?"

"I played on his sympathies for a young girl new to the area and with no other relatives to care for her."

I raised an eyebrow. "And he bought that?"

"He didn't like the idea of having to put Sophie into foster care."

I didn't buy it. I'm guessing Zack called in a favor or two from one of the alphabet agencies he swears he has no connection to, but I kept my mouth shut. We'd been down that road too many times, and the story never changed.

"The judge has final say, but the D.A. had no objections as long as Shane can come up with the money, agrees to house arrest, and turns over his and Sophie's passports."

"How much money?"

"Three million cash bond."

"I suppose that means Shane stays behind bars for the foreseeable future."

"You'd think so, but Shane said the money wasn't a problem."

Now both my eyebrows shot up toward my hairline. "Curiouser and curiouser."

"I'll say. How's Sophie?"

"Borderline catatonic but she finally fell asleep about an hour ago. With any luck, she won't wake until morning."

"We should get a few hours shuteye." He laced his fingers through mine and led me toward the bedroom.

I left the bedroom door ajar and listened all night, expecting Sophie to wake at some point. At least I needn't worry about Lucille returning at this late hour and causing a fuss over Sophie asleep in the spare bed. By now Lucille would be deep in snore mode—most likely at Harriet Kleinhample's apartment.

I couldn't imagine any of the other Daughters of the October Revolution allowing her to spend the night. As far as I knew, none had previously extended an invitation. Then again, I found it hard to believe even Minion Number One would put up with Lucille's nocturnal noise. At Casa Pollack earplugs often made the difference between a sleepless night and one of sound sleep.

~*~

At five I heard Sophie stir. After a few minutes she shuffled down the hall to the bathroom. Not wanting to startle her, I waited until she returned to the bedroom before slipping out of bed.

Zack rolled over and propped himself up on an elbow. "Did you get any sleep?"

"Not a wink. I'm going to check on Sophie."

"I'll start a pot of coffee."

After a quick trip to the bathroom, I made my way down the hall to Lucille's room. I called quietly from the other side of the curtain, "Sophie?"

When she didn't answer, I swept the curtain aside, discovering an empty room. Had she crawled into bed with Alex? I dreaded finding her in the boys' room. Taking the cowardly way out, I decided to check the other rooms first and found her curled up on the couch in the den. Mephisto sprawled next to her, his head resting on her thigh as he exhaled doggie snores.

"I thought I heard my dad, but..." She stroked the dog's back. "I didn't know dogs snore. I've never had one." Her lower lip quivered, and tears swam in her eyes. "Dad's in jail, isn't he?"

At the sound of her voice, Devil Dog raised his head, opened one sleep eye, and snorted at the interruption. Not noticing anything of interest, he settled back down on Sophie's leg and fell back to sleep.

The heat hadn't kicked on yet, and a chill filled the house. I grabbed a crocheted afghan from the back of the sofa and draped it across our laps, taking care not to cover Mephisto's snout, as I joined her. "Your father has to go before a judge later this morning."

Her voice brightened with hope. "Then he'll come home?"

"If the judge agrees to release him on bail."

"He didn't kill that woman. My Dad wouldn't kill anyone." She beseeched me with her red-rimmed eyes. "You believe me, don't you?"

I cupped both of her hands in mine. I wanted to believe her. Whether I did or not, didn't matter. Right now Sophie needed reassurance that her world wasn't falling apart around her. "Of course." My brain swam with a myriad of questions about Shane Lambert, but I kept them from his daughter.

For one thing, Sophie had no idea the police believed the dead woman was Shane's ex-wife. She and the boys joined us in the school lobby after Spader had dropped that bombshell.

Was Dawn Heathwood, aka Tammy Arnold, also Sophie's mother? According to Shane's timeline, that made sense. And if so, it certainly wasn't my place to break the news of her mother's death to Sophie. Whether Shane had killed her or not, I didn't envy him that conversation.

Zack entered the den carrying two steaming mugs. He handed me a cup of coffee and gave Sophie a cup of cocoa. "I'm going to start breakfast," he said.

"I've decided to call in sick today and also let the kids stay home."

He nodded as he headed back to the kitchen.

"What about me?" asked Sophie.

"What about you?"

"Do I have to go to school today?"

"No, of course not."

She released a shuddering sigh before placing the mug to her lips and taking a tentative sip. Poor kid. Did she really think I'd force her to go to school after her father's arrest last night?

When she finished her cocoa, I said, "Why don't you try to get some more sleep?"

She tossed the afghan from her lap and stood. "I'll try."

~*~

66

A few hours later Zack was about to leave for the courthouse when Sophie ran into the kitchen. Alex followed behind her. "I want to go with you," she said.

Zack shook his head. "I don't think that's a good idea."

"Please! You have to take me!"

I had no idea if a seventeen-year-old would be allowed in the courtroom during an arraignment, but I suspected Sophie would be barred from the proceedings. Besides, given her emotional state, her presence might do her father more harm than good. What if she blurted out something the prosecution could use against him?

"They won't allow a minor in the courtroom during the proceedings," I said. Sophie didn't have to know I was winging it.

"But I could see Dad before or after, couldn't I?"

"No, not unless he's released on bail."

"And if that's the case," said Zack, "I'll bring him right home to you."

"I could wait in the car," she said.

"Sophie, you need to stay here. Zack will call as soon as we know what the judge decides."

She stared at both of us for the longest time, her hands clasped in front of her, silently begging us to reconsider. But neither Zack nor I would cave. Finally Sophie's shoulders slumped and her head bowed. I nodded to Alex, and he gently coaxed her from the room.

~*~

Zack called from the courthouse later that morning. "The judge allowed bail. They're fitting Shane with an ankle monitor now. We'll leave shortly."

"Should I meet you there with Sophie?"

"No, we'll pick her up but not for a few hours."

"I thought Shane was under house arrest."

"He is, but because he's a single parent, he's confined to within the town limits."

"You said you were leaving shortly. Why the delay in picking her up?"

"The cops had a warrant for the house. Sophie's traumatized enough. She doesn't need to walk in on the aftermath of a police search. I'm going to give Shane a hand straightening up first."

"Should I come help?"

"No, stay with Sophie. I'll call when we're finished. How's she doing?"

"About to jump out of her skin but the boys and I are handling it."

I hung up from Zack, turned to leave the room, and nearly collided with Sophie. She bounced up and down on her toes. "I heard the phone ring. Was it Zack? Is my Dad coming home?"

"Yes and yes."

Joy filled her face. "I'll get my coat." She turned to rush out of the room.

I grabbed for her hand. "Hold on."

"Why? What's wrong? You said he's coming home."

"He's going to pick you up here but not for several hours."

Joy segued into worry. "Why?"

"Paperwork. Lots of legal paperwork." It wasn't exactly a lie, merely a manipulation of the timeline. Unfortunately I'm incapable of fibbing with a straight face. I crossed my fingers and hoped Sophie interpreted the smile on my face as one of happiness over her father's release. "Zack said he'd call as soon as they're on their way home."

~*~

When Zack finally called to say he and Shane were on their way,

Sophie took up a position in front of the window. The moment Zack pulled into the driveway, she shot out of the house, not even bothering with a coat, and launched herself at her father as he stepped from the car. Father and daughter clung to each other, neither moving for the longest time.

Zack left them alone and joined me in the house. "How's Shane holding up?"

"Not good. He wants to speak with us before he tells Sophie about her mother."

"He doesn't intend to tell her in front of us, does he?"

"I don't think he's in a state of mind to do it on his own. The man is falling apart."

"Did he tell you anything else?"

Zack shook his head. "He said he'd tell us everything once we got here."

Still wrapped arm-in-arm, Shane and Sophie joined us in the house. "Why don't the two of you go into the living room? I'll make some coffee and hot cocoa."

Shane had other ideas. He placed his hands on either side of his daughter's face and in a voice filled with forced lightheartedness, said, "Why don't you find Alex, Soph? I'd like to speak to Zack and Anastasia alone for a few minutes."

Sophie's brows knit together. "But—"

"Please, Sophie. Only for a few minutes. I promise."

She nodded. "Okay, Dad." Reluctantly she pivoted and exited the kitchen.

Shane removed his coat, draped it over the back of a chair, and took a seat at the kitchen table. He lowered his head into his hands. Zack sat opposite him and waited patiently, not pressuring him to talk, while I made a pot of coffee.

When the coffee finished brewing, I poured three cups and

brought them to the table. After grabbing milk from the fridge, I settled next to Zack.

Shane wrapped his hands around the warm mug. He inhaled a deep breath, releasing it slowly, as if giving himself time to fit together a complex jigsaw puzzle in his mind before offering up any words. After taking a sip of coffee, he started to speak but immediately faltered. He uttered a few words, stopped abruptly, then tried again. "I'm sorry," he finally said. "This is complicated. I'm not sure where to start."

"How about with Dawn Heathwood?" I said. "How could you not recognize your ex-wife? Or did you?"

He stared at me from across the table and shook his head. "I was telling the truth—to both of you and Detective Spader when he interrogated me Sunday night."

"Interrogated?" My eyes widened at the mention of the word. "I thought they just wanted to ask you a few questions at that point."

"In hindsight it was certainly more an interrogation than a friendly Q and A. Especially after he showed me the photo of the two of us together and suggested I had something to do with her death. You can't imagine my shock when he told me last night that Dawn was Tammy. I swear that woman didn't look anything like Tammy. I told him he'd made a huge mistake."

"How did Spader find out?" asked Zack.

"He realized the ID identifying his victim as Dawn Heathwood was bogus. So he ran her prints, and Tammy's name popped up."

"Tammy has a record?" I asked.

"Not necessarily," said Zack. More and more companies require their employees to submit to fingerprinting. She could work for the government or in education or any one of a number of other professions."

"But that's not the case," said Shane. "Apparently Tammy racked up quite a rap sheet over the years, mostly petty crimes like shoplifting, but she was also convicted of embezzlement and spent three years in federal prison."

"*To prison with her!*" squawked Ralph, flying into the kitchen and coming to roost on his favorite spot atop of the refrigerator. "*Measure for Measure.* Act Five, Scene One.

The color drained from Shane's face as he stared wide-eyed and mouth agape at Ralph. "That bird...he—"

"Quotes Shakespeare," I said, thinking back to Shane's earlier visit and realizing he hadn't come in contact with Ralph Sunday night.

"How is that possible?"

"African Greys are quite intelligent," said Zack. He walked over to the refrigerator and offered Ralph his arm. When Ralph hopped on, Zack returned to the table, pulled a sunflower seed from his pocket, and offered it to the bird. Ralph grabbed the seed with his beak.

Shane continued to watch in fascination as Zack fed Ralph from his pocket stash. "But Shakespeare?"

"Ralph spent decades listening to my great-aunt's college lectures," I said. "I suspect he knows every line from every play by heart."

"Fascinating. Have you had him tested?"

Was Shane stalling, or was he deliberately trying to change the subject? I decided the time had come to redirect the conversation back to the more pressing issue. "No, but getting back to Tammy, you knew nothing about her run-ins with the law?"

"I haven't seen or heard from Tammy since she walked out on

us."

"How did Spader learn you were living under an assumed name?" asked Zack.

"I'm not. I legally changed my name and Sophie's."

"Why?" I asked.

"Mostly to protect my daughter."

"From her mother?"

Shane shook his head. "No, Tammy was out of our lives."

"Then from whom?" I asked.

"Others." He turned to Zack. "To answer your question, when Tammy stumbled against me, she dropped her purse. The contents spilled out. I helped her retrieve the items."

"You didn't mention that earlier," I said. "Did you tell Spader about this when he first interviewed you?"

Shane lowered his head. "I didn't think it was important at the time."

"So Spader figured you were hiding something from him."

He sighed. "Big mistake on my part. Tammy's purse was found with her body. My prints were all over the purse and its contents. I'm a former teacher. My prints are in the system. I also had to be fingerprinted again for the name change. When the detective ran the prints, I came up as both Shane Lambert and Shane Arnold. That's all he needed for an arrest warrant."

A chill of foreboding skittered up my spine. This did not look good.

"Even if Sophie never had a relationship with her mother, you have to tell her Tammy is dead," I said. "You don't want her finding out from someone else." Tammy's murder had all the earmarks of making national news. If the media hadn't already gotten wind of the case, they soon would. It was only a matter of time before the vultures set up camp on Shane's front lawn.

"I know." He stared directly at me. "But I need your help."

"It's not my place to tell your daughter her mother is dead."

"No, of course not, but I've overheard some conversations between Alex and Sophie."

"Meaning?" I had no idea how much Alex had told Sophie about Karl's death and its aftermath, but apparently he'd told her enough.

"How did you handle telling your kids about their father when he died?"

"Anastasia's husband wasn't murdered," said Zack. "He suffered a massive heart attack."

"I know."

"He wasn't estranged from his sons," I said. "He loved Alex and Nick and was very much a part of their lives." Only he didn't love them as much as he loved Lady Luck. However, I didn't want to discuss Dead Louse of a Spouse with Shane. Karl's deceit had no bearing on Shane's situation.

Shane raked his fingers through his hair, then lowered his head into his hands again. "Please, just tell me what to say to her. I don't know how to do this."

If Shane was guilty of his ex-wife's murder, he played the wrongly accused quite well. I wanted to believe him, for Alex's sake more than anything. I'd already dealt with a murderous stepfather. The thought of my son involved with a girl whose father might be a cold-blooded killer sent my protective Mama Bear instincts into overdrive.

My gut told me Shane Lambert was a good guy, but could I trust my gut? After all, even good guys sometimes make really bad decisions in the heat of the moment. Is that what had happened between Shane and Tammy on Sunday? I barely knew the man. Maybe it was time to learn more about him. "Tell me about your relationship with Tammy. How did the two of you meet?"

With his head still lowered, he said, "We were in high school together. It's your typical cliché story—mix one senior quarterback and one head cheerleader. Crown them king and queen of the prom. Celebrate with a combination of contraband vodka and raging hormones."

He lifted his head and stared directly at me, his jaw set tightly.

"If you're worried about Sophie and Alex—" I began.

"I hope we have nothing to worry about. I don't want those two making the same mistake Tammy and I made."

Neither did I.

"Anyway," he continued, "the next thing I knew Tammy announced she was pregnant. She never considered abortion. I manned up and did the right thing. We married a week after graduation. Sophie was born nearly eight months later."

Upon first meeting Shane, I pegged him at around fifty, but given his timeline, he couldn't be older than thirty-five or thirty-six. "How long did the marriage last?"

"Not long. I think Tammy had starry-eyed expectations about marriage and motherhood. She quickly realized the reality didn't match her dream. She chafed at being tied down to a husband and baby."

"She never tried to contact you in all these years?" asked Zack.

"Not once."

"And never showed up out of the blue?"

"Never. When we divorced, Tammy made it clear she wanted nothing to do with either Sophie or me."

Tammy may have felt that way at eighteen, but who hasn't regretted a decision from our teen years? At some point she may have had second thoughts about leaving Sophie, especially if someone had pressured her into that decision. "Was she coerced into giving up her parental rights?"

Shane barked out an ironic laugh. "Not only didn't I coerce her, she freely offered. I didn't even have to ask." He shook his head and heaved a loud sigh. "That's why none of this makes any sense. As I said earlier, Dawn Heathwood looked nothing like Tammy. But even if I had recognized her, what possible reason would I have for killing my ex-wife?"

"That woman was my mother?"

NINE

Sophie, flanked by Alex and Nick, stood wide-eyed in the doorway. Hands on hips, she stared at her father.

In a tight, measured voice Shane said, "Sophie, I asked to speak privately with Anastasia and Zack. How long have you been eavesdropping?"

"Long enough to learn the truth. Were you going to tell me?"

"Of course. I was asking Anastasia for advice on how to do that."

"Too late. What was she doing here? How did she find us?"

"I have no idea, Soph. Maybe she hired a private investigator to track us down."

Zack and I both stared at Shane. "Track you down?" asked Zack.

"It's nothing cloak and dagger," he said. "Just more about maintaining our privacy and protecting Sophie."

"You said that was the reason for the name change," I said. "Protecting Sophie from what? If you haven't heard from Tammy since the divorce, what were you afraid of?"

Sophie folded her arms across her chest. "Tell them, Dad."

She walked over to the table and plopped onto the chair next to her father. She stared intently at him, her expression seeming to dare him to divulge a secret they shared.

I turned my attention to Alex. He avoided eye contact with me, quickly pivoting toward the refrigerator. Whatever their secret, Alex knew about it.

I glanced at Nick. His expression showed no evidence of collusion, but he quickly followed his brother to the fridge. After scanning the contents, he walked over to the pantry and pulled out a bag of cookies. "Yo," he said to his brother, indicating the Oreos.

Alex nodded and closed the fridge.

"Try again," I said, aiming a *Mom Look* at both of them.

Alex returned to the refrigerator and retrieved a bowl of apples while Nick substituted the cookies for a jar of peanut butter, grabbing a cutting board and two knives before the two of them settled into the two remaining kitchen chairs. They busied themselves cutting apple slices and spreading them with the peanut butter, pretending a lack of interest in the conversation. They failed miserably in their lame attempt to fool me.

I wasn't pleased with my sons' involvement in the Lambert family drama, but if I didn't allow them to stay, they'd only hear everything later from Sophie. I glanced over at Alex. He definitely knew far more than I did at this point.

Shane nodded in agreement with his daughter. He then turned his attention to Zack and me. "After Tammy and I split, Sophie and I moved back in with my parents. During the day I worked in construction, attending classes at night. Teaching seemed the logical profession because Sophie and I would have similar schedules."

This certainly explained why he looked so much older than he was. Rugged good looks only went so far. A physical life working outdoors and burning the proverbial candle at both ends had taken their toll, prematurely aging him.

"As you can imagine," he continued, "it took quite a few years, but I finally graduated. Once certified, I secured a position teaching history and economics at a high school in a neighboring town."

"Where was Tammy all this time?" I asked.

Shane shrugged. "I have no idea. Like I said, as soon as the divorce was final, she left town."

"What about her family?" I asked. "She never returned to visit them?"

"Her folks had died in a car crash our junior year. A local minister and his wife took her in, but I think they were relieved when we married. Tammy didn't exactly follow their rules—or anyone else's rules."

"And she had no other family? Grandparents? Aunts and uncles?"

"Not that she ever mentioned."

"You said you were protecting Sophie," said Zack. "What did you mean?"

"I was getting to that," said Shane. He stood and walked to the coffee maker to pour himself another cup before continuing. "Years ago I'd gotten in the habit of buying a lottery ticket once a week. Never won more than a few dollars until last summer when I hit it big."

"Wow!" said Nick, practically jumping out of his chair. "How much did you win?"

"Nick!"

He flashed me a sheepish grin. "Sorry, Mom, but aren't you curious?"

Sophie bowed her head to avoid eye contact with anyone and nibbled on a wedge of apple. "Really, really big," she mumbled.

My assessment of Shane immediately skyrocketed. Here's a guy who scored a huge lottery windfall, yet his teenage daughter worked part-time at Starbucks. According to Alex, Sophie was saving to buy a car. Shane Lambert definitely understood the finer points of parenting.

Too many parents—Ira being a prime example—give their children everything on a platinum platter and wind up creating spoiled offspring with huge senses of entitlement. I had no doubt that the day Ira's twins Melody and Harmony turned sixteen, they'd each get their learner's permits and their own cars.

"Were you worried about someone kidnapping Sophie?" asked Zack.

Shane returned to his seat. "Exactly. Don't ever let anyone tell you the day you win the lottery your worries are over."

The guy had obviously never faced the prospect of setting up housekeeping in a cardboard box. A lottery windfall would certainly solve my financial problems. I'd considered the risk worth taking—if only I could afford to play.

"We had moved to North Dakota a few years earlier," Shane continued, "after both my folks passed. Sophie took their deaths hard, especially my mom's. She was diagnosed with cancer. Her death was slow and painful."

"She was the only mother I've ever known," said Sophie.

Alex reached for Sophie's hand. They exchanged sympathetic smiles.

"Even though North Dakota is one of the few states where winners can remain anonymous," said Shane, "word quickly spread in the small town where we lived."

"I think it was the owner of the luncheonette where Dad bought the ticket," said Sophie. "He knew he sold the winning ticket. He probably scanned his video surveillance and compared it with his lottery sales for the week."

"Or it could have been someone at the lottery commission," said Shane. "Or the law office where I set up a trust for Sophie and established a charitable foundation with the proceeds. There's no way to know how the information got out."

"So much for remaining anonymous," said Alex.

"All of a sudden the phone didn't stop ringing," said Shane. "Day and night. Strangers with sob stories, scammers with investment deals, people claiming to be long-lost relatives, even the parents of some of my students—everyone wanted a piece of my winnings. But that wasn't the worst of it. I started receiving anonymous threats against Sophie."

"That's why you moved here?" I asked.

"We packed up a few things in the middle of the night and left without telling anyone," said Sophie. "We even smashed our cell phones and tossed them into a Dumpster. Dad was afraid some hacker would track us. He bought us new phones with new numbers once we stopped in Minneapolis."

"Is that why you're not on any social media?" asked Nick.

"And she won't be," said Shane. "Ever."

Sophie turned to Nick. "You looked me up?"

"Hey, you're dating my brother. I was curious about you."

"Dad made me delete all my accounts."

"That's also why I changed our names," said Shane. "We established residency in Minnesota while I dealt with that. A legal name change now involves far more time and red tape than it once did. Then we headed east. I wanted to put as much distance as possible between our old life and our new life."

"And yet Tammy found you," I said.

"My guess is she somehow got wind of my lottery winnings and hired someone to find me."

"Why?" asked Nick.

"Probably to worm her way back into our lives so she could get her hands on the money."

Zack and I quickly exchanged a knowing look. Shane claimed he had no reason to kill Tammy, but that sure sounded like motive to me.

Shane must have caught our quick exchange. "I would have gladly given Tammy money had she asked."

"Why?" asked Sophie.

"Because I'm responsible for screwing up your mother's life."

I inwardly scoffed. Tammy screwed up her own life. Yes, Shane's sperm cavorted with one of her eggs and produced Sophie, but Tammy was complicit in that act and also responsible for every decision she'd made afterwards. No one forced her into a life of crime.

"It's only money," said Shane. "We have more than we'll ever need. Although…" He grew thoughtful.

"What?" I asked.

"Maybe money wasn't the reason Tammy showed up. Given her physical transformation, she spent a fortune on plastic surgery." He paused again before adding, "That costs megabucks, right?"

"Unless she went broke from all those surgeries," I said. "Insurance wouldn't have covered any of it."

Sophie turned to her dad. "What was different about her?"

"You've never even seen a photo of your mother?" I asked.

She shrugged. "Dad kept a few pictures in case I ever asked

about her, but I ripped them up when I was in kindergarten."

"Why?" asked Nick.

She shrugged. "I really don't remember. I guess I was angry with her for leaving me. All my friends had mothers. I only had a grandmother."

Shane frowned. "You didn't just rip them up; you systematically tore them into smaller and smaller pieces until there was nothing left but a mound of confetti."

"Did I?"

"You don't remember?"

Sophie shook her head.

Shane turned to me. "Sophie had anger issues back then, but we worked through them."

Given my own sons' reactions to their father's duplicity, I certainly understood. At least Alex and Nick were older at the time and could voice their anger. I may not have taken any psychology courses in college, but I knew enough about the subject to realize at such a young age Sophie may even have subconsciously blamed herself for Tammy's desertion.

"Whatever," said Sophie. "So if my mother didn't look anything like the dead woman, what did she look like?"

Shane squinted up at the ceiling as if trying to remember. "Your mother was small-breasted with an athletic build. No curves. And she never had high cheekbones or pouty lips like the woman at the crafts fair. You can change hair color for a few dollars with a box from the drug store, but if that was Tammy, she underwent a total reconstruction from her face down to her butt."

Alex had sat silently listening throughout the conversation, probably because he already knew so much, but now he said, "Just because she turned out to be Sophie's mom doesn't mean her dad killed her."

On the surface Shane's story made sense. However, no one knew why Tammy had shown up after so many years, and that was a huge missing element. In addition, why had she kept her identity from Shane? Or had she? We only had Shane's word that she merely thanked him once again for breaking her fall, then left.

In my non-expert opinion, either Detective Spader had more evidence against Shane and was keeping mum about it, or he had an extremely weak case. Knowing Spader, I doubted he'd make an arrest based on an extremely weak case.

"Someone out there is going to get away with murder, and Sophie's dad will go to prison unless we find the real killer," said Alex.

"*We?*" I stared at my son.

"Alex told me you'd solved some murders, Mrs. Pollack. Would you help prove dad's innocence?"

"Please, Mom," said Alex. "You have to help."

"Mom," said Nick, "you promised!"

Alex turned to his brother. "Promised what?"

"That she'd stop putting herself in danger."

"Nick is right," said Zack. "This is a matter for the police."

"But that man is going to put Dad in prison, and he didn't do anything wrong," said Sophie. Tears began streaming down her face again. "You have to help him!"

"Sophie," said Shane. He leaned over and wrapped his arm around his daughter. "Listen to me. I've hired a very good defense attorney with a staff of experts at his disposal. They'll find a way to prove my innocence. We don't need to get Anastasia or anyone else involved."

"No, Dad!" She slammed her palms onto the table, startling Ralph. He squawked once, flapped his wings and took flight, heading into the dining room.

"Sorry," said Sophie. "I didn't mean to startle him."

"Ralph is used to sudden outburst," I said. "Don't worry about it."

She nodded. "But innocent people do go to prison, don't they?"

I ached for Sophie, but I had to think of my own kids. If I kept sticking my nose where it didn't belong, at some point my luck would run out, and I'd leave them orphaned.

I looked down at my bandaged wrist. If Zack hadn't come home when he did Saturday, my family would be planning my funeral right now. "I don't know that there's anything I can do to help, Sophie."

"Mom," said Alex.

"Mom," said Nick.

Both boys pleaded with me for opposing reasons. I turned to Zack. "Is there anything you can do?"

"I'll make a few calls first thing tomorrow morning."

"I don't understand," said Shane. "What can you do? You're a photographer."

"Zack has certain connections," I said.

"What sort of connections?" asked Shane.

"Ones he doesn't talk about."

Making eye contact with me, Zack shook his head. "You never give up, do you?"

I shrugged. "Someone's jumping to conclusions. I was thinking of Patricia." Patricia Tierney was Zack's ex-wife. Like Shane and Tammy, they'd married too young and quickly split. However, unlike Shane and Tammy, they never had children and have continued to maintain a friendly relationship. Patricia's twins even call Zack Uncle Zacky.

Zack shot me a wry smile. "Sure you were."

Busted. But I simply smiled back at him. He'd never convince me he didn't have a side gig as one of the good guys on the government's payroll. Or perhaps photojournalism was the side gig—AKA his cover.

Truthfully, I'd love to believe him. Every time he jetted off on assignment I worried I'd never see him again. Zack spent far too much time in remote Third World nations filled with drug lords, terrorists, or civil unrest—often all three. The needle on my Skepticism Meter had frozen permanently in the red zone, and no matter how often he denied living a clandestine life, that needle refused to budge.

"How can this Patricia person help?" asked Shane.

"She's an assistant DA in Manhattan," said Zack. "And I don't know that she can, but she has connections on this side of the Hudson River. She may be able to learn why Spader has his sights set on you."

"I doubt she'd find something my lawyer's people won't find," said Shane.

"You might be surprised," I said, but as the words tumbled from my mouth, another thought struck me. "We've overlooked something," I said.

Everyone stared at me. "What?" asked Shane.

"You assumed Tammy had tripped and fallen into you. Given the circumstances, doesn't that seem far too coincidental to be believable?"

"Now that you mention it," said Shane. "What are the odds?"

"Exactly. What if you were set up?

TEN

"You may be onto something," said Zack.

"Set me up for what?" asked Shane.

"What if Tammy never intended to divulge her identity to you?" I suggested. "What if her plan was to have you fall for Dawn Heathwood?"

"And marry her?" asked Shane. "I'm not following you. She had her chance and walked away."

"Million of dollars might have made her reconsider," I said.

"It's one possibility," said Zack. "Maybe that's also why she was lurking near us at the Armory and why she later struck up a conversation with Sophie. She was laying the groundwork for establishing a relationship."

"She may have deliberately tripped and fallen into you," I said. "It's the classic 'cute meet' that happens all the time in romantic comedies."

"Only her scheme wouldn't have worked," said Shane.

"Never underestimate the power of a woman on a mission,"

said Zack.

Was that a dig over my refusal to believe Zack had no secret life as a government operative? I glanced in his direction; he offered me a catbird smile. Yup, definitely a dig.

I turned back to Shane. "What makes you so sure her plan would fail?"

"The Tammy I remember looked like the girl next door, even if her rule-breaking personality didn't match that wholesome image. I'm not into plastic Barbies. Besides, if she showed up after all these years to try to get her hands on my money, she'd have been sorely disappointed."

"I'm confused," I said. "Didn't you say you would have been happy to give her some?"

"Enough to help her out, but the bulk of the estate is tied up in a trust for Sophie and a charitable foundation I administer. I can't touch the principal of either."

"If she was after your money," said Zack, "she wouldn't have settled for a token handout. She'd keep coming back for more."

"Marrying you would have given her far more access to a steady income stream," I said.

"True," said Shane. "I hadn't thought of that."

Or had he? Reluctantly, I took a baby step toward Slater's camp. Maybe he knew something I didn't. What if Shane had lied about not realizing Dawn was Tammy? He may have offered her money, only to have her demand far more.

I studied Shane. I wanted to believe him, but doubt blasted me from all angles. What did we really know about the man? Next to nothing other than what he'd told us, and we had no way of knowing how much of that was true.

However, as his ex-wife, Tammy knew about Shane's past. Did skeletons lurk in his closet? Had she tried to blackmail him? Is that what got her killed?

I kept these thoughts to myself for now, preferring to believe in the man until concrete evidence proved otherwise.

"So who killed her?" asked Alex.

"And why?" added Sophie.

"That's the multi-million-dollar question," I said, no pun intended. "We don't know where she went after leaving the Armory. She may have hooked up with the wrong person Sunday evening or been the victim of a random mugging gone wrong."

Anything could have happened to Tammy after she left the Armory, another reason why I suspected either Detective Spader had jumped to the wrong conclusion, or he had additional evidence leading him to zero in on Shane to the exclusion of all other suspects. Too many unanswered questions moved me back to straddling the line between Spader and Shane.

Not only didn't we know Tammy's true motive, we knew nothing of her whereabouts prior to showing up at the holiday crafts fair. When had she arrived in the area? Had she come alone or with someone? Was that someone an accomplice in her scheme or simply a means to an end? Where was she living? Had she rented an apartment, or was she staying at a local hotel?

I looked around the table. None of us had any answers, only questions, and the more we pondered over the situation, the more questions arose. A man's life hung in the balance. His daughter was devastated. My sons were pulling me in opposite directions.

Someone had to do something. Since Spader didn't seem inclined to delve elsewhere, how could I uncover the truth while appeasing both of my sons and keeping all my body parts safe and sound?

And what if the truth led me to agree with Spader?

Before I had a chance to dwell on that disturbing thought for too long, the doorbell rang. Lucille wouldn't ring the bell. Neither would Mama. Besides, she'd never pop in at this hour of the day. She'd expect me to be at work. "I'll get it," I said, foreboding churning in my belly.

As I left the kitchen, I held my breath, hoping I'd find a gaggle of proselytizing pamphleteers standing on the other side of my front door rather than my not-so-friendly neighborhood detective. On my way through the living room, I glanced out the front window and breathed a sigh of relief when I didn't see Spader's unmarked police car at my curb. Instead I saw a black Mercedes SUV with dealer plates parked at the end of my driveway.

I knew only one person who drove vehicles with dealer plates—Ira. Worse yet, he wasn't alone. Wearing huge scowls of utter disdain, Melody, Harmony, and Isaac stood several feet behind their father.

What in the world were they doing here this time of day? I thought back to my last conversation with Ira. Not only do I distinctly remember telling him I'd let him know about his plan for a celebratory dinner, I definitely remember telling him weeknights were out of the question.

I didn't realize I'd groaned out loud until Zack came to investigate. "What's wrong?"

"Ira and his kids are here. Any chance we can all sneak out the back door and hide in your apartment?"

Zack speared me with the kind of look I usually reserve for my kids when I'm not pleased with them—in other words, a *Mom Look*. Since Zack has never had kids, he apparently picked up the look from me. Sometimes I'm not a very good influence.

"He knows we're home. Our cars are parked in the driveway in front of his."

"I suppose that's as obvious as a flashing neon sign."

"Pretty much."

By this time Nick, Alex, Shane, and Sophie had joined us at the window. "Why are they all here?" asked Nick.

There was only one way to find out. I stepped into the foyer, tried to force the annoyance from my features, and swung open the front door.

A huge smile filled Ira's face. "Anastasia, how wonderful! I didn't expect to find you home."

"What are you doing here, Ira?" When his expression of happy surprise morphed into a frown of concern, I realized I'd failed miserably at masking my annoyance.

Ira being Ira, he pasted a smile back on his face and stepped inside without being invited. "I brought the kids to see the new house." He motioned for them to follow him. "I thought if Alex and Nick were home, they might like to join us. This is great. You can come, too, and we'll all go out to dinner afterwards."

"Do they have to?" asked Melody, her arms crossed over her chest. Or maybe it was Harmony. I can't tell the two of them apart. Whichever twin it was, she speared me with an evil eye that rivaled any I'd ever received from my mother-in-law or her cohorts. Her sister and brother joined her in a triple whammy glare.

"Of course, they do," said Ira. "Don't be rude." He pulled his phone from his pocket. "I'll call Flora. We'll pick her up on the way."

"Wait." I placed my hand over his phone to prevent him from making the call. "Tonight is not going to work out, Ira. I told you on Sunday that weeknights aren't good for us."

"But you're home, and the twins and Isaac did their homework in the car on the way over. So there's no problem. Although, we'll have to take two cars. Mine only holds seven people. What do you feel like eating?"

"Ira, we're busy this evening," said Zack, stepping into the foyer.

Ira turned to face him. That's when he noticed Shane and Sophie standing in the living room with Alex and Nick. Ira immediately broke into car dealer mode and strode past Zack toward Shane. He extended his hand. "Hello, I'm Ira Pollack, Anastasia's brother-in-law."

"*Half*-brother-in-law," I said, following him.

Shane accepted Ira's hand and forced a smile, his discomfort obvious to everyone except Ira.

"And you are?" he asked Shane, ignoring my comment.

Before Shane could answer, Zack placed his hand on Ira's upper arm and drew him away from Shane. "He's a neighbor."

"Well then," said Ira. "That makes us neighbors as well. My kids and I are moving to Westfield. I recently bought a home on Prospect Street."

Prospect Street? Ira hadn't previously mentioned the location of his new house. Shane and Sophie lived on Prospect Street. And a sold sign was stuck in the lawn of the newly constructed McMansion next door to them. The last thing Shane Lambert and his daughter needed right now was Ira Pollack and his three brats as next-door neighbors.

Alex apparently had a similar thought. His features clouded with worry as he wrapped a protective arm around Sophie's shoulders. "Where on Prospect Street?"

"Near the border with Scotch Plains," said Ira.

Alex exhaled his relief. Ira's new home was more than a mile from Shane and Sophie.

"Would you like to come with us to see it?" asked Ira.

"Can't," said Alex. "We're sort of in the middle of something right now."

Ira turned to Nick. "What about you, Nick?"

"I'm right in the middle of that something along with Alex."

"Now can we get out of here?" asked Harmony. Or Melody.

"Yeah, I'm bored," said Isaac. "Let's go already."

Perfect timing. I placed my hand on Ira's arm. "Go show your kids their new home. And please, next time call first before dropping by. We really need to continue what we were doing before you arrived."

Ira shifted his gaze between Shane, Zack, and me. I could tell he was dying to know what was going on, but it was none of his business. Besides, I really resented him barging in on us.

"I didn't call because I wasn't expecting you to be home, Anastasia. What if I take the twins and Isaac to see the house and come back to pick you all up for dinner?"

"Not tonight," I said, urging him toward the front door.

"I could order something in, then."

I shook my head. "Not tonight," I repeated more forcefully.

He looked like I'd just informed him Santa Claus, the Easter Bunny, and the Tooth Fairy don't exist. His kids had the exact opposite reaction. Isaac opened the front door, and the three of them raced outside.

"Another time, then?" asked Ira, pausing at the door.

"Another time. But please, call first."

His shoulders slumped as he stepped outside and walked toward his car, glancing back once as I shut the door.

As always, when it comes to Ira, I'm conflicted. One part of me feels sorry for him, but the other part of me is growing increasingly angry from the way he tries to insert himself into my life. "Why is it that every time I turn him down," I asked

Zack, "I feel like I've kicked a puppy?"

"Ira isn't as pathetic as he appears. He's a master of manipulation. It's probably what makes him such a successful salesman."

"People buy cars from him because they feel sorry for him?"

"He plays on their sympathies."

"But I turned him down."

"This time. He knows he'll get his way eventually. You're a soft touch."

I raised an eyebrow. "Really?"

"Didn't you open your home to a woman who's never had a kind word for you in two decades?"

I sighed. "Point taken. Maybe I need to grow a backbone."

He kissed the top of my head. "No need. Your big heart more than compensates."

"Hey, Mom," said Nick. "Any chance of cooking dinner before things get too mushy?"

Dinner! I reached for Zack's wrist to check the time.

"We should get going," said Shane. "It's been a long day, but we'll need a lift home."

"Stay," said Zack. "We'll order in."

"Only if you let me pay," said Shane.

~*~

After dinner Alex offered to drive Shane and Sophie home while Nick, Zack, and I cleaned up. Not that there was much to clean up after a dinner of take-out Thai. I was once seventeen, too, but all I said was, "Don't stay too long. It's a school night."

"Yes, ma'am." He gave me a peck on the cheek and grabbed his coat and keys, happy to play chauffeur to his girlfriend and her father.

"I'll kick him out by nine-thirty," said Shane. Then he added,

"Thank you both...for everything. I don't know how Sophie and I would get through this on our own. Your kindness means so much to both of us right now."

Before leaving, Sophie hugged both Zack and me, then Nick. "Thank you for believing in my dad," she said.

But did I? I mentally crossed all my digits and smiled, hoping my eyes didn't betray me.

Ten minutes later while Nick walked Mephisto and Zack lugged the trashcans to the curb for the morning pick-up, my phone rang. When I checked the display, my heart plummeted to my stomach.

Is it just me, or are all mothers genetically conditioned to worry from the moment their children leave the womb? Each time my son gets behind the wheel, I live in fear that he won't arrive home in one piece. I told myself that if Alex was well enough to place a call, whatever had happened couldn't be that bad. But just in case, I also sent up a quick prayer to the God of Worrywart Mothers and their Seventeen-Year-Old Sons-With-Drivers-Licenses before I answered the call.

"Just tell me you're okay," I said without so much as a hello.

"I'm fine, Mom. And so is the car if that's your next question."

I exhaled a huge sigh of relief. "But?"

"Sophie and her dad were robbed."

ELEVEN

"The place looks trashed," said Alex.

"Get out of the house now, Alex!"

"Relax, Mom. We're not in the house."

Relax? My son may have walked into a home where armed robbers were lurking, and he's telling me to relax? I don't think so. "Where are you?"

"In the car. As soon as Sophie's dad opened the door and saw what happened, he wouldn't let us in. He said the robbers might still be inside. He even made me move the car off the driveway and park it across the street and down a few doors."

"Good. Did Shane call the police?"

"He's on the phone with them now."

"Lock the car doors. We're on our way."

I grabbed my coat and spun Zack around the moment he walked back into the house, leaving the door unlocked for Nick. I knew his dog-walking route. We'd pull up alongside him on our way and let him know what had happened. As we drove down the street, the first snowflakes began to fall. "Are we supposed to get a storm tonight?"

"Not unless the forecast changed," said Zack. "Last I heard, the prediction called for only a light dusting."

"Do you think the break-in is a coincidence?"

He shrugged. "Possibly, but I doubt it."

"That makes two of us." At least a break-in, if connected to Tammy's murder, lent credibility to Shane's story. He'd spent last night in jail. Once released on bail, Zack had helped him clean up the mess from the police search of his home. He had no opportunity to stage a robbery in order to redirect Spader onto a wild goose chase hunting for a phony suspect.

"One thing puzzles me, though," he said.

"Only one thing?"

"Shane has an alarm system, and I remember him setting it as we left the house earlier."

"You saw him punch in the code?"

"I stood right next to him. The alarm was definitely enabled when we left the house."

"Then why didn't it go off and notify the security company?"

"Good question."

We arrived to find two squad cars, their lights flashing, parked in front of Shane's house. Detective Spader's black unmarked sedan idled behind them. Two officers walked the property, sweeping the area with powerful Maglites, catching snowflakes in their beams. Under normal circumstances, I might have remarked on the dancing fairies imagery. Not tonight.

Spader stood on the sidewalk speaking with Shane. Alex and Sophie hovered nearby. Curious neighbors had gathered across the street. This was a part of town where residents viewed police activity on their street as a threat to their property values.

As we approached, two other officers exited the house. "All clear, Detective. No sign of anyone inside."

Spader nodded and said, "Canvas the neighborhood."

One officer headed across the street to speak with the neighbors while the other hopped into his squad car and slowly drove down the street in search of suspects. Spader turned back to Shane. "Come with me, Mr. Lambert. We're going to do a walk-through. I want you to tell me what you notice missing."

The wind picked up and the temperature dipped as Zack, Alex, Sophie, and I waited on the sidewalk. Icy flakes stung my cheeks; snow swirls whipped around our feet. None of us wore hats or boots, and I'd rushed out of the house without gloves. "Let's wait in the car," I said.

Zack and I had driven over in his Boxster, so the four of us piled into Alex's Jeep. He turned on the engine and cranked up the heat. "How bad did it look in the house?" I asked.

"Hard to tell," said Alex. "We only made it as far as the foyer when we saw the mess in Mr. Lambert's office."

"Papers everywhere," said Sophie. "The file cabinet and desk drawers were pulled out and dumped. Dad rushed us out of the house."

"Someone was looking for something," said Zack.

"Well, if they're looking for money, they're out of luck," said Sophie. "Dad doesn't keep very much in the house."

"The intruder wouldn't know that," I said.

Sophie shuddered. "Still cold?" asked Alex. He reached over and cranked up the heat another notch.

She shook her head. "No, it's just..." She turned around to face Zack and me. "What if whoever broke into our house is the person who killed my...killed Tammy?"

Although I had my doubts about the random nature of the

break-in, I didn't want to add to Sophie's mounting fears. "Most robberies that occur in town are kids looking to steal prescription pain killers or small items they can easily pawn to buy drugs. The cops catch them very quickly."

Sophie looked skeptical. "But what if it wasn't? He could come back."

"Let's wait until we learn what was taken," said Zack. "That will give us better insight into the culprit's identity."

Twenty minutes later Shane emerged from the house. When Alex flashed the Jeep's lights to let him know our location, he waved to us, indicating we should join him. The four of us exited the Jeep, hurried across the street, and entered the house. Spader stood in the foyer.

"Nothing of value is missing," said Shane.

"Nothing?" asked Sophie. "Somebody just decided to break in and trash our house for the fun of it?"

"It happens occasionally," said Spader. "Juvenile delinquents mostly but sometimes drug addicts."

Or psychotic Mafia loan sharks out to make a point. However, Ricardo, the Mafioso who had not only trashed my house but nearly killed me last winter, now cooled his heels in an out-of-state federal prison and would remain locked up for life. Same for Lawrence Tuttnauer, my mother's ex. If either had orchestrated revenge from behind bars, they'd target me directly. Or worse yet, they'd go after my loved ones, inflicting a pain far greater than any physical harm they could cause me. As I looked at my son, I fought to suppress the shudder of fear threatening to course through my body.

Shane and Sophie weren't family. Besides, I'd only met them several days ago. Neither Ricardo nor Lawrence would know or care about Shane and Sophie.

"When they don't find alcohol, drugs, or money," continued Spader, "they get angry and make a mess before they leave. This is minor compared to some damage I've seen. The crime scene unit is on their way to dust for prints."

Shane ran his hands through his hair. "I can't believe I forgot to set the alarm."

"You didn't forget," said Zack. "I saw you set it."

That caught Spader's attention. "Are you sure?"

"Positive."

Spader frowned. He turned to Shane. "Did you change the password from the default setting? Too many homeowners don't."

"I'm not one of them."

Spader grimaced. "Then I doubt we'll find any fingerprints or other evidence of the intruder's identity."

"Why?" asked Sophie.

"Our alarm is state-of-the-art," said Shane. "The only way to disable it is by hacking into the system."

"And anyone skilled enough to do that," said Zack, "isn't going to be dumb enough not to wear gloves."

"Which means we're not dealing with a random break-in," said Spader. "The perp only hit a couple of rooms, and he didn't take any valuables. At first I thought maybe something spooked him, and he fled before he finished. But in light of this information about the alarm, it's obvious the guy was looking for something specific. Any idea what that something might be, Mr. Lambert?"

We all turned to face Shane. He held his arms akimbo and shook his head. "I don't have a clue."

"Then it could have been the same person who killed Tammy," said Sophie.

Spader opened his mouth to say something, but when I glared at him, he pursed his lips into a tight line.

Sophie took a step toward him. Hands on her hips, she bristled. "This proves my dad didn't kill Tammy. I told you, but you wouldn't believe me."

Shane drew Sophie back. "The detective has to do his job, Sweetheart."

Tears welled in Sophie's eyes and spilled onto her cheeks. "Then he sucks at his job. The real killer is still out there, and now he's coming after us."

"Out of the mouths of babes," I muttered.

Now it was Spader's turn to glare at me. "You have something to say, Mrs. Pollack?"

"Don't," said Zack under his breath.

He was right. No good would come from antagonizing Detective Spader. Instead of going on the offensive, I calmly suggested a possible alternate theory. "If the intruder wasn't interested in money, drugs, jewelry, or electronics, is it possible he was searching for information? Maybe a computer file? Can you log on and check the history?"

"No," said Shane.

"Why not?"

"Detective Spader is currently in possession of all our computers."

"*What!*" Sophie's voice climbed several octaves. She glared at Spader. "You took my computer?"

Shane placed his hand on her shoulder to restrain her, but she shrugged it off and moved well into Spader's personal space. "I don't believe this. How am I supposed to do my schoolwork?"

"You'll get the computer back as soon as forensics is done with it," said Spader.

Sophie stamped her foot. "Not good enough. I have three papers due before Christmas break. All my research and notes are on my computer."

"I'll see what I can do about speeding up the process."

"While you're at it, you can also see about dropping the charges against my dad and go find the real killer."

Shane grabbed her arm and pulled her away from Spader. "That's enough, Sophie. This isn't helping."

She jabbed a finger in Spader's direction. "Neither is anything he's doing."

~*~

For the second time in two days the crime scene unit descended on Shane's house, but they kept their search to the two rooms where the intruder had rifled through Shane's possessions—his office and the master bedroom.

At first we waited in the foyer with Detective Spader, but as the snow continued to fall, I grew antsy. The earlier light dusting of flakes had morphed into wet, heavy snow. The increasing winds suggested an impending blizzard that the weather report had failed to note. Alex had experienced limited driving during snowy conditions. My protective Mom Gene kicked in. "We need to leave before the weather gets worse," I said.

Sophie reached for Alex's hand. Her eyes, filled with fear, darted between her father and me. "What if the burglar comes back while we're asleep?"

"I'll change the password on the alarm," said Shane. "You don't need to worry, Soph. We'll be safe."

Sophie wasn't convinced. "But what if he hacked in without needing the password? He could do it again."

A far more disturbing thought grabbed hold of me. While Shane continued to calm his daughter, I surreptitiously indicated to Spader that I'd like a private one-on-one.

He nodded before pointing toward the kitchen and saying, "Mrs. Pollack, a word? The rest of you wait here."

Zack wrinkled his brow and was about to say something, but I shook my head and held up my hand to stop him from objecting. Then I followed Spader.

When we arrived in the kitchen, he heaved himself onto one of the bar stools at the island. After running his hand over the five o'clock shadow—now grown to nine o'clock—covering his jaw, he indicated I should take a seat. I deliberately placed an empty stool between us to avoid any thigh fraternization. Although Spader had lost some weight recently, shrinking his triple chin to double, he hadn't lost enough to prevent excess poundage from spilling over the edges of the stool.

"What's on your mind, Mrs. Pollack?"

"How likely is it that a burglar would have the tech skills to bypass a state-of-the-art alarm system?"

He raised an eyebrow. "You don't think it was a burglary, do you?"

"Are you aware that Shane received threats against Sophie prior to moving here?"

He nodded. "After he won the lottery. He claims that's why he changed their last name and moved east."

"You don't believe him?"

"I never said that. Where are you going with this?"

"Suppose the intruder wasn't after information?"

"You think he wanted to kidnap the kid?"

"Isn't it possible? Maybe he trashed the house out of frustration when he found no one home."

"If that were the case, why didn't he wreak havoc? Topple furniture? Break things?" Spader shook his head. "No, he was definitely after something specific, something he suspected he'd find in a file, either paper or digital. I figure he didn't expect not to find any computers in the house. That's why he ransacked the file cabinet and desk drawers. On the surface it might look like he trashed the place, but I'm guessing he executed a methodical search."

"Then why would he leave evidence of his search?" I asked. "Especially if he came up empty?"

"To send a message? Scare the crap out of Lambert?"

"So you agree with me?"

"It's a working theory, Mrs. Pollack. I won't dismiss it, but I like mine better. Lambert's hiding something. I think he knows what the guy was after but isn't saying."

"I have another working theory."

He sighed. "I'm not surprised. You don't think the guy's guilty of murder, do you?"

"I don't."

"The evidence points to him."

"But it's all circumstantial, easily explained."

"Except for the eyewitness."

TWELVE

Good thing I was sitting because at that moment my legs never would have supported my body. "What eyewitness?"

"The one who places Lambert near where the body was found."

"Meaning Tammy was killed someplace other than where her body was discovered?"

"I didn't say that."

So far Spader had managed to keep a lid on his investigation. Even the news media hadn't yet picked up the story. As far as I knew, Shane wasn't told the location of Tammy's body, let alone the existence of an eyewitness that placed him near the scene. Or maybe he was told, and if so, why had he failed to share that information with us?

Spader eyed me for a moment, scowled, then shrugged. "You might as well know. The story will be all over the eleven o'clock news tonight. I held a press conference earlier."

"I don't suppose you thought of Sophie and what that would do to her?"

"That's where you're wrong. I feel for the kid, but once Lambert was arraigned, I had no choice."

"And?"

"The body was found in a wooded area off Route 22, behind the motel where the deceased was last seen with the suspect."

"Which explains your theory of a planned rendezvous between Shane and Tammy."

"It does."

"Was Tammy staying at that motel?"

"She checked in two days earlier."

"Alone?"

"Alone."

This didn't bode well for Shane. "How credible an eyewitness?"

"He had no reason to lie."

"Unless he did. Have you considered your eyewitness might be your killer?"

"I didn't attend the Acme School of Detecting, Mrs. Pollack. We checked out the guy's alibi. It's solid."

"I wasn't accusing you of sloppy investigating."

"Really? Forgive my skepticism."

"This is New Jersey, Detective. You know as well as I do that alibis can be bought."

"Fair enough. But not this time."

"Why is that?"

"The guy was from out of state, here for a job interview and staying in the room next door. My men canvassed the motel guests. He picked Lambert out from a photo array. Said he saw him walking into the motel room with the victim."

"Was Tammy killed at the motel?"

"We have no conclusive evidence one way or the other.

Nothing to indicate a scuffle."

"And no evidence of Shane having been in the room?"

"Nothing other than the eyewitness account."

"No video surveillance?"

"Only at the front door and inside the office."

"Isn't that unusual these days?" Cameras are everywhere. Pick your nose, and you run the risk of becoming the next YouTube sensation.

"Not really. It's the kind of motel known for protecting their customers' privacy."

I raised an eyebrow.

"They offer hourly rates."

"Oh." This definitely fell under the heading of TMI. I suddenly had an overwhelming urge to jump into a scalding hot shower. "Why would a man here for a job interview book a room at such a place?"

Spader answered with a shrug. "Like I said, he's from out of town."

"Did he hear Tammy scream? Call for help?"

He shook his head. "He was leaving his room as they arrived at hers."

"So he only saw the man for a second or two?"

"Correct."

"I have one word for you, Detective."

"What's that?"

"*Rashomon.*"

His eyebrows drew together as the corners of his mouth dipped down. "The movie?"

"Exactly. The one where four people witness a murder and no two accounts are the same. Surely you learned about the Rashomon Effect in detective school." After all, I'd heard of it, and

I've never gone to detective school.

"Yeah, I know about it. Your point?"

"You're basing your entire case against Shane on one eyewitness who briefly saw a man and a woman enter a motel room."

"Not entirely."

"You have additional evidence against Shane? What?"

"I can't share that with you."

There it was, Spader's standard ongoing investigation disclaimer. Maybe he'd be more forthcoming about something else. "How did you find out about the body?"

"Anonymous tip."

"Forgive *my* skepticism, Detective."

He shrugged. "Happens all the time. People are civic-minded, up to a point. They'll report a crime but don't want to get involved beyond tipping us off. You can't blame them. They worry about their own safety. The caller was out walking his dog."

"On Route 22? Who walks a dog on one of the busiest highways in the state?"

"Probably no one, but there's an apartment complex on the other side of the woods. The dog picked up the scent of the body."

"So your theory is Shane killed Tammy and dragged her body into the woods behind the motel without anyone seeing him?"

"More likely he killed her in the woods."

"Because couples always go for a stroll in the woods in freezing temperatures after having sex?"

"I never said they had sex. He could have forced her into the woods."

"But even if Shane did follow Tammy to the motel—and I don't believe for one moment that he did—she could have been killed by someone else after he left."

"You missed your calling, Mrs. Pollack."

"How so?"

"You'd have made one heck of a defense attorney. What makes you so damn sure he's innocent? You said yourself you barely know the guy."

"Call it feminine intuition. What makes you so damn sure he's guilty?"

"Call it decades of experience."

"Meaning?"

"Ninety-nine percent of the time the most likely suspect turns out to be the killer."

"But not *always*?"

"No, not always." As reluctant an admission as I'd ever heard but an admission, nonetheless. He nodded toward the front of the house. "Didn't you want to get home before the snow got worse?"

"Is that your way of saying this conversation is over?"

Spader hoisted himself off the stool. "It is." He swept his hand in front of him to indicate I should precede him back to where the others waited.

When we arrived in the foyer, I noticed Sophie maintained a two-fisted death grip on Alex's hand. I turned to face Spader. With a slight tilt of my head to indicate the teens, I asked, "Can you post a patrol car in front of the house?"

He approached Sophie. Foregoing his usual gruff tone, he said, "We'll keep you and your father safe tonight, Miss Lambert."

Sophie stared at Spader, as if weighing the truthfulness of his words. "Promise?"

When he nodded, she loosened her grip on Alex. Shane wrapped his arm around her shoulders and drew her close to him. "We're in good hands, Soph."

She twisted her neck to make eye contact with him. "Really,

LOIS WINSTON

Dad? There's a killer out there, and those good hands want to lock you up for a murder someone else committed."

"Don't worry, Sophie," said Alex. "My mom's going to find the real killer."

Five pairs of eyes stared at me. Three conveyed hope, one conveyed fear, and one—belonging to the detective—shot me an angry don't-you-dare-go-there warning.

~*~

In near blizzard conditions that no one predicted and with only a few feet of visibility in front of me, I inched home in Alex's Jeep. Zack followed in his Boxster.

Alex flipped on the radio in time to catch the weather reporter saying, "Our bad, folks. All the computer modeling showed this storm staying well off in the Atlantic. Looks like we're in for at least a foot of snow in the city and as much as a foot and a half for the surrounding suburbs." He chuckled. "Mother Nature sure played a joke on us."

"Glad he thinks it's funny," I said. "He's safe in his studio while we're risking life and limb to get home."

As it turned out, that was no exaggeration. The normally five-minute trip through town—ten during rush hour—lasted half an hour. I spun out once, missing a parked car by inches, coming to a stop perpendicular to the road. Luckily, Zack had stayed far enough behind me to avoid T-boning the Jeep.

"This is why I didn't want you driving home," I told my son after swallowing down the rush of adrenaline that had surged through my body and offering up a prayer to the God of Antilock Brakes.

"You never told me you raced at Daytona, Mom. I'm impressed."

"Wise guy."

112

His phone signaled a text. He pulled it from his pocket to check the display. "School's canceled tomorrow."

A surge of relief swept over me once I pulled into the driveway. I turned off the engine, took a deep breath, and said, "I hate snow."

Then I stepped out of the car—and landed ankle deep in the cold white stuff. Of course, I hadn't bothered to slip into a pair of boots before leaving the house, thanks to the incompetent meteorologists who failed to warn us of an impending storm. "And I *really* hate weathermen!"

Alex and I trudged a path through the snow to the back door. Nick met us in the mudroom, a stack of towels in his arms. We removed our coats, shoes, and socks. As we dried off our feet, I heard Zack pull into the driveway.

I stared out the window as he approached the house. "Days like this make me seriously consider moving to Florida."

"You hate Florida," Nick reminded me. "All that heat and humidity."

"At this moment I wouldn't mind a little heat and humidity."

"Except Florida has a *lot* of heat and humidity," said Alex. "And alligators."

"Remind me of that tomorrow when I'm thawing out my frostbitten fingers and toes from hours of shoveling."

Zack entered the house, bringing with him a rush of frigid air. "Nice maneuver back there," he said.

"All those years racing the NASCAR circuit finally paid off," I said.

Nick knit his brows together. "Huh?"

"Mom nearly got us killed," said Alex.

"I did not! I was in total control at all times."

From the expressions on their faces neither Alex nor Zack believed me. Barefoot, I stormed off toward my bedroom to strip out of my wet jeans.

Zack joined me a few minutes later. Ralph sat perched on his shoulder.

"You can't ever leave me," I said eyeing the bird nuzzling his beak against Zack's jaw. "You'd break Ralph's heart."

"That's the only reason I stay."

"Nice to know where I stand in the pecking order."

"Speaking of pecking..." He dipped his head and planted a kiss on my lips before heading over to the armoire to retrieve a pair of sweatpants. Little by little Zack's wardrobe was making its way from his apartment to what used to be Karl's armoire.

"What were you and Spader discussing?" he asked as he stepped out of his jeans and donned a pair of sweatpants.

I filled him in on the conversation. "He insinuated he's got more evidence against Shane."

Ralph squawked in Zack's ear. "*I'll see their trial first. Bring in their evidence. King Lear.* Act Three, Scene Six." Then he lifted off from Zack's shoulder and flew to the top of the armoire.

Zack shook his head and stared at the parrot for a moment before returning to the conversation. "Spader gave you no clue as to what sort of evidence?"

"Not even a hint. It's possible the eyewitness may only have seen a man with a similar build and coloring as Shane, but Spader seems convinced this other evidence clinches the case for him."

"Maybe it does."

"I hope you're both wrong."

"I hope so, too. I like the guy."

"Won't the district attorney have to share whatever he has with Shane's attorney?"

"Eventually."

I plopped face up on the bed and bit down on my lower lip as I stared at the ceiling.

"I know that look. Out with it."

I heaved a deep sigh before speaking. "You're probably going to think this is crazy, but another thought had occurred to me."

Zack settled in next to me. "I'm all ears."

I turned and propped myself up on my elbow to face him. "What if none of this has anything to do with Shane?"

"I'm not following. The guy's ex-wife was murdered. He's the prime suspect. Plus, someone broke into his home today."

"Yes, but what if Lawrence has something to do with all of it?"

Zack sprang up. "Are you suggesting he's orchestrating these crimes from his prison cell? To what end?"

"To mess with me."

"That's crazy."

"Is it? After all, thanks to me, the guy is going to spend the remainder of his life behind bars."

"If that were the case, wouldn't he have his goons go after you and not Shane?"

"You'd think. But Lawrence is so twisted. Maybe this is his way of toying with me for his own amusement. What if he's had someone watching me—watching us—and reporting back to him? Messing with Shane's life could be the first step in a long tail plan to target anyone in my life—even casual acquaintances—to turn me into a cursed pariah. No one would want to have anything to do with me for fear of becoming the next target."

Zack whistled under his breath. "Sounds pretty sick, even for Lawrence."

"Given his prior crimes, I'm not so sure."

"Have you suspected someone's been watching or following you?"

I shook my head. "Only Sunday when Tammy hovered near us during the crafts fair."

"She had her eye on Shane."

"Maybe finding Shane was pure coincidence. Didn't he say Spader told him Tammy spent several years in prison?"

"Are you suggesting Lawrence somehow had a connection to Tammy and hired her to stalk you?" Zack shook his head. "I think your imagination has shifted into overdrive."

I wrinkled my nose. "When you put it like that, it does sound far-fetched. Besides, the government seized all of Lawrence's assets. Where would he get the money to hire a stalker?"

"The Feds seized what they could find. I'm guessing Lawrence has plenty of money stashed in offshore accounts. Having a connection to Tammy seems a stretch, but what isn't so far-fetched is Lawrence keeping tabs on you and your family. You should mention it to Spader."

"At this point I'm sure Spader is fed up to his double chin with my theories."

Zack reached for my hand. "But this one isn't out of the realm of possibilities, even if it has nothing to do with Shane's troubles. Lawrence is a twisted psychopath."

I pulled a deep frown. "Nick is right."

"About what?"

"Ever since Karl died, I've become a magnet for deadly creeps."

Zack matched my frown with one of his own. "Present company excepted, I hope."

I smiled. "Most definitely."

I forced myself off the bed. As physically and emotionally drained as I was from the day's events, I needed to stay awake long enough to catch the eleven o'clock news. I wanted to see what Spader had told the media about Tammy's murder and Shane's arrest. If I turned on the bedroom television, I'd probably fall asleep before the announcer finished his promo pitch for the upcoming stories.

Zack and I left the bedroom and headed for the den. We found Alex and Nick already camped in front of the TV awaiting the start of the newscast. Mephisto snored between them, his head on Nick's thigh.

Our local murder didn't even rate one of the headline teasers, thanks to various national stories and a major drug bust that occurred earlier in the day on Staten Island. The story finally appeared after the second commercial break.

Spader and the Union County district attorney stood before a bank of microphones set up in front of the courthouse in Elizabeth, but instead of broadcasting their comments, we heard a summary of the events as a voiceover from the reporter on the scene.

"An arrest has been made in the murder of Tammy Arnold, a tourist whose body was discovered in the woods behind the Staying Inn Motel in Union Township Sunday night. Westfield resident Shane Lambert, the victim's ex-husband, has been charged in her death and released on three million dollars bond after surrendering his passport and agreeing to wear a monitoring device.

The reporter then sent the telecast back to the anchor, who moved on to the next story.

"That was a total waste of sleep," I said, punctuating my words with a yawn.

"Busy news cycle," said Zack. "Spader and the D.A. probably gave more details during the press conference, but they didn't make it into the piece."

"I guess busting drug dealers on Staten Island trumps a murder in Westfield," said Nick.

"That's a good thing," said Alex. "On a slower news night they might have splashed pictures of Sophie and her dad across the screen and gone into all sorts of stuff about them."

I patted him on the leg. "Absolutely. Now which one of you boys is going to do your exhausted mother a huge favor and walk Devil Dog before going to bed?"

"He will," they both said at the same time, pointing to each other.

"I walked him last," said Nick.

Alex muttered something under his breath as he patted the dog's rump. Then he added, "Is Grandmother Lucille ever coming back, or are we permanently saddled with caring for her dog?"

"Good question," I said.

"Where is she?" asked Nick. "Not that I want her back any time soon. It's really peaceful around here without her."

Peaceful was an odd choice of word, given the recent murder, but I understood what my son meant. "I have no idea," I said. I turned to Zack. "Do you think I should call around to the local hospitals? File a missing person's report?"

"Are any of her clothes missing?" asked Zack. "Medications? Toothbrush?"

"I didn't think to look."

While Alex walked Mephisto, Zack and I searched Lucille's room. Even before all of my mother-in-law's earthly possessions fell victim to an arsonist, she'd maintained a sparse wardrobe consisting mainly of polyester pantsuits that harkened back to the nineteen seventies. After the fire, she'd replaced her wardrobe with half a dozen nearly identical polyester pantsuits purchased at secondhand shops. I swung open the door to the bedroom closet. Six empty hangers hung from the clothes rod.

One by one Zack pulled out the dresser drawers. "All empty," he said.

I walked down the hall to the bathroom she shared with the boys and opened the medicine cabinet. Her meds and toothbrush were gone.

Lucille had indeed flown the coop.

THIRTEEN

Whenever a snowstorm hits Westfield, our street is one of the last visited by the town's plows. I cynically believe the reason has everything to do with the size of the lots and the age of the homes on our street. We pay far less in property taxes than the residents of the sprawling McMansions in other parts of town. However, the upside of an unplowed street is my inability to drive to the office, thus allowing me to work from home—after breaking my back shoveling out my car, the driveway, and the walks. My wrist had healed enough over the last four days that I refused to use the injury as an excuse not to share in the snow removal detail.

"The boys and I can handle it," said Zack.

"I'm fine," I insisted.

"I don't believe you."

I held up my arm and wiggled my wrist back and forth. "See? No pain."

"What if you rip open your stitches?"

"Won't happen. The doctor is taking the stitches out on Friday."

Zack pursed his lips, heaved a sigh, and shook his head, but what could he do? File a restraining order preventing me from going within fifty feet of a snow shovel?

However, even with four—technically three-and-a-half—able bodies tackling all the white stuff on the ground, Zack, Alex, Nick, and I spent nearly two hours cleaning off the cars and clearing the driveway, the sidewalk, and the paths to the front and back doors.

Wet, heavy flakes had continued to fall all night. When the storm had finally ended before dawn, it was obvious the weather dude's updated forecast had erred on the low side of estimated total accumulation. He was off by seven inches.

Even though my wrist no longer throbbed from coming into contact with Virginia Owens' teeth, my muscles raged in protest at every one of those additional inches—not to mention the pain of shoveling the first eighteen. I also seriously doubted I'd ever get complete feeling back in my fingers and toes.

"Getting old sucks," I said as Zack and I watched my sons, unfazed by the physical assault to their own limbs, head off in search of neighbors willing to pay someone else to shovel their properties.

"How's your wrist?"

"No worse than every other muscle in my body. My aches have aches." Then again, if I exercised occasionally, maybe I'd only feel half-dead right now instead of totally dead.

"If the garage didn't look like the set of a *Hoarders* episode," said Zack, "we could park two of the three cars inside, eliminating at least some of the work."

Besides all the typical lawn paraphernalia, my garage housed most of Mama's life prior to moving into her condo. Along with paying for her new digs, Ira had handed her and Lawrence his Amex card to furnish the place. My garage now served as Mama's private, rent-free storage unit for all the old furniture she refused to sell or give away.

"Cleaning off the cars was a piece of cake compared to the shoveling," I said.

"I have two words for you."

"And that is?"

"Snow blower."

"Lovely word. Too bad I can't afford one."

"Merry Christmas."

My jaw dropped. "Are you serious?"

"Completely. Your muscles aren't the only ones complaining. I'm not getting any younger, either."

"You?" Zack's body came equipped with built-in flab and fat repellant. Forget six-pack abs. The guy had a full case.

"Yeah, must be all that spy stuff," he teased.

"So you finally admit it?"

He laughed. "Seriously, though, it's only the beginning of December. If last night's storm is any indication of the next few months' weather, at this rate, I'm not sure either of us will survive the winter."

Most women would prefer gold, diamonds, or a surprise winter vacation to the Bahamas for Christmas. I'd take a gas-powered snow blower over any of those—although a diamond engagement ring would be nice. But not yet. Someday. As much as I was head-over-heels in love with Zack, I was still too raw from Karl's deception to leap into a commitment of that magnitude. I rubbed my lower back. A snow blower was just what the doctor ordered.

"Let's go inside," said Zack. "The boys should be gone for a few hours. I'll rub your back if you rub mine—but only with your good hand. For the record, I don't believe a word you said about your wrist no longer hurting."

I hate when he sees right through me, but all I said was, "Deal."

~*~

An hour later one of the town's plows finally made several passes down our street, clearing the road but leaving in its wake a four-foot mountain of snow that blocked my driveway. With the boys still out earning shoveling money, Zack and I once again donned snow gear—even though he tried to persuade me he needed no help—and began to clear a path from the end of the driveway to the street.

We'd whittled away half the mound when a patrol car pulled up to the curb and Officers Harley and Fogarty stepped from the vehicle. I quickly scanned up and down our street, catching a glimpse of Alex and Nick working on a house at the end of the block, and willed my heart rate to cease racing with fear. However, other scenarios—all involving Shane and Sophie and none of them good—forced their way into my brain, keeping my adrenaline pumping. "Unless they're selling tickets to the annual Patrol Persons Ball, this doesn't bode well," I said.

"I doubt it's a social call," said Zack.

With their standard issue winter patrol jackets covering bulletproof vests, the heavy-set Harley and his lumbering partner Fogarty now resembled members of the law enforcement division of the Michelin Man. Although, even with all that extra padding, neither man exerted undue effort in scaling the mound of snow to join us on the other side.

Harley, the more senior of the two officers got right to the point. "Your mother-in-law never showed up for her court date, Mrs. Pollack. If she was snowed in, she should have called to reschedule."

"What court date?" I asked, relieved that their visit had nothing to do with Shane and Sophie. Lucille's run-ins with the law happened so frequently that they no longer shocked me.

"On the charge of assaulting an officer," said Fogarty. He jabbed a gloved thumb on his chest to indicate he was that officer.

"The incident last week?" Lucille had attacked Fogarty when he and Harley attempted to arrest Harriet Kleinhample for a hit-and-run. I had no idea Lucille was scheduled for court today.

"Right," said Harley. "The judge issued a bench warrant for her arrest. Said he's reached his limit with her antics."

"I don't blame him," I said. I'd reached my limit with Lucille long ago. Unfortunately, I was stuck with her as a permanent houseguest.

"She inside?" asked Harley, jutting his chin toward the front door.

"No."

"Know where we can find her?" asked Fogarty.

I shook my head. "She hasn't been home in several days. Have you checked Harriet Kleinhample's apartment? I assume she's holed up there."

"Ms. Kleinhample didn't show up for court, either," said Fogarty, "and she didn't answer her door. We even had the superintendant unlock the apartment for a wellness check. The place was empty. We thought she might be here with your mother-in-law."

Suddenly Lucille's missing clothes made sense. "I don't believe it!"

"Believe what?" asked Harley.

"They've pulled a Thelma and Louise." Thank goodness I'd refused to post Lucille's bail this time. I had no idea who had forked over the funds—perhaps the other Daughters of the October Revolution had pooled their Social Security checks—but the poor sucker or suckers were now out a bundle.

Fogarty raised both eyebrows until they disappeared under the brim of his hat. "You think they're on the lam?"

"I'd bet on it." I told them about Lucille's empty closet and dresser drawers.

"We'll put out an APB," said Harley.

"This won't sit well with Judge Roland," said Fogarty.

"Copy that," said Harley. "He said he's through cutting her slack due to her advanced age. This time he'll throw the book at her."

Couldn't happen to a more deserving scofflaw.

Did I care such a callous thought dubbed me Evil Daughter-in-law Extraordinaire? I did not. The woman had sucked every ounce of kindness and caring from me. I'd spent years offering honey in response to the vinegar she spewed at me. When Karl died, she replaced the vinegar with pure venom. If she could find a rationale, I'm certain she'd blame me for his death. Even Goody Two-Shoes had her limit.

"Kleinhample, too," added Fogarty.

With any luck, it would be months before the law caught up with Thelma and Louise and far longer before they set foot out of prison. I wouldn't even mind taking care of Devil Dog in the interim.

"Any idea where they'd go?" asked Harley.

"I suppose there's always the possibility that they're hiding out at the home of one of the other Daughters of the October Revolution. However, I doubt it."

"Why's that?" asked Fogarty.

"I believe they all either live in senior housing or with their children. I don't know whether any of them would have room for both Harriet and Lucille."

"We'll check them out all the same," said Harley. "I don't suppose you have addresses?"

I shook my head a second time. "I don't even know all their last names, but as soon as we finish shoveling, I'll search her room and contact you if I find anything."

"I'd appreciate it." Using his teeth, he gripped the tips of two fingers of his leather glove and yanked the glove off his hand. Then he reached into his pocket, pulled out a business card, and handed it to me. "You can call or text me at this number."

I didn't bother telling him I already had his cell, as well as Fogarty's and Spader's, programmed into my phone, thanks to numerous encounters with them over the past year. Instead, I nodded and placed the card in my coat pocket as I stamped my feet. Between the time we'd already spent shoveling the mountain at the entrance to the driveway and now standing in one place for several minutes, my toes had grown so numb I feared frostbite.

I grimaced at the expanse of cold white stuff surrounding us. "If I were in my mother-in-law's shoes, I'd head south. Somewhere warm and sunny with no chance of ever again having to shovel a single snowflake." Not that Lucille had ever picked up a shovel in her life.

"You're probably right," said Harley. "If they took off several days ago, I'll bet by now they're sunning themselves on a Florida beach." He raised his hand in a friendly gesture. "Thanks for your help, Mrs. Pollack."

I wanted to tell him to take his time sending out that APB. The longer Lucille was AWOL, the lower my blood pressure, but

I bit my tongue. Thinking evil thoughts is one thing; voicing them to the police reached an entirely different level. Given what they say about Karma, I thought it best not to tempt fate any further than I already had.

~*~

After Zack and I finished shoveling for the second time and warmed up with steaming cups of coffee, we headed to Lucille's room to search for any paperwork listing the full names and addresses of the other octogenarian revolutionaries. Since all of Lucille's books, files, and assorted other papers went up in flames a year and a half ago, I had little hope of finding anything that might help the police. Still, I had promised to look.

Zack swept the curtain aside, and we stepped into the room. When Lucille had been forced to share the space with Mama, the room resembled an overstuffed storage unit, thanks to Mama's financial ménage a trois with Mr. Lord and Mr. Taylor. A jam-packed eight-foot portable metal clothes rack had filled the floor space between the double windows and her bed. Dozens of plastic tubs, stacked nearly to the ceiling, contained the remainder of her clothes and covered all but a small path of floor space on her half of the room.

Mama's expansive wardrobe now resided in her condo's master bedroom walk-in closet, a space larger than her former shared bedroom. Having gotten rid of Lawrence's clothes, between the closet, the triple dresser, and chest, she now had *almost* enough room for all her clothes. The overflow she stored in the den closet.

The only furniture in the room consisted of the twin beds, a dresser, and a nightstand. Nick had moved his desk into his brother's room when he was forced to give up his room to Lucille.

Zack began the search by pulling open the dresser drawers to double-check that he hadn't overlooked anything in his initial search. "Completely empty."

"We're not going to find anything," I said, scanning the closet floor and finding nothing besides a pair of rain galoshes and a dozen dust bunnies.

I periodically search Lucille's room for contraband wine. She's not supposed to mix alcohol with her meds. However, she constantly ignores her doctors' orders, secreting bottles of merlot and burgundy in her room. The galoshes had doubled as wine storage. "I don't remember ever seeing any paperwork related to her not-so-merry band of minions. If they keep files, someone else in the group stores them."

Zack joined me at the closet and checked the shelf. "Nothing up here."

That left the nightstand, which I'd never bothered with previously because the drawer wasn't deep enough to hide a wine bottle. I pulled open the single drawer and gasped. Then I laughed.

"What's so funny?"

I reached into the drawer and pulled out a dog-eared copy of *Fifty Shades of Grey.* "Maybe Mama left it here," I said. Although, if the book belonged to Mama, why would Lucille hold onto it?

"Or maybe when they're not fomenting revolution, your mother-in-law and her pals are sitting around reading S and M."

I wrinkled my nose. "As long as they're just reading about it and not doing it."

"Find any books by the Marquis de Sade? Any sex toys?"

"I'm afraid to look."

Zack pulled the drawer out of the nightstand and dumped the contents onto the bed. "Just your run-of-the-mill nightstand junk."

"You sound disappointed." I fished through the remainder of

the items scattered on the bed. "This looks promising." I picked up a small spiral-bound notepad and flipped up the cardboard cover. "Bingo!"

The notepad was a makeshift address book. Along with the names, addresses, and phone numbers of each of the Daughters of the October Revolution, Lucille had recorded members' birthdates. "I wonder if she throws parties for them," I said, handing Zack the notepad and pointing out the birth dates. "She's never once remembered her grandsons' birthdays."

"For which you should be grateful."

"Grateful for what? That she's always ignored her grandchildren?"

"Think about it. What would Lucille give Alex and Nick for their birthdays?"

"How should I know?" Then it dawned on me. Sometimes it takes a minute or two before my neurons fire up and kick-start my brain cells. "A copy of the *Communist Manifesto*."

"Or a biography of Karl Marx. Or Lenin. Or any other book from The Socialist Workers Press. Do you really think she would have bought them LEGOs or a Millennium Falcon?"

"Point taken."

Zack flipped the notepad closed and handed it back to me. I fished my phone from my jeans pocket. "I'll give Officer Harley a call, but I'd be surprised if he finds her hiding out at any of these homes."

"You really think they drove to Florida?"

"Wouldn't you?"

"Hell, no. If I jumped bail, I'd head for a country without an extradition treaty with the U.S."

We looked at each other for a split second before we both blurted out. "Russia?"

"Does she have a current passport?" asked Zack.

"I have no idea. Wouldn't she also need a visa?"

"Yes, but it's a lengthy process. She would have had to plan well in advance. In addition, the visa would list an entry and exit date. Russian visas aren't open-ended, and there are no exceptions. If she overstayed her welcome, she'd face serious consequences."

"What kind of consequences?"

"Major ones, and the Russian government won't allow the U.S. embassy to intervene in visa violations."

For someone who claimed no alphabet agency affiliation, Zack knew a great deal regarding travel to Russia. "I take it you've gone there on assignment?"

"A few years ago for a *National Geographic* spread on nineteenth century dachas."

"I see. So it seems unlikely they've hopped on an Aeroflot flight."

"Unlikely but not impossible, especially if they plan to seek asylum."

For all of Lucille's constant complaints about our country and government, I never thought she'd leave. Did she even speak Russian? I had no idea. "I'll let Officer Harley know."

I was about to call the patrolman when my phone rang. "Naomi," I said, reading my editorial director's name from the screen. I answered the call. "Hi, Naomi."

"Anastasia, we have a problem at work. The power is down over half of Morris County."

"What happened?"

"I'm not sure. The power company is offering few details at this point other than the problem is storm-related and will require a major repair. We were told not to expect power restoration for several days. We'll all be working from home for at least the remainder of the week. Do you have anything at the office you need?"

"You're still there?"

"Only for a few minutes more, but I can grab some things for you before I leave."

"Am I able to access our cloud?"

"Yes."

"Then I'm good. I have plenty of supplies here."

"I'll check in with you on Sunday evening to let you know if the office will reopen on Monday."

I hung up from Naomi and passed along the news to Zack before placing my call to Officer Harley. Along with telling him I had the addresses he requested, I suggested if he didn't find Lucille staying with one of the other Daughters, he should check the manifests of all international flights to Russia from either Newark Liberty or JFK during the last few days.

"I hope she did fly to Russia," said Harley.

"Why is that?"

"She's a drain on our resources, not to mention our budget. If she's in Russia, she's Moscow's problem."

A part of me (albeit, an extremely small part) felt sorry for the Kremlin.

FOURTEEN

Harley said he'd swing by within the hour to pick up the notepad. When I mentioned this to Zack, he said, "Let's make copies of the pages before you hand it over to him."

"Why?"

"You might need that contact information at some point."

"Good idea." And one I obviously wouldn't have thought of on my own. We grabbed our coats and headed to his apartment.

I had first moved my home office and studio from the garage apartment to my basement when I rented out the apartment to Zack. Little had I realized that Lucille and her cohorts would avail themselves of my office equipment and supplies whenever I wasn't home. Of course, they never replaced or reimbursed me for the reams of paper and multiple ink cartridges they used. So just as Zack's clothes were migrating from his apartment to my bedroom, my office had migrated back to his apartment.

Once we placed the notepad on the scanner bed, we realized we had a problem. The notepad's metal spiral prevented a clear scan of the pages. Frustrated, I suggested tearing the pages from the notepad.

"I wouldn't," said Zack. He pulled his phone from his pocket and began snapping photos of each page.

When all else fails, leave it to the photographer—or the spy—to find a solution. I wondered how often Zack had performed similar tasks, but I didn't ask. I already knew both the look and the answer he'd give me.

Harley and Fogarty arrived half an hour later. When I handed over the notepad, Harley flipped it open and quickly leafed through the pages. "I guess we know what we're doing this afternoon," he said to Fogarty.

"Will you let me know if you find her?" I asked.

"Of course."

Shortly after the two officers left, notepad in hand, Zack received a call from Shane Lambert. After a brief conversation in which Zack did little more than respond with a word or two, he hung up and said, "Shane wants to speak to us."

"About what?"

"He didn't say, but he sounded extremely angry and upset."

A bowling ball landed in the pit of my stomach. Logically, my first thought should have centered on Shane's arrest for the murder of his ex-wife. However, my mind immediately zeroed in on something far closer to home. "You don't think Sophie's..." I stood momentarily paralyzed with fear, unable to give voice to the word I dreaded hearing most in connection with my son.

"Pregnant?"

I vigorously shook my head. Tears clogged my throat. "No, it can't be. We've talked about this. He assured me they weren't...hadn't—"

Zack wrapped his arms around me. "And you believed him?"

"Of course." Not only because I wanted to believe Alex but because I'd raised my kids to understand the consequences of their actions and trusted them to make decisions accordingly. "What was he thinking?"

"Speaking as a former teenage boy, I can state unequivocally that as a species, we don't think, at least not with our brains and not until we're much older. Until then we're ruled entirely by the area below the belt."

"Not all boys all the time." I'd dated my share of teenage boys. I knew all about raging hormones. But this was my son. Frustration and anger consumed me. I wanted to smash something. "How could they be so careless?"

"Maybe they weren't. No birth control is a hundred percent effective."

"Not that it matters now," I muttered. If there was a bun in the oven, what difference did it make if it got there through carelessness or failed birth control?

"Maybe you're jumping to conclusions."

I heaved a fearful sigh. There was only one way to find out. "I'll get my coat."

Alex and Nick were playing a video game in the den. Before leaving the house, I stopped to tell them Zack and I were going out, but all I could do was stand in the doorway and numbly stare. Alex eventually noticed me and paused the game. "Something wrong, Mom?"

"Why do you ask?"

Nick turned his attention to me, his brow wrinkled. "You have a strange look on your face. Like you're both sad and angry at the same time."

"Is it Grandmother Lucille?" asked Alex. "Has she gotten into more trouble?"

"No, Zack and I have to run out for a little while. We should be back in an hour."

"Okay," they both said in unison.

"You sure you're okay?" asked Alex.

"Why wouldn't I be?"

"Because you don't *look* okay?"

"I'm fine." I pivoted on my heels and hurried to the front door. My sons had obviously inherited Mama's knack for seeing right through me.

~*~

When we arrived at Shane's home, he greeted us at the door. The guy looked like he'd aged another ten years overnight. "Thanks for coming," he said, ushering us inside and taking our coats.

"Where's Sophie?" I asked.

"In her room. She doesn't know about this yet. I'd like your advice on how to tell her."

Sophie didn't know she was pregnant?

Shane shook his head. "No, that's not true." He cast pleading eyes at both of us. "My lawyer called earlier. I need some backup support, and I have no one else to turn to."

I clasped Zack's hand, and we exchanged a quick look. I had taken a flying leap, plummeting headfirst into the land of erroneous conclusions. Relief flooded through me. Whatever had upset Shane was obviously bad, but it had nothing to do with my son's sperm cavorting with one of his daughter's eggs.

We followed Shane into the kitchen. "Coffee?" he asked.

Zack and I nodded. We took seats at the island and watched as he busied himself pouring three cups. After pulling a container of milk from the refrigerator, he joined us, but instead of taking a seat on one of the barstools, he stood on the opposite side of the island, directly in front of us.

Shane clutched his mug with both hands, his grip so tight that his knuckles turned white, but it did little to stem his trembling. He focused on the steaming contents of his cup as he spoke. "When I told Detective Spader I hadn't had contact with Tammy since the divorce, I lied."

I lifted an eyebrow. "Then you had seen her prior to Sunday?"

He shook his head. "No, that part was the truth. Other than to finalize the divorce, the last time I saw her was the day she walked out on us."

"But you'd spoken with her?" asked Zack.

Shane shook his head again. "Remember how I told you about Sophie's anger issues as a child?"

I nodded. "When she destroyed the photos of Tammy."

"Yes. Seeing her systematically cut up those photographs into smaller and smaller pieces made me suspect that her behavior issues all centered around not having a mother.

"I spoke with the school psychologist at the high school where I taught. She suggested that in the ensuing years, Tammy might have come to regret her decision to give up her parental rights. If that were the case, a relationship between the two of them might benefit both mother and daughter."

"I thought you didn't know where Tammy had gone," said Zack.

"I didn't. But I figured her divorce attorney might know. I wrote her a letter, gave it to my divorce attorney, and asked that he pass it along to her lawyer to give to her."

"This was back when Sophie was in kindergarten?" asked Zack.

Shane nodded. "Twelve years ago."

"Did you ever hear from her?" I asked.

"No, but according to my attorney, she did receive the letter."

"That's hardly having contact," said Zack.

"The problem is..." Shane paused for a deep breath, releasing it slowly. "...Detective Spader found the letter in a zippered compartment of Tammy's purse."

"I still don't see the problem," I said.

"Just the letter, no envelope with a postmark, and I didn't bother to date the letter. It could have been written years ago or a week ago."

"So you wrote to your ex-wife asking if she'd changed her mind and would like to have a relationship with her daughter. What difference does it make when you wrote the letter?" Maybe I was missing something, but I didn't see why the letter posed a problem for Shane.

He raised his coffee cup to his mouth and drained the contents before continuing, keeping a firm but shaky, two-fisted grip on the mug. "In the letter I made a veiled threat about how one day Tammy would regret her actions. I wasn't threatening her with harm; I only meant she'd regret not having a relationship with Sophie. But that's not the way the district attorney is interpreting it."

This was the additional evidence Spader alluded to when we spoke yesterday. Without proof of the letter's age, Shane's uphill battle to prove his innocence had now grown even steeper.

Shane slammed the empty coffee cup onto the island hard enough that I was surprised when the mug didn't break. I glanced down at the marble countertop but saw no damage from the force of the impact. Broken mugs and chipped counters were the least of his worries, though. He could afford to replace both, but his wealth wouldn't help him escape a murder conviction.

He leaned over, propping his elbows on the counter and lowering his head into his hands. "I need to prepare Sophie for the worst case scenario. How do I tell my daughter her father may spend the rest of his life in prison?"

"Don't you think I already know that?"

Shane straightened, his jaw dropping, his eyes widening, as we all turned to find Sophie standing at the entrance to the great room. Her arms crossed over her chest, she approached her father. "I'm not stupid," she continued. "Why do you think I've been so upset, Dad? This isn't like a parking ticket."

"I know, Soph."

"So what are you going to do about it?"

"I'm working on it."

Sophie threw her arms up in the air, then slammed her fists down on the island. "Work harder!" She whipped her head around to confront Zack and me. "All of you!"

I reached over and covered her fists with my hands. I didn't know what to say, but it didn't matter. My touch had drained Sophie of her bravado. Her jaw trembled. She sucked in a ragged breath and in a near whisper said, "No one else cares what happens to us." Then she ran out of the room. We heard her race up the stairs and slam her bedroom door.

"Excuse me," said Shane. He hurried from the room and bounded up the stairs.

"Well, that went well," said Zack.

"Not." I threw my hands up in the air, then slapped them on my thighs. "I feel so helpless."

"Are you still convinced he's innocent?"

I nodded. "Aren't you?"

"If he isn't, he's the world's greatest actor. Unless we're unaware of some crucial details, I don't see what Shane would gain by killing Tammy. He has no motive. If not for the eyewitness, the D.A. has no case."

"Unless the eyewitness has a motive."

Zack knit his brows together. "And what would that be?"

"Beats me. Now that I knew I wasn't about to become a premature grandmother, I returned to my current pastime of pulling ideas out of the stratosphere. Have you heard from Patricia?"

"She made a few calls. Nothing jumped out that raised any suspicions on her part."

"What we need is for a suspect to jump out. Is there any way we can access Lawrence's phone and visitor logs?"

"You still think he has something to do with this?"

"I don't know, but I'd like to turn over every available stone to see what crawls out. Nothing is too far-fetched when it comes to Lawrence. After all, he put out a hit on two innocent strangers to keep my nose out of his business." Which in my mind made my mother's ex-husband more a boulder than a stone. I might need a crowbar. "Maybe if I paid a visit to the prison—"

"Absolutely not! I don't want you anywhere near that man. Talk to Spader. As the detective on the case, he should be able to find out who Lawrence has spoken with since his incarceration."

"Unless he gave orders to one of his henchmen before the feds locked him up. Or arranged with someone on the inside to get word out for him. What else does he have to do in max other than plot revenge?"

"Talk to Spader," Zack repeated.

"I'll talk to Spader."

Shane had been upstairs with Sophie for ten minutes when his doorbell rang. "Do you think he heard it?" I asked after waiting a few seconds without hearing him come downstairs.

"Maybe we should answer it," said Zack.

We both stood and headed for the front door. I crossed all my available digits, hoping not to find the police on Shane's doorstep. Or if they were there, it was to say they'd found the real killer."

After looking through the peephole, Zack swung open the door. Trey Krause, the food bank board treasurer who had introduced himself to Shane at the crafts fair on Sunday, stood on the front step. He wore a wool cashmere tailored camel coat. The turned-up color exposed a lining of classic Burberry plaid that matched the scarf peeking out from behind his lapels. The man's outerwear telegraphed success.

The expression on his face telegraphed surprise. "Oh...I'm...uh...here to see Shane Lambert. Is he at home?"

"Come in, Mr. Krause," said Zack as he stepped aside to usher him into the foyer.

Krause's forehead wrinkled, his surprise segueing to puzzlement. "Have we met?"

"Not formally," said Zack. "We were standing with Shane at the crafts fair on Sunday when you introduced yourself to him. I'm Zachary Barnes, and this is Anastasia Pollack. Her son is on the high school community service committee that raised the funds for the food bank."

Krause extended his hand, first to Zack, then to me, his sleeve hiking up slightly to expose the king's ransom he wore around his wrist. "A pleasure to meet you both. The food bank is indebted to this year's graduating class. And of course to Mr. Lambert for his generous offer to match the amount they raised."

"Is that why you're here?" I asked.

"Why, yes." The corners of his mouth quirked up slightly. "I thought I'd save him the price of a stamp."

"Really? How thoughtful." A man about to donate thousands of dollars to charity would hardly care about spending an additional fifty cents on postage. And, Trey Krause, with his two-thousand-dollar overcoat and fifty-thousand-dollar Rolex, didn't strike me as a man who would worry about saving another man fifty pennies.

"Well, that and having the opportunity to thank him once again in person, of course."

"Of course." Still not buying it. Something about the man told me he had an ulterior motive for dropping in on Shane.

Then again, if he'd caught Spader's press conference and knew of the indictment, he may have panicked that Shane might renege on his promised donation. Shane had staggering legal fees looming, and even though such expenses would bankrupt the average person, given Shane's enormous lottery win, those expenses hardly put a dent in his net worth, not that Krause had any way of knowing that.

My gaze darted from the overcoat that cost twice my monthly mortgage payment to the still visible watch that cost more than the average new car. Perhaps I'd simply allowed my innate dislike for ostentatious people to cloud my judgment.

I tabled my inner musings as Shane descended the staircase. "Mr. Krause," he said, stopping halfway down the stairs, his voice filled with surprise at seeing his unexpected guest. "Did we have a meeting?"

"No, forgive me," said Krause. He offered Shane a huge smile as he stood at the bottom of the staircase and extended his hand. "I was in the neighborhood, so I thought I'd stop by to pick up your donation."

Shane descended the remaining steps and shook his hand. "Of course. Give me a minute."

He stepped into his office, which showed no signs of the chaos from last night's break-in. Shane must have stayed up all night sorting and filing several thousand sheets of paper and shelving hundreds of books to return order to the room. He settled into the chair behind his desk, pulled a ledger from the top drawer, and flipped it open.

Krause stepped away from Zack and me and walked over to the office entrance. He glanced around the room as if appraising it. Then without waiting for an invitation, he strode across the hardwood and hovered over the desk as Shane filled out the check.

"How rude," I whispered to Zack. After all, Shane had implied Krause should wait in the foyer with us. At least that's how I had interpreted his "give me a minute" comment.

We watched as Shane paused his pen, glanced up at Krause, and frowned. "Was there something else, Mr. Krause?"

"Please, call me Trey."

"Was there something else, Trey?"

"As a matter of fact..." He reached into his breast pocket, removed a business card, and offered it to Shane. "Since you're relatively new to the area, I thought I might be of service."

Shane glanced at the card. "Thank you, but I'm not in the market for a broker."

Krause placed the card on the desk. "I'll leave this with you in case you change your mind. Feel free to call at any time."

Shane ripped the check from the ledger and folded it in half. Before handing it over, he said, "According to the long-range meteorological forecasts, we're in for a brutal winter."

Krause didn't respond at first, most likely puzzled by the comment. Then it hit him. "Yes, of course. The staff is worried we won't have enough resources to help everyone who will need our services over the next few months."

Shane handed him the check. "I've added a bit extra for that reason."

"That's quite generous." Krause unfolded the check and stared at it. "Exceedingly generous." He studied the check closer. "You have your own foundation? I had no idea."

Shane stood. "Spend it wisely, Mr. Krause. I have auditors."

The man paled for a split second before saying, "Trey."

Shane nodded. "Now if you'll excuse me, I have guests."

"Of course."

Shane ushered Krause from his office and walked him toward the front door. When he swung open the door, Krause extended his hand, his coat sleeve once again hiking up to expose his Rolex, and said, "I hope we'll be seeing much more of each other, Shane."

Shane accepted his hand, but all he said was, "Good day, Mr. Krause." He closed the door the moment Krause stepped over the threshold. *Don't let the door hit you on your way out.*

"That guy is a real tool," said Sophie.

The three of us glanced toward the staircase to find her sitting on a step.

"He hopes to see more of you?" she continued. "Give me a break! He hopes to see more of our money."

"The money isn't for him," said Shane. "It's to feed the homeless and people who are having a hard time making ends meet. You know that."

Sophie bounded down the stairs and joined us in the foyer. "I know, Dad, but they're lucky the committee didn't meet that guy before we chose the food bank as our charity. Did you guys see his wrist bling? How many poor people would that watch feed?"

I had wondered the same thing, but I didn't want to insert myself into the middle of this conversation. After everything that had happened over the last few days, Shane and Sophie needed as much father/daughter time as possible, I turned to Zack and said, "We should leave."

Zack walked over to the foyer closet and retrieved our coats.

"Do you have to go?" asked Sophie, her eyes begging me—or us?—to stay.

I certainly hadn't expected that, but perhaps I should have. All Sophie had was her father. She'd lost her mother before she ever knew her. Her grandparents had died years ago. She had no aunts, no uncles, no cousins. And now she might lose her father, the only family she'd known for most of her life. The poor kid was desperate for family connections.

After Zack helped me into my coat, I could no longer help myself. I wrapped my arms around Sophie and said, "If I don't make a trip to the supermarket, your boyfriend and his brother will starve to death. But how about if you and your dad join us for dinner this evening?"

Sophie turned to Shane. "Can we, Dad?"

"You sure?" Shane asked me. "I don't want us to impose."

"We'd love to have you join us."

"Thank you. We'll bring dessert. Sophie and I make a mean brownie."

When he opened the front door, we discovered Detective Spader, poised to ring the doorbell.

FIFTEEN

Spader cradled a silver MacBook Air under one arm. He stepped inside the house and offered the laptop to Shane. "I wanted to return this to your daughter as soon as possible."

Before Shane could take possession, Sophie pushed her way past her father. Scowling at Spader, she snatched the device from his hands. She was about to run off when Shane reached out and grabbed hold of her shoulder to stop her. "Don't you have something to say to Detective Spader, Sophie?"

She turned back and eyed the detective. "Yes, as a matter of fact, I do. What about my Dad's computer?"

"That's not what I meant," said Shane.

Sophie continued staring at Spader without saying another word. Maybe she was waiting for him to answer her question. Shane gave her shoulder a squeeze, and she finally offered a contrite apology. "Thank you, Detective."

"You're welcome. I'm sorry we had to take it."

That set Sophie off again. "Really? Do you honestly think if my father had killed my mother—which he didn't—he would have left evidence on *my* laptop?"

"Sophie!"

Shane looked like he wanted the floor to open up and swallow him while Spader looked like he was regretting not sending a patrol officer to deliver the computer. To his credit, though, instead of addressing Sophie's outburst, he said, "Get an A on those school papers."

Clutching her laptop to her chest, she answered, "I always get A's." Then she sprinted upstairs.

Shane apologized to Spader for Sophie's lack of manners. "She's not normally like this. Thank you for returning her computer."

Spader nodded. "No problem."

Zack and I left the house with Spader. "Tough kid," he said as we walked with him down the front path toward our cars.

"Do you blame her?" I asked.

"No, I don't, but I have a job to do."

"We know that," said Zack.

"But Sophie's world is crumbling before her eyes," I said.

"And she blames me," said Spader.

"Why wouldn't she?" I asked. "If you want to get in her good graces, find the real killer."

We had come to the curb where Spader's unmarked sedan sat idling. As he opened the car door, he said, "I'm not ignoring other leads, Mrs. Pollack. There are none."

"Well, I may have one for you."

Spader closed the door and turned around to face me. "I'm listening."

I explained my Lawrence theory to him, how Tammy may have fallen victim to Lawrence's twisted idea of revenge in much the same way my neighbors, Betty Bentworth and Carmen

Cordova, had wound up dead, simply due to their proximity to me. "After all, if someone has been stalking me, he could have seen Tammy standing near me at the fair. She hung around us for quite some time, but if he was keeping his distance, he might not have been close enough to see if she and I spoke. The fair was extremely crowded. If he thought she was a friend, he may have chosen her as his victim and followed her back to the motel."

When I'd finished, Spader scrubbed at his jaw for a moment as if digesting my theory. Finally, he heaved a deep sigh and said, "You realize how cockamamie this sounds, don't you?"

"Except that he's done it before."

"Which is why I'm not dismissing it."

"You're not?"

Spader looked me in the eye and said, "If it's one thing I've learned, Mrs. Pollack, it's not to underestimate you. I'll contact the feds to check the prison phone and visitor logs. I'll let you know if anything turns up."

"That's all I ask."

On the way home, guilt reared its ugly head. I'd spent so much time the last few days worrying about Sophie, Shane, and Lucille, that I hadn't thought to check in on Mama. In her sixty-five years on the planet my mother had never lived on her own until now. As a young bride, she went from her parents' home to living with my father. After he died, she sold their home and moved in with me while she searched for my first stepfather.

The pattern repeated with each new stepfather, the only difference being none of my four prior stepfathers owned their own homes, much less anything else. Mama had an uncanny knack for picking men whose purported wealth didn't live up to either their exaggerated claims or her expectations.

Because Mama couldn't afford to live on her own, thanks to

her need to support Mr. Lord and Mr. Taylor, she moved back and forth from my home to a rental apartment to my home as each subsequent stepfather met his maker. Then along came Lawrence Tuttnauer and his son-in-law Ira, the New Jersey King of Car Dealers. Upon Lawrence's arrest and incarceration, Mama became queen of her own condo.

I pulled out my phone and called her.

"I was wondering if you'd ever get around to checking to see if I was still alive," she said by way of greeting.

"Hello to you, too, Mama."

"Sarcasm is never becoming, Anastasia."

Except for her? "Is everything all right, Mama?"

"Of course, everything is all right. Why wouldn't it be?"

I decided to ignore the question. It was either rhetorical or a landmine waiting for me to step on it. "Zack and I are on our way to the supermarket. Do you need us to pick up anything for you?"

"I'm almost out of food for Catherine the Great." She rattled off the name of some high-priced organic, grain-free gourmet brand sold in the refrigerated section of the pet food aisle. "One of each flavor but not the one with pumpkin. Catherine the Great doesn't care for pumpkin."

"Finicky feline," I muttered under my breath. Mama's corpulent Persian ate better than I did.

"What's that, dear? I didn't hear you."

"I asked if there's anything else you need."

"Now that you mention it, I have had a craving for Beluga caviar lately."

I turned toward Zack, shook my head, and executed an eye roll. Good thing Mama couldn't see me. "I don't think ShopRite carries caviar, Mama."

Zack's eyes widened as he mouthed, "Caviar?"

"Beluga," I mouthed back.

He responded with a headshake and eye roll of his own.

"I'm sure they do," she said. "Look in the gourmet food section."

"Cat food and caviar. Check."

I hung up the phone, wishing I hadn't bothered to call. "I can't remember if she's always been this self-absorbed or has gotten worse with age."

"I read somewhere once," said Zack, "that as people age, their negative traits become more pronounced."

"Not comforting," I said. Mama might live another thirty years. Or more. *Would I survive?*

"By the way, do you have any idea what Beluga caviar costs?"

I shook my head. "It's not exactly a staple in my pantry."

"Google it."

I pulled out my phone and asked Siri. Several websites popped up on my phone. My eyes bugged out as I scanned them. "Holy mackerel!"

"Sturgeon," said Zack, as he pulled into the supermarket parking lot and searched for an empty parking space.

"Not in this lifetime." Mama also occasionally had an empty wallet when it came time to reimburse me. No way was I footing the bill for Beluga. Gourmet cat food was bad enough.

Given the packed aisles, it seemed half the town had descended on ShopRite to replenish their bare cupboards. As we slowly made our way down one row of food and up another, filling our shopping cart, I stopped in front of the gourmet food section. Zack raised an eyebrow.

"Just curious," I said. As expected, the shelves were devoid of Beluga caviar. "And now at least I can say I tried." No way did I want Mama catching me in a lie.

Thirty minutes later we stuffed the small trunk of Zack's Boxster with four bags of groceries. A fifth bag, holding twenty dollars worth of overpriced cat food, sat on the floor between my legs as we drove to Mama's condo.

"Want me to wait in the car while you run in?" asked Zack after he pulled into a parking spot in front of the condo.

I'd love nothing better than to hand Mama her cat food and dash back to the car, but that would really set her off. "We'd better go in, even if only for a few minutes."

Zack cut the engine, and we exited the car. As we walked up the shoveled path, I noticed the curtain flutter on the front-facing kitchen window. A moment later Mama swung open her condo door before I had a chance to ring the bell.

"Hello, Mama." I handed her the grocery bag. "The cat food came to twenty dollars."

"Come in," she said. "I just finished brewing a pot of coffee."

Of course, she completely ignored my not-so-subtle hint for reimbursement as we stepped inside the apartment. I expected no less. "We can't stay long, Mama. We have perishable food in the car."

"Well, you certainly don't have to worry about anything spoiling in this weather, dear. Take your boots and coats off."

As Zack and I complied with the order, she glanced in the bag and frowned. "No caviar?"

I tugged a boot from my foot. "Sorry. Not a single tin on the shelves. Maybe you can satisfy your craving with a can of salmon or tuna."

"Really, Anastasia, how can you compare caviar to canned salmon and tuna?"

I yanked off my other boot. "They both come from fish, don't they?"

Mama appealed to Zack. "Do you believe her?"

"She does have a point," he said.

"And this is why I keep him around."

Mama shook her head at both of us. Then she uttered a deep sigh, turned on her heels, and marched into the kitchen. As we followed her, I fought the urge to stick out my tongue. Mama had succeeded in resurrecting my inner twelve-year-old.

However, as long as we were here, I decided to ply her for information about her ex-husband. So I quickly morphed back into the obedient daughter and helped her by pouring coffee while she placed Catherine the Great's pricey gourmet meals in the fridge.

After the three of us were seated around her kitchen table, I asked, "Mama, have you had any contact with Lawrence?"

"Why on earth would I want to have anything to do with that man after what he did to me?"

"You haven't spoken to him since his trial?"

"I haven't spoken to him since his arrest!"

"And he hasn't tried to contact you?"

She hesitated for a moment. "He's tried, but I haven't accepted his calls."

"How often does he call?"

"Once a week."

My Spidey senses tingled from my scalp down to my toenails. "Why haven't you told me?"

She set her coffee cup on the table and waved a hand in dismissal. "What's there to tell? When the Caller ID displays a call is from the prison, I don't answer. I want nothing to do with that man."

"Have you told anyone about the calls?" I asked.

"Like who?"

"The police? Your attorney? The D.A.?" asked Zack.

"I saw no reason to. Why are you asking me about Lawrence?"

"I was worried he might be harassing you," I said.

She raised an eyebrow. "He hasn't called you, has he?"

"No." Receiving phone calls from an inmate at a federal penitentiary wasn't what concerned me, but I refused to burden Mama over my suspicions regarding Tammy's murder. One worrywart insomniac in the family was more than enough.

After we finished our coffee, I said, "I hate to drink and run, Mama, but I'm supposed to be working from home today."

"Then you'd better get home," she said, following Zack and me as we headed toward the coat closet.

Her purse sat on the foyer console table. As I slipped on my boots, she retrieved her wallet. I waited for her standard excuse about not having any cash, but to my surprise, she pulled out a twenty-dollar bill and handed it to me. "Thank you, dear."

Mama often surprises me, but rarely is it a pleasant surprise.

On the ride home I pulled out my phone and placed a call to Detective Spader. He answered on the first ring. "Mrs. Pollack, always a pleasure."

"Good to know you don't dread my calls, Detective."

"What can I do for you?"

"Have you contacted the prison yet?"

"It's on today's to-do list. Why?"

"I just learned Lawrence Tuttnauer has been placing calls to my mother once a week."

"About?"

"Mama said she's ignored all the calls."

"Good. Tell her to keep ignoring them. I'll be in touch if I learn something."

He hung up before I had a chance to say more.

~*~

Shane and Sophie arrived for dinner with a pan of freshly baked chocolate chip brownies and a half-gallon of salted caramel and chocolate chip ice cream.

"How about if we skip dinner and go right to dessert," said Nick.

"No chicken and asparagus, no dessert," I said, forcing a *Mom Look*.

"You're no fun," he grumbled under his breath.

"I'm your mother. It's part of the job description."

Before I had a chance to place the ice cream in the freezer, the doorbell rang again. Zack checked out the newcomers through the peephole. "Harley and Fogarty."

I saw Sophie stiffen and grab Alex's hand. "Are they alone?"

Zack nodded. Noticing the fear that had spread across Sophie's face, he said, "I don't think they're here because of your dad, Sophie."

"Why else would they be here?" she asked, her voice trembling.

"Grandmother Lucille is missing," said Alex. "She hasn't been home in several days."

"That's terrible," said Shane.

"Not really," said Nick.

"Nick!"

"Well, it's true, isn't it?" he asked. "Don't tell me you wouldn't be happy if she never came back, Mom."

All I could do was emit a huge sigh and shake my head at him.

Zack opened the door. Both Harley and Fogarty showed surprise at being greeted by a contingent of six, one of whom cradled a pan of brownies and another who held a half-gallon of ice cream.

Fogarty pointed to the food. "For us?"

"Depends," I said. "Do you come bearing good news or bad?"

"That depends how you look at it," said Harley. He handed me the spiral notepad. "I added all the names and addresses into a database. Sooner or later we'll probably need the information again."

"Did you find them?" I asked.

He shook his head. "Not only didn't we find your mother-in-law and Ms. Kleinhample, we couldn't find any of them."

"They're *all* missing?"

"Every last Daughter of the October Revolution," said Fogarty.

"Where did they go?"

They both shrugged. "No one seems to know," said Harley. "We checked flight manifests, as you suggested, not only those going to Russia but all domestic and international flights leaving Newark Liberty, LaGuardia, and JFK the last few days. They didn't fly anywhere."

"Unless they drove to Philly and took a flight from there," I said.

"We didn't think of that," said Harley. He pushed a button on his shoulder-mounted walkie-talkie and relayed a message to have someone check the flight manifests for not only the Philadelphia Airport but also Atlantic City and Westchester.

"If those come up cold," he said, "you're probably right about them heading down to Florida."

"Or they've all been abducted by aliens," said Fogarty, peppering his words with a chuckle.

"Cool!" said Nick. "Either way, that means she won't be coming home any time soon, right?"

"Nick!" I thrust the ice cream at him. "Put this in the freezer."

I then turned back to the two officers. "So what happens now?"

"We've put out both a nationwide APB and a Silver Alert," said Harley. "Thirteen female octogenarians riding around in a vintage VW minibus shouldn't be too hard to spot."

"And once you find them?" I asked.

"We extradite them back to New Jersey," said Harley. "Your mother-in-law and Kleinhample are fugitives. The others will be charged with aiding and abetting."

My evil twin wondered if they might deport them all to Russia.

~*~

School reopened the next day, but since I didn't have to rush off to work, thanks to the Morris County power outage, our morning routine was less frenetic. I spared the boys their morning Mephisto and Ralph chores, taking on the duties of walking Devil Dog and filling water and food bowls myself, while Zack whipped up a breakfast of egg and Canadian bacon sandwiches. Nick and Alex wolfed theirs down in two bites before donning boots, hats, coats, and gloves; grabbing their backpacks; and rushing out the door.

With Lucille still MIA, a peaceful calm descended over the kitchen as Zack and I took our time with our own breakfast sandwiches and sipped our morning coffee. Mephisto had retreated to his spot under the coffee table in the den while Ralph quietly observed us from his perch atop the refrigerator. "I could get used to this," I said.

"Being a lady of leisure?"

"Enjoying an unhurried weekday breakfast." I didn't eat and run each morning; I only ran, grabbing for breakfast whatever I could find in the break room once I arrived at work. And those

157

offerings always consisted of massive amounts of sugar and calories.

Was it any wonder after seventeen-plus years I still hadn't shed the baby weight I'd gained from two pregnancies? At this stage of my life nothing short of a starvation diet, coupled with the exercise routine of a triathlete, would shed those excess pounds. Unfortunately, diet and exercise continually lost out to the temptation of morning muffins, pastries, and croissants.

Zack drained his coffee cup, then rose from the table and carried his dishes to the sink. "Do you have a packed work schedule today?"

"No more than usual but working from home I won't have any interruptions. I should finish early." I watched as he rinsed his dishes and loaded them into the dishwasher. "Are you suggesting we ditch our responsibilities and enjoy the day?"

Ralph flapped his wings, squawked once, then said, "*Consent with both that we may enjoy each other. As You Like It.* Act Five, Scene Two."

Zack glanced at Ralph, then turned toward me and shook his head. "Don't look so eager."

"Do I look eager?"

"You look like a woman itching to play hooky."

"We do have the house to ourselves."

Zack shook his head again. "You have the house to yourself. I'm off to a meeting in D.C."

"Oh." I frowned. "Did I know that?"

"With everything that's happened the last few days, I may have forgotten to mention it."

Or he'd deliberately kept his travel plans to himself up until the last possible moment. Was he really going to a meeting in Washington, or was that a cover for a more clandestine trip?

"When will you be home?"

"Most likely by eight o'clock."

"Most likely?"

He shrugged. "You never know with Amtrak and the weather."

"Right." At least if he expected to return this evening, he wasn't flying off to someplace where the U.S. only has a covert presence. No way could Zack travel to Africa, the Middle East, or any other overseas hotbed and return within twelve hours, assuming he really did plan to arrive home later this evening.

I pasted a smile on my face, swallowing down my fear and insecurity and forcefully reeled in my overactive imagination. I didn't even bother to ask about his destination in D.C. He'd say the World Wildlife Federation or the Smithsonian or National Geographic, even if he planned to meet with the CIA, FBI, or NSA. I'd never know the truth. Or I'd know but refuse to believe it.

No matter how often or how vehemently he protested otherwise, something about Zack's day job refused to add up in my mind. I doubt it ever would. But was my skepticism justified, or was I suffering from post-traumatic Karl syndrome, the aftermath of marriage to a pathological liar? I honestly didn't know.

A few sessions with a psychiatrist probing my psyche might provide me with answers, but I had more pressing expenses. For now—as well as the foreseeable future—I'd have to take Zack at his word and make peace with my suspicions. I had no other choice.

After Zack left, I placed Ralph in his cage, locked up the house, and climbed the stairs to the garage apartment where I planned to spend an uninterrupted day in front of my computer.

Two hours later, as I proofed the craft pages for the *American*

Woman issue about to go to press, I heard heavy footfalls making their way up the stairs. I froze. My heart pounded in my ears.

Had Lawrence sent one of his goons to kill me?

I had no escape. As quietly as possible, I made my way into Zack's bedroom and opened the closet door, reaching up to the top shelf in search of his gun case. I'd never fired a gun in my life, but if ever there was a time to learn by doing, this might be it.

Except the gun was missing.

Zack lied to me!

Someone pounded on the door. Fear shot waves of tremors through my limbs. I grabbed the closet doorjamb to keep from collapsing onto the floor.

I'm going to die.

"Mrs. Pollack? You in there?"

Spader? I'd never been so happy to hear that gruff, tobacco-damaged voice.

I opened my mouth to answer, but my words came out as a squeak. I closed my eyes and took a few deep breaths to steady my nerves and tried again. "Be right there." Then I exited the bedroom and made my way across the living room.

"You okay?" he asked when I swung open the door. "You look like you've seen a ghost."

Not a ghost, just my life flashing before my eyes. "Come in, Detective. I'm fine."

He eyed me up and down, skepticism written all over his face. "If you say so."

I offered him a seat. After he settled into a chair, I sat opposite him on the edge of the sofa and asked, "What can I do for you?"

"I looked into your theory regarding Tuttnauer."

I hoped Spader was about to alleviate my fears by telling me he found no evidence Lawrence wasn't up to his old tricks. However, if that were the case, wouldn't he have called rather than making a special trip? I clasped my hands together to stem the shaking and leaned forward. "And?"

SIXTEEN

When Spader didn't immediately respond, I repeated my question. "And?"

"Since contraband is a huge problem in prisons," he said, "random searches are routinely performed. When I notified the warden of my concern—"

"*Your* concern?"

Spader raised one of his bushy salt-and-pepper eyebrows. "He wasn't going to toss a cell block based on *your* suspicions, Mrs. Pollack. The request had to come from law enforcement."

"I see."

"No, I don't think you do. Can you imagine the chaos if anyone could insist a prison be searched at any time for any reason, whether valid or not? Not to mention the cost, let alone the legal ramifications? The courts would be tied up in lawsuits for years."

"Because prisoners' rights supersede victims' safety?"

Spader glared at me, his brow wrinkling, his mouth forming a tight line before he spoke through gritted teeth. "Because in this country we don't trample on the Constitution."

I sighed. "Point taken. Did they find anything?"

"A burner phone."

"Mama said the calls she received from Lawrence came from the prison. She declined to accept them."

"Tuttnauer used the prison phone system for his legitimate calls, the ones to your mother and his lawyer. He used the burner for other business."

"What kind of other business?"

"The illegal kind. Over the last month he'd placed three calls to someone from the burner."

"Who?"

"The name Tommy Gravino ring a bell?"

I shook my head. "Should it?"

"He's a low-level hood living in Weehawken. Dumb as dirt."

"How so?"

"For one thing he's too stupid to know he should be using a burner phone."

"That must put a huge smile on the D.A.'s face."

"Damn straight. Certainly makes my life a heck of a lot easier. Anyway, his name and number popped right up in the history on Tuttnauer's confiscated cell. My guess is Gravino's doing Tuttnauer's bidding to earn points with the mob. The Feds rounded up quite a few of his cronies when they nabbed him. It's a good time for up-and-comers to make their mark."

"Lots of recent job openings in the family business?"

"Exactly. But only for those not dumb as dirt." Spader pulled out his phone, thumbing it for a moment before handing it to me. "This guy look familiar?"

I stared at the mug shot on the screen. The face in the photo scowled back at me, his lips pursed, his eyes narrowed slits under unruly eyebrows that had formed into a "V". An overabundance of gel sculpted his blue-black hair off his face, exposing either a high forehead or early-onset male pattern baldness. "Gravino?"

Spader nodded.

"He's a kid."

"Nineteen but don't let his age fool you. Seen him around?"

"Not that I recall."

"Keep your eyes open. If your suspicions are correct, this is the guy Tuttnauer has dogging you."

"You think he killed Tammy?"

"*You* think that. My money is still on Lambert."

"You're wrong, Detective."

"So you've said." He ran his hands through his closely cropped, thinning hair. "Look, Mrs. Pollack, I'm willing to give you the benefit of the doubt. That's why I contacted the prison, but you have to admit, it's pretty far-fetched."

It was my turn to raise an eyebrow. "Is it? The man put out a hit on two of my neighbors to distract me from questioning his daughter's accidental drowning. Two innocent people died because of that twisted psycho. And that was *before* I was instrumental in sending him to prison. Why is it so hard for you to believe that he's up to his old sick tricks?"

"It's not. Like I said, I'm giving you the benefit of the doubt." He shrugged. "You could be right. Stranger things have happened, especially when it comes to cases that involve you."

I didn't know whether to take that as a compliment or not, but I decided against rising to the bait. "Then you'll check out Gravino's alibi?"

"Already on it. And I've got someone tailing him just to be on the safe side."

I handed the phone back to Spader. "What about Lawrence?"

"Getting caught with that phone landed him in solitary for a month. Other than his lawyer, he won't be seeing or speaking to anyone."

"How'd he get the phone?"

"The same way they all get contraband, either from their crooked lawyers or corrections officers on the take." He rose to leave. "Keep your eyes open, Mrs. Pollack. Just because Tuttnauer is in solitary for the next few weeks doesn't mean he hasn't already set future events in motion."

After dropping that comforting bomb on me, Spader departed, leaving me jumping at every unexpected sound and constantly running to the window to scan the street for unfamiliar parked vehicles. Twice I noticed a patrol car cruise down the street and wondered if Spader had requested periodic drive-bys. If so, rather than allaying my fears, knowing the cops were keeping an eye on me only confirmed my suspicions about Lawrence and raised my anxiety level by a few hundred notches.

Shortly before noon I heard a car pull into the driveway. I ran to the window, hoping to find Zack had returned early. Instead I watched as Ira cut the engine and exited a shiny new silver Mercedes with dealer plates. Even though I'd admonished him countless times to call before dropping by, this time I breathed a sigh of relief at the sight of my half-brother-in-law. That alone spoke volumes about my current anxiety level. Talk about desperation!

I opened the apartment door, stepped onto the landing, and waved to let him know I wasn't in the house. His face lit up in a broad grin as he waved back. I stepped inside and closed the door before the whipping December winds turned me into a Popsicle. (Or would that be a *Momsicle*?) A moment later Ira bounded up the staircase and entered the apartment.

"I had a feeling you might be working from home today," he said. "I heard on the news most of Morris County is without power." He glanced around the apartment. "Zack's not here?"

"He's out of town today."

"That's too bad," he said, but something in his expression told me his private thoughts didn't match his spoken words.

"What brings you across the state, Ira?"

"I had a meeting this morning in Elizabeth. Figured, if you were working from home, I'd swing by on my way back to see if I could convince you to join me for lunch."

"I'd be delighted."

"Really?"

"Don't look so surprised."

Ira lowered his head and mumbled to his boots. "You've been avoiding me lately. I thought maybe you were angry about something."

I sighed. There was so much about Ira that angered me, but I didn't want to hurt his feelings, and I certainly didn't want a confrontation—especially today. I opted for the coward's way out. "It's been a rough week, Ira. I have a lot on my mind."

He reached for my hands and clasped them in both of his gloved ones. "Is it Zack? Are the two of you having problems?"

Did I detect a note of hope in his voice? Every so often I got the uncomfortable feeling that Ira would like nothing better than to learn Zack and I had broken up. I pulled my hands away and took a step backwards. "No, of course not. Why would you think that?"

Two crimson spots sprouted on his already ruddy cheeks. "I don't know...I just...what can I do to help? Do you need money?"

Ira lived by the philosophy that if you threw enough money

at a problem, it disappeared. You'd think by now he'd realize such an approach had serious flaws. Money hadn't kept his second wife from cheating on him, and all the gifts he showered on his children only made them prime candidates for a Willy Wonka comeuppance. "This has nothing to do with finances, Ira, and there's really nothing you can do to help."

"You know I'd do anything for you, Anastasia."

"I know."

"Then let me help you. Please."

"How about we get that lunch, okay?"

"You'll tell me what's going on once we arrive at the restaurant?"

I'd never met a man with such a need to be needed. I wasn't about to tell him anything regarding Shane, and I saw no point in divulging the latest incident with Lawrence. Why worry him? Besides, from what I'd seen, Lawrence had a soft spot when it came to Ira, or at least for Ira's money. Even with everything Lawrence had done, I never believed for a moment he'd set his goons on Ira or his children. I was the psycho's prime target.

I saw no harm, though, in tossing Ira a proverbial bone by filling him in on Lucille's latest escapade. Perhaps knowing more about the real Lucille would open his eyes to the truth.

When it came to his father's first love, Ira was totally clueless. He kept trying to win Lucille over, refusing to understand that the mere sight of him was like a steel hammer and sickle to her commie heart. Lucille looked at Ira and saw the only two people she'd ever loved, both of whom she'd lost.

I grabbed my coat and said, "We'll talk over lunch. I promise."

Ira and I had never spent any one-on-one time together, something that suited me just fine but obviously bothered him. Instead of picking a local restaurant, he drove us into Millburn.

"How lucky is this?" he asked as he parked the Mercedes at the curb on Main Street. "We couldn't get any closer."

I turned to look at the restaurant and swallowed back a gasp as I read the name emblazoned on the plate-glass window. "Ristorante Gravino?"

"Ever been here?"

I shook my head and sent up a quick prayer to the God of Coincidences, hoping there was no connection between the restaurant and Lawrence's mob wannabe. Talk about leaping from the frying pan into the fire! I had only agreed to lunch with Ira because Spader's visit had turned me into a basket case.

I stared at the name on the window. Was Gravino a common Italian surname? I desperately hoped so. "How do you know about this place?"

"I grew up in Millburn. I'm sure I mentioned it."

"I don't think so." Spader had said Tommy Gravino lived in Weehawken. He never mentioned Millburn. Maybe it was nothing but coincidence.

Ira shrugged. "The Gravinos lived next door to us. Great family. Tommy Two took over the restaurant after his father retired."

"Tommy Two?"

"Tomas, actually, like his father, but everyone always called him Tommy Two. We went to school together. He's grooming his son, Tommy Three, to take over the business some day, but he's got his work cut out for him." Ira punctuated his last statement with a frown.

"Why is that?"

"From what I can see, Tommy Three hasn't shown much interest in becoming a restaurateur. He's a bit of a rebel."

"In what way?"

Ira shrugged. "He wants to do his own thing, whatever that is. I'm not sure even he knows."

If Tommy Three was the same Tommy Gravino as the one in cahoots with Lawrence, I knew his career of choice. However, I had no way of probing without raising Ira's suspicions. It's not like I could come out and ask him if Tommy Three now lives in Weehawken.

Ira had offered up very little information regarding his life prior to our meeting last summer. I ticked off in my mind the few facts I'd learned about him: He and Karl had had the same father. His parents were both deceased. He had three kids by his first wife. She died of cancer several years ago. I couldn't remember if he'd ever mentioned her name or the type of cancer that had killed her. Neither he nor his kids ever spoke of her.

In addition, Ira owned half a dozen car dealerships throughout the state, and his second wife was murdered. However, the murder occurred after we met.

That was the nutshell sum total of my Ira knowledge. Not only did he shy away from talking about himself, I made a point of not encouraging him. Too much of Ira's life had already flowed into mine. I refrained from asking questions to stave off a dam breach.

We exited the car and entered the nearly empty upscale northern Italian restaurant. The ambiance struck me as better suited for lovers. High-backed booths separated the tables, affording diners intimate privacy.

"They have a strolling violinist and guitarist in the evenings," said Ira as a hostess led us to a table and handed us menus.

As soon as we were seated, he said, "This is nice, isn't it?"

I glanced at his eager expression, nodded without saying

anything, and turned my attention to the menu, trying to focus on the day's offerings. The task proved nearly insurmountable. I not only had to worry about a possible connection between Tommy Gravino and the Ristorante Gravino, I also had to fend off Ira's subliminal messages without hurting his feelings.

I had no desire to encourage any unrealistic fantasy Ira might harbor about me. Even if Zack and I weren't a couple, I'd never marry Ira, not if he were the last eligible man on the planet. I'd rather take a vow of celibacy for all eternity.

I thought about playing matchmaker, but I wouldn't wish Ira's kids on a total stranger, let alone someone I knew. Ira would have to find the next Mrs. Ira Pollack on his own. And good luck to her. She'd need it.

After the waitress took our orders, Ira leaned forward, his forearms resting on the table, his hands clasped around his water glass. "What's going on, Anastasia? You can tell me. I'm here for you."

I took a sip of water. The time had come to muster my inner actress. I needed to compose myself, place the Gravino coincidence on hold for now, and toss that bone to Ira. "Lucille is missing."

His jaw dropped open, his eyes grew wide. He pushed back from the table with both hands and flattened his spine against the back of the wooden booth. For a moment he stared at me, not uttering a sound. Finally, he said, "Missing? As in kidnapped?"

I bit my lower lip to keep from laughing. If someone had kidnapped Lucille, I'd gladly pay him to keep her. "As in she's skipped bail and is on the run."

Ira's brows knit together. "I don't understand."

As I explained the events leading up to Lucille and her communist minions going on the lam, Ira's eyebrows shot higher and higher toward his receding hairline. "Let me get this straight. You're saying your mother-in-law has been arrested previously?"

"Multiple times."

"For what?"

I counted off on my fingers her various recent illegal acts. "Disorderly conduct, vandalism, protesting without a permit, and assaulting an officer. That's just a few of her offenses from this past year and before they slap her with these newest charges."

"I had no idea. I knew she was involved in various social justice causes...but...I...I'm flabbergasted."

Ira had originally found me after he saw a news clip of Lucille being interviewed at a protest in Westfield. He put two and two together and eventually showed up on my doorstep, announcing he was Karl's half-brother. "Lucille believes in the Law According to Lucille," I said. "She often crosses the line from peaceful protest into anarchy."

"Where do you think she's gone?"

"My guess is she and her Bolshevik brigade are headed south."

"To Cuba?"

"Most likely Florida." I hadn't considered Cuba as their final destination. Perhaps their plan was to ditch the VW minibus once they arrived in the Keys and charter a boat to Havana. I made a mental note to contact Officer Harley about this new theory.

Did the Daughters of the October Revolution have a Key West branch? Were there chapters all along the I-95 corridor to aid fleeing commies?

Ira withdrew his phone. "I'll hire a private investigator to find her."

I reached across the table and placed my hand over the phone. "No."

"Don't worry. I know someone. He's discreet."

Had Ira engaged the services of a private detective when Cynthia ran off with the pool boy? I didn't ask. I already knew far more than I cared to about that sordid affair and its deadly outcome. "The police are on it, Ira. They have an APB out for them. You don't need to do anything."

"But what if they don't find her?"

"A bevy of octogenarian women driving around in a fifty-year-old VW minibus won't be hard to spot."

"But what if they refuse to surrender? What if there's a shootout?"

Was he kidding? "Trust me, their deadliest weapons are Lucille's cane and Harriet's mouth."

"Are you sure?"

"Positive. If she and her misguided sisterhood were armed, they would have accidentally shot themselves or each other long ago." That not-so-merry band of commie anarchists would give new meaning to The Gang Who Couldn't Shoot Straight—assuming any of them had the strength to lift a loaded weapon.

Ira mulled that over for a minute. "I suppose you're right, but my offer stands. If there's anything I can do to help—whether concerning Lucille or anything else—I'm here for you. We're family, Anastasia. Never forget that."

"I won't forget, Ira." How could I when he reminded me every chance he got?

The moment I saw the restaurant name, I'd lost my appetite, but when our food arrived, I forced myself to eat the salad I'd ordered. Throughout the meal as Ira made small talk and I listened with half an ear, I tried to convince myself that I was worrying over nothing. Mere coincidence.

While Ira waited for the check, I excused myself to use the

ladies' room, which was situated down a long oak-paneled corridor. Three generations of Gravino family photographs covered the walls. I stopped in front of the most recent one, a photo of Tomas Gravino handing the restaurant keys over to his son. A bronze plaque on the frame identified the other people in the photo. Tomas's wife Rose stood to his left. Standing beside Tommy Two was his wife Angelica and their three children—Angelina, Rose Marie, and Tommy Three, his gel-drenched blue-black hair looking like an oil slick atop his head.

I ran into the bathroom and lost my lunch.

SEVENTEEN

As I hovered over the porcelain throne, a thunderbolt hit me: Did Ira know of the connection between his childhood friend's son and his murderous ex-father-in-law?

I rewound the tape in my head and played back everything I knew about Ira. Had he ever told me how he and Cynthia met? I couldn't remember.

What if Ira met Cynthia through Lawrence and not the other way around? If so, that brought up a host of disturbing questions, including Ira's connection to the mob, and whether he knew of Lawrence's plan to eliminate Cynthia. That thought sent another wave of nausea coursing up my esophagus.

After several more minutes I finally exited the stall and headed for the sink to clean myself up. One thought kept playing over and over in my head: had Ira been playing me from the moment he entered my life? Did a much darker person lurk behind that affable, needy exterior? If so, what did that say about my ability to judge character?

I took a shuddering breath and studied my reflection in the mirror above the sink. Amazingly, given the circumstances, I only looked half-frightful. I could work with half-frightful.

After rinsing out my mouth and splashing cold water on my face, I ran a comb through my hair and applied lip gloss. Then I rooted around in my purse for a pack of Tic Tacs and popped two into my mouth. After a final deep breath for courage, I summoned my inner actress before returning to the table.

Ira stood as he saw me approach. "Everything all right?"

So much for my acting ability. "Why wouldn't it be?"

"You were gone for quite some time."

"Women always take longer than men, Ira. You should know that."

"Of course." His cheeks flushed as he held my coat out for me. "Ready?"

"Yes, I need to get home to finish some editing."

"Oh." The corners of his mouth dipped. "I thought we'd take a short detour so I can show you the new house."

"You've made settlement already?"

"No, but we can do a drive-by. It's not all that much out of our way."

When I agreed, his face brightened. Ira was either a master of manipulation or an insecure puppy in need of constant petting. I'd always assumed the latter, but in light of today's events, I no longer had faith in my own judgment. Therefore, as soon as I returned home, I'd place a call to my very own law enforcement Rottweiler, Detective Samuel Spader.

On the other hand, maybe I had no need to worry about Ira. I'd gone to school with dozens of Mafia princes and princesses. Some later went into the family business. That didn't make me complicit in any of their crimes. By the same logic, having a friend whose son yearned to make his mark in the mob didn't prove Ira was guilty of anything. Still, the coincidence unnerved me.

Once we arrived back in Westfield, Ira cut through the shopping district and down Prospect Street, stopping in front of a sprawling three-story Craftsman-style McMansion with a sweeping cobblestone driveway that led to a three-car garage. "What do you think?" he asked.

I gaped at the structure. "That's a lot of house, Ira. Four-thousand square feet?"

He puffed out his chest. "Five. Do you like it?"

I forced a smile, hoping he wouldn't pick up on my insincerity. "It's perfect." A perfect example of conspicuous consumption. My nineteen-fifties modest rancher would get lost within Ira's new abode.

"Wait until you see the media room. We're going to host some fabulous movie nights."

"I'm happy for you, Ira." Then for emphasis I glanced at my watch. "Now I really do need to get home."

"Of course." He shifted into Drive, pulled away from the curb, and executed a U-turn.

As we drove down the street, I thought I caught a glimpse of Trey Krause standing on the sidewalk across the street from Shane's house.

~*~

After Ira dropped me off at home and before I called Detective Spader, I sat down at my computer to search for any information I could find on both Ristorante Gravino and Tommy Three. Dozens of review sites praised the restaurant for its food, service, and ambience with hardly any complaints from disgruntled diners. With very few exceptions, everyone who ate at Ristorante Gravino sung its praises.

I dug deeper, clicking page after page. Other than a local article about Tomas Gravino retiring and turning the business over to his son, I came up cold. If Ristorante Gravino and the first two generations of Gravinos had any connection to the mob, they'd managed to stay under the radar of both the police and the news media.

I turned my attention to Oil Slick Tommy. Several articles popped up detailing three arrests—one for driving under the influence, one for assault during a bar brawl, and one for attempted rape. Each time the charges had been dropped. A host of red flags flapped furiously on the horizon.

Finally, I Googled Ira, something I should have done after he showed up on my doorstep months ago. But I never doubted Ira's story, mostly because he was a younger, less-balding spitting image of my dead husband. Once I accepted him as Karl's half-brother, I accepted everything else about him.

The Internet contained a vast amount of information pertaining to Ira's automotive empire, along with an obituary for his first wife and several dozen articles detailing the events surrounding Cynthia's murder and her father's conviction. The only other mention of Ira that popped up concerned a college alumni event Cynthia had hosted. Still, to keep myself from going crazy, I needed confirmation that the guy was as squeaky clean as I once thought.

I picked up the phone and punched in Spader's number. His phone rang five times before he answered. His tone conveyed his joy at hearing from me. "What now, Mrs. Pollack?"

"Are you busy, Detective?"

"Always."

"I'm sorry to disturb you, but I thought you should know what I discovered today."

"Didn't I tell you to keep your nose out of this investigation?"

"My nose—along with the rest of me—wasn't anywhere it didn't belong; I was out to lunch with my husband's half-brother—Lawrence's former son-in-law."

"How nice. Did you enjoy yourself?"

"As a matter of fact, I most definitely did not." I proceeded to tell him about Ira's connection to the Gravino family. "I'm more than a little freaked out by this."

"You think he was sending you a message?"

"I don't know. What do you think?"

"I think there's a rotten apple in every family barrel. I know the Gravinos from my time in Essex County. They're good people. Tommy Three is their rotten apple."

"So you're saying I don't need to worry about Ira?"

"Probably not."

"*Probably* not?"

"There are no guarantees in life, Mrs. Pollack."

Except for death and taxes. Thanks to my deceased husband, I constantly worried about paying off the latter. Now, thanks to his half-brother, I needed to add the former to my ever-mounting list of fears.

~*~

The boys and I were about to sit down to dinner when a car pulled into the driveway and a pair of headlights lit up the kitchen. "Zack's home," said Alex, glancing out the window.

A moment later the spy-who-claims-not-to-be-a-spy came in from the cold. He dropped his backpack on one of the kitchen chairs and planted a quick peck on my lips.

"You're early," I said, turning away from him to remove dinner from the oven. I placed the roasting pan filled with chicken, carrots, and baby potatoes on top of the stove and covered it with a glass lid to keep the contents hot.

"The meeting ended in time for me to catch the 3:50 Acela."

With my back still turned toward him I said, "You should wash up for dinner."

Zack grabbed me by the shoulders and spun me around. "Something wrong?"

My eyes darted to my sons. Where did I begin? You lied to me? Where's your gun? Lawrence is after me again? Ira may be connected to the mob?

Zack followed my gaze. The next thing I knew, he took hold of my hand and said to the boys, "We'll be right back." Then he dragged me out of the kitchen.

Once we were in the bedroom, he closed the door, turned to me, and said, "Out with it. What's wrong?"

"Where were you today?"

Confusion settled over his face. "What do you mean? I had a meeting in D.C. You knew that."

"Where in D.C.?"

Zack sat on the edge of the bed and crossed his arms. "At the Smithsonian. What the hell is going on?"

Everything spilled out in a torrent. "After you left this morning, I went up to the apartment to work. I heard someone climb the stairs. I panicked. I thought for sure one of Lawrence's goons had come after me. I went into the bedroom to grab your gun from the closet, but it wasn't there."

Stunned, Zack stared back at me without saying a word.

I moved toward him. "Why did you need to bring a gun with you for a meeting at the *Smithsonian*?"

When he didn't answer immediately, I jabbed a finger at him. "I knew it," I said. "I was right all along. You are a spy."

He smiled. "Really? You came to that conclusion on the basis of not finding my gun?"

"Why else would you take a gun to Washington?"

"I didn't."

Either he was lying to me again, or he was telling the truth, and if he was telling the truth... "Oh my god! Someone broke in and stole your gun!"

"No one stole my gun."

"Then where is it?"

"Where I've been keeping it—"

"No, it's not. I just told you—"

"—in one of the darkroom cabinets. I did some reorganizing a few weeks ago."

I blinked. "The darkroom?"

He nodded. "Would you like to check?"

I collapsed onto the bed next to him and lowered my head into my hands. "I feel like such a fool."

He wrapped his arm around my shoulders and drew me to him. "But a lovable fool. So who was climbing up the stairs?"

I sighed. "Spader."

"What did he want?"

I told Zack about the burner phone, Tommy Gravino, and my lunch with Ira. "Now I'm second-guessing everything I thought I knew about Ira."

"You've had a busy day jumping to so many conclusions."

I turned to face him. "Can you forgive me? I'll make it up to you. I promise."

He gave me a peck on the cheek. "I'll take you up on that but later. I'm starving." He pulled me to my feet. "Let's eat first."

On the way back to the kitchen he said, "By the way, the gun is in a combination lockbox. You need the code to open it."

"Now you tell me."

~*~

Later that evening while the boys tackled homework at their desks, Zack and I camped out on the den sofa. Mephisto snored away under the coffee table. Ralph flew into the room and landed on Zack's shoulder, his perch of choice ever since man and bird first bonded.

Zack studied me as if he either planned to paint my portrait or pronounce a fatal diagnosis. I squirmed under his intense gaze. "What?" I asked.

"You doing okay now?"

"Stress-wise?"

"And otherwise."

I heaved a sigh. "Let's just say I've taken a few steps away from the ledge, but I'm still teetering on the brink."

He reached for my hand. "You need to walk yourself back about a mile."

"Rather difficult under the circumstances but I promise, I'll try."

Ralph squawked. *"If circumstances lead me, I will find where truth is hid. Hamlet.* Act Two. Scene Two."

Zack reached into his shirt pocket and rewarded Ralph with an almond sliver. "Try harder."

"Me or Ralph?"

"You."

"Right." Easy for him to say. "However, as long as you've brought up the subject—"

"The Smithsonian is not a cover for the CIA."

"Good to know, although not the subject I had in mind. I was about to ask your thoughts on Ira."

"Ira, huh?" Zack chuckled. "Ira is an open book; what you see is what you get. The man allows his own kids to run roughshod over him. Do you really believe a guy like that is leading a double life in organized crime?"

"I suppose when you put it that way..."

"Besides," he continued, "the Feds turned over every rock in their investigation of Lawrence and his cronies. They rounded up all the cockroaches that scurried out. With everyone they indicted and convicted, if Ira had more than a marital connection to the mob, what are the chances he would have evaded detection? The guy is no Keyser Söze."

Zack made sense, especially once he referenced *The Usual Suspects*. "All right. You've convinced me. I took a flying leap and did a face-plant into a totally ridiculous conclusion."

Using his index finger, he executed a checkmark in the air. "One down. Shall we move on to the next?"

I raised both eyebrows. It would take much more than a relocated gun to convince me the guy didn't juggle both an overt and a covert career. One battle did not a war win. So I lobbed him a curve ball. "Trey Krause."

"What about him?"

I told Zack how I thought I had seen the food bank board treasurer as Ira and I drove down Prospect Street. "I can't be one hundred percent certain, but it looked like him. He stood on the opposite side of the street, his arms crossed over his chest, glaring at Shane's house."

"Glaring?"

"That's what it looked like to me."

"Maybe he showed up unannounced again to try to sell Shane on his brokerage services."

"I think Shane made it quite clear at the time exactly what he thought of Krause."

Zack shrugged. "Some people are dense. Others don't like to

take no for an answer."

"Which category do you think Trey falls into?"

"Definitely the latter."

"I can't help but think something more is going on with him."

"Surely you're not suggesting he killed Tammy?"

"Of course not. That makes no sense."

"Good. Because that would be one huge leap, even for you."

"Agreed."

"Keep in mind," he continued, "Shane and Trey first met at the crafts fair last Sunday."

"As far as we know."

Zack raised both eyebrows. "Haven't you jumped to enough conclusions today?"

EIGHTEEN

The next morning I awoke to a cacophony of metallic clanging and banging punctuated by shouting. I rolled over to find Zack's side of the bed empty. The clock on my nightstand read a-quarter-past-too-early-for-so-much-noise. I pulled on my robe, and after a quick trip to the bathroom, made my way to the kitchen.

As I passed the boys' bedroom, I pounded on the door to wake them. "Rise and shine, gentlemen."

Twin groans answered back.

I found Zack preparing breakfast smoothies. "What's all that noise outside?" I shouted over the whirring blender.

"Betty Bentworth's house is coming down."

"In the snow?"

Zack shrugged. "The quicker they get new homes built and sold, the more profit they make. With the house gone, they can dig the foundation and pour concrete at the first thaw. Once that's complete, they can start framing, no matter how cold it gets."

I retraced my steps into the living room and pulled up one of the shades covering the bay window that looked out onto the street. A flotilla of construction vehicles filled every available curbside parking space on both sides of the road. An oversized Dumpster sat parked on Betty Bentworth's driveway. Half a dozen men scurried back and forth, hauling items from the house and unceremoniously tossing them into the Dumpster.

"We're about to get our first McMansion on the street," said Zack, coming up behind me. He handed me a smoothie.

"I'm not surprised," I said. "I suspect everything inside that house is original, including the seventy-year-old wiring and plumbing."

"Starting from scratch is probably much cheaper than attempting a renovation," he said, "but it's a shame. That house had character. At best something cookie cutter will spring up in its place."

"At best? What could be worse?"

"An eyesore."

I sighed. "Beauty is in the eye of the beholder." Some of the new-builds kept to the original Victorian and Craftsman style of many of the original Westfield homes built prior to the cape cods, ranchers, and split-levels of the fifties and sixties. However, some of the builders buying up older properties possessed an extremely skewed sense of beauty, which resulted in the construction of garish, nouveau riche monstrosities. I hoped we weren't about to see one of those rise across the street.

"Betty's kids probably wanted to unload the house as quickly and easily as possible," said Zack. "Selling to a builder means no inspections and haggling over repairs."

I watched as workers continued to toss away all remnants of my deceased neighbor's life. "Under the circumstances, I can't blame her children. I'm sure they want no reminders of their mother."

"Not that she had much. The only valuable items in that house were the copper pipes, which the work crew already removed."

I turned to look at him and noticed one of his cameras dangling from a leather strap around his neck. "How do you know?"

To my knowledge Zack had never entered Betty's home. I'd lived across the street from her for nearly two decades and had only set foot in her entryway and living room once, the day I discovered her dead from a gunshot wound to the head.

He held up his camera. "I slipped the foreman a few bucks to allow me to walk through the house to document it," said Zack.

"Why?"

"To preserve the memory of a home that will be gone by the end of the day. I also plan to capture the work crew bulldozing the house and hauling away the remains. I see the makings of a photo essay." He shifted the camera so I could view the screen and began scrolling through the shots he'd taken. "As you can see, each room contained very little in the way of furnishings."

No photographs or artwork decorated the walls. No knickknacks lay on the limited horizontal surfaces. No books lined the built-in bookshelves. "Makes you wonder why she moved into the house in the first place," I said.

"And what she did all day," added Zack.

"That I can answer. She spent her days seated in front of her living room window, spying on her neighbors. When she wasn't doing that, she was pestering the police over nonsense. She once demanded they arrest a six-year-old for drawing a chalk hopscotch board on her sidewalk."

Zack rolled his eyes.

"I often wondered how she could afford that house, but maybe she inherited it along with the silver."

"What silver?" asked Zack.

"The pieces in the living room, an ornate pair of candlesticks and a matching five-piece silver tea service. They seemed so incongruous with the sparse, threadbare furnishings in the room. Didn't you notice them?"

"Where were they?"

"The candlesticks were on the mantle, and the tea service was on her coffee table."

Zack scrolled back to the photos he'd taken of the living room. Both the mantle and coffee table were empty.

I shrugged. "Looks like someone walked off with them." A long list of suspects flipped through my head—any one of dozens of first responders who traipsed in and out of Betty's house the night of her murder—the attorney her children had hired, the realtor who'd sold the house, the builder who'd purchased it, the men currently working across the street.

"Do you think we should notify the police?" I asked.

"I wouldn't bother," said Zack. "If they were the only items of value in the entire house, most likely they weren't stolen."

"Then what happened to them?"

"My guess is someone in authority took them to send to her children."

That made sense.

"Besides," he added. "Even if that's not the case, those candlesticks and tea service no longer exist."

"Melted down?"

"At the going rate for an ounce of silver? Definitely."

I drained my glass and turned from the window. The aroma of

fresh-brewed coffee drew me toward the kitchen. The boys entered as I finished pouring two cups. "Where's Mephisto?" I asked.

"Still snoring in the den," said Nick.

Once again I offered to spare the boys morning pet duty. They rewarded my generous offer with dual cheek pecks. "You're the best," said Alex.

"Ditto," said Nick.

"Don't get too used to it," I said, filling Ralph and Mephisto's food and water dishes. "I expect the office will reopen Monday morning. Then it's back to dog and parrot chores for both of you."

After gulping down their smoothies, they donned their coats and grabbed their backpacks. As they dashed out the back door, they offered Zack and me an over-the-shoulder wave accompanied by a sing-song, "Bye, Mom. Bye, Zack."

After Zack and I finished our coffee, he headed back outside to take more photos. I jumped into a quick shower while Mephisto continued to snore away under the den coffee table.

Ten minutes later, showered and dressed, I popped my head into the den once more and found the room minus one sleeping dog. I discovered Mephisto in the kitchen where he was chowing down on his kibble.

I stepped into the mudroom to retrieve his leash. The next thing I knew, my legs flew out from under me, and I landed with a splat in a puddle of piddle. Devil Dog paused, lifted his head from his bowl, and stared at me. I swear I could read his mind.

I glared back at him. "You did that on purpose, didn't you?" And here I thought Lucille's dog and I had entered into a détente of sorts. After all, he had saved my life over the summer, but I suppose détente—and bladder capacity—only go so far. "See if I allow you to sleep in ever again."

Mephisto barked once before returning to his breakfast. I

growled at him as I grabbed a handful of rags and began sopping up his mess. Then I washed the mudroom floor with bleach before returning to the shower.

I had just finished dressing for the second time when Zack returned. "Why does the house smell of bleach?"

"Because timing is everything, and mine sucks."

"I think I'm going to need more of an explanation than that."

I glanced over his shoulder and discovered the peeing perpetrator hovering in the hallway outside my bedroom. "I thought Devil Dog and I had reached an understanding, but apparently he was merely waiting for the right moment to strike."

Zack followed my gaze. "With bleach?"

"With pee." Although, I suppose I got off lucky this time, considering he used fluid ammunition on a tile surface. Maybe Mephisto's liquid landmine was a warning. If I didn't heel, he'd amp up his attacks.

Zack studied the culprit in question. "How old is he?"

I thought for a moment, trying to remember when Lucille's previous dog had passed on to that fire hydrant in the sky. Karl had kept his mother at arm's length for much of our marriage. Even though she lived less than an hour away, we only saw her a few times a year prior to her coming to live with us. I could only offer a rough estimate of the dog's age. "At least ten years, maybe twelve."

Zack bent down and scratched Mephisto behind the ears. "Ever have a dog as a kid?"

I shook my head. "My father had allergies."

"In doggy years this guy is a senior citizen. I don't think he broke the truce, at least not deliberately. You should schedule an appointment with the vet."

"Great." Just what I needed, footing another of Lucille's expenses. She still owed me for the last time I hauled her pooch to the vet. Now with a prison sentence looming once the police caught up with her, I'd never get reimbursed.

The vet charges more than the pediatrician, and pets aren't covered under our family health plan. What if Mephisto needs expensive meds? Or worse yet, surgery? I didn't know which I dreaded more—Devil Dog breaking our truce or having to deal with his leaky bladder syndrome.

Did Pampers make doggy diapers?

~*~

I called the vet and scheduled an appointment for later that afternoon. In the meantime, we commenced on a schedule of walking Mephisto hourly to avoid any further surprises.

"Is this your way of telling me I need more exercise?"

I asked the dog after I bundled up and we made our way outside for our third trip of the day. This time Devil Dog and I braved the elements minus Zack who'd run off to a dentist appointment.

Heaven only knew what I'd do from now on with no one home for hours each day. I suppose I'd have to hire a dog walker. Yet another Lucille-incurred expense.

The sweet gum tree several doors down the street momentarily captured the dog's attention, but after a few sniffs, Lucille's picky pooch changed his mind and continued on his search for the perfect peeing spot. He took his sweet time while the chill air invaded my bones.

"Aren't you cold?" I asked. His legs were so short that his belly skimmed the surface of the snow, but it didn't seem to bother him.

Mephisto finally chose to grace a red maple in front of the next house, but instead of trotting back home, he maintained a soldier-like stance at the tree. He pulled back his jowls, emitting a low growl as he focused on a gray Ford pickup parked directly across the street.

I followed his laser stare, expecting to see a squirrel, a cat, or another dog lurking somewhere near the truck, but all thoughts of four-legged beasts disappeared when I noticed the oil slick black hair of the two-legged animal in the driver's seat.

Tommy Three held a phone to his ear, his left elbow propped against the driver's side window. He faced straight ahead. Although he couldn't have missed me as I ambled down the sidewalk with Mephisto, given the way his arm blocked his peripheral vision, he obviously hadn't noticed me catching sight of him. Since he had no idea I knew who he was, I'm not sure it would have mattered.

Had Mephisto's heightened doggy senses picked up some sort of malevolence emanating from Tommy Three? Was he warning me? He'd already saved my life once before.

"Good dog," I whispered as I yanked on his leash. Despite my racing heart, I forced myself to continue strolling to the end of the block. I then turned around and retraced my steps, ushering Mephisto back toward the house, but as I approached the pickup, I zeroed in on the license plate. As much as I wanted to, I hesitated to pull my phone out and snap a photo. I didn't want to tip my hand and alert Tommy Gravino I was on to him. Instead, I committed the plate to memory.

After I'd put enough distance between the pickup and myself, I pulled out my cell and called Detective Spader. "Tommy Gravino is parked on my street," I said when he answered.

"I know."

"You know? How do you know? And why aren't you doing something about it?"

"We're keeping an eye on him, Mrs. Pollack."

"Really? I don't see any unmarked cars on the street."

"Thank you. That's a testament to our fine police work."

I glanced skyward. Did Union County now employ drones? I neither heard nor saw any. And if so, were those drones armed? Because as far as I could see, at this moment absolutely nothing and no one prevented Tommy Gravino from rolling down his window and shooting me. "Instead of 'keeping an eye on him' how about if you arrest him?"

"And charge him with what?"

"Stalking?"

"Has he been following you, Mrs. Pollack?"

"I don't know. Maybe. This is the first time I've caught sight of him."

"Then I don't have enough evidence for a stalking charge."

"Fine. What about loitering?"

"Loitering is a misdemeanor. He'd walk in five minutes. Besides, he hasn't been sitting there long enough for a loitering charge."

"How do you know?"

"Like I said, we've been keeping an eye on him."

"Then arrest him for burglary."

"Did he break into your house?"

"No, but I'm pretty sure he broke into Betty Bentworth's house."

"What makes you suggest that?"

"Her silver is missing." I explained how I knew.

"Tommy Gravino didn't take Mrs. Bentworth's silver."

"How can you possibly know that?"

"Because I took it."

"You?" I knew every police force had an occasional bad apple cop, but I never would have suspected Spader of being one of them. "How could you? You're supposed to be one of the good guys!"

"I am."

"Not if you stole Betty's silver."

"I didn't steal it."

"You just admitted you took the silver."

"Took it, yes. Stole it, no."

"That makes no sense."

"If you'll stop making accusations, I'll explain."

"This I've got to hear."

"The silver was the only thing of value in that entire house. I took it for safekeeping, tagged it, and locked it in the evidence room until we found Mrs. Bentworth's next-of-kin."

"Oh." Chalk up another leap for the Queen of the Conclusion Jumpers. If I had a tail, it would now be firmly tucked between my legs as I ran off to bury myself in the nearest hole. "I'm sorry I jumped to the wrong conclusion, Detective." Yet again.

"Apology accepted, Mrs. Pollack. I know you're under a bit of stress lately."

A bit? Lately? Talk about gross understatements!

"Bottom line, Detective, my life is in danger. How do you plan to keep Tommy Gravino from killing me?"

"He's not going to kill you, Mrs. Pollack."

"I suppose you saw that in your crystal ball?"

He let loose an enormous sigh. "In a manner of speaking. Look, Tuttnauer doesn't want you dead; he wants to make your life miserable."

"So I'm a thorn in his side."

"Exactly."

"Until he gets tired of toying with me and decides to put me out of his misery."

"I don't think so."

Mephisto and I had reached the house. I unlocked the back door and stepped in out of the cold. "Why is that, O Soothsayer?"

"Because he's still got feelings for your mother, and he wouldn't cause her that kind of pain. You're safe. Your kids are safe. If he wanted you dead, you'd already be dead."

"I'm not sure how comforting that is, but I suppose you have a point." I paused for a moment as I bent to unclip Mephisto's leash, then added, "But if you're correct, that gives more weight to my theory."

"Which one of your numerous theories is that?"

"The one about Shane Lambert's innocence in the murder of his ex-wife."

Spader let loose another sigh, this one gruffer than the last. "I'd like nothing better than to exonerate the man."

"You would?"

"Yes. I actually like the guy. But until I uncover evidence to the contrary, he's my prime suspect."

"I guess that means I need to dig up some evidence for you, Detective."

"No, Mrs. Pollack. That means you continue to keep your nose out of my investigation and allow me to do my job. Have I made myself clear?"

"As clear as mercury glass, Detective." I held my breath, waiting for him to comment on my snide remark. However, much to my delight, the detective had limited knowledge of crafts, thus no idea of mercury glass's lack of clarity. "Don't be a stranger, Detective."

Spader ended the conversation by saying, "Wouldn't think of it, Mrs. Pollack," before hanging up.

~*~

An hour later Zack still hadn't returned from the dentist, so I bundled myself up and hauled Mephisto into the car for his trip to the vet. As I drove down Central Avenue toward the We Care Animal Clinic, I glanced in my rearview mirror. A white Honda Civic followed behind me. A gray Ford pickup trailed the Honda. The Civic blocked my visibility. I could see neither the driver nor the license plate of the pickup. "There must be tens of thousands of gray Ford pickups driving around New Jersey, right?" I asked Mephisto.

He barked once. Too bad I didn't speak dog. I could have used some reassurance.

At the next intersection the Civic turned right, but the pickup stayed too far behind for me to make a positive identification. Two blocks later I slowed as I approached a red traffic light. The pickup swung around and pulled alongside me. I glanced to my left. An older man with a full salt-and-pepper beard sat behind the wheel.

Five minutes later I pulled into the parking lot of the animal clinic. Mephisto took one look at our location and refused to budge from the car. I finally had to haul him out in my arms and carry him into the waiting room.

I took a seat, wrestling the lummox of a dog to stay put on my lap. I knew if I allowed him onto the floor, he'd bolt for the door, most likely dislocating my shoulder in the process. However, the longer I sat with my arms firmly around his body, the greater my risk of receiving a golden shower.

Finally, after twenty minutes we were ushered into the examining room. I needed the aid of two veterinary assistants to hold Mephisto in place on the table while the vet examined him. "I'd like to keep him overnight to run some tests," he said.

In my mind I saw hundred dollar bills sprouting wings and

taking flight, but I had no choice. "Do you have any ideas at this point?"

"He's old. It's not uncommon for dogs to begin experiencing incontinence at this age, but we have treatments."

"What sort of treatments?"

"Meds. In more severe cases, surgery."

A flurry of additional Benjamins flew off toward the horizon.

"We'll call when we have the test results."

I thanked him and left the office. As I walked across the parking lot, I noticed a gray pickup parked next to my silver Jetta.

NINETEEN

Detective Spader stood, arms crossed over his chest, between the two vehicles. As I drew closer, he strode across the parking lot to meet me. "Unfortunately the officers didn't arrive soon enough," he said.

"Soon enough for what?" I glanced over at my Jetta. "Tell me he didn't key my car." Could this day get any more expensive?

"A bit worse than that, I'm afraid."

I sidestepped Spader and jogged the remainder of the way across the parking lot to where I'd parked. The Jetta's front end was jacked up on the driver's side, and my tire and wheel were missing.

"He slashed your tire," said Spader, coming up behind me. "At least we got him before he destroyed all four."

Was that supposed to make me feel better? "Did you arrest him?"

"I will."

"When?"

"After Officers Harley and Fogarty return with him."

"From where?"

"They escorted him to the Volkswagen dealership where he's purchasing a new tire for you and having it mounted and balanced. Then he's going to place it back on your car before we haul his keister to booking."

"He agreed to this?"

"Let's say we gave him no choice. Would you like to wait in my car until they return?"

Since I couldn't sit in my own car, and I didn't relish the thought of freezing my buns off while I waited for the Jetta to be put back together, I accepted Spader's offer.

As it turned out, we didn't have long to wait. Harley and Fogarty arrived with Tommy Gravino and my brand new mounted tire ten minutes later.

I jumped out of Spader's car and confronted the vandal, stepping so close to him that he cringed as I screamed in his face. "Lawrence Tuttnauer is playing you for a fool, you stupid Soprano wannabe. You think doing his dirty work is going to make you a made man? All it makes you is a freaking moron."

Spader placed his hand on my arm. "Mrs. Pollack—"

I shrugged off his hand. "No. This snot-nosed juvenile delinquent needs to understand exactly what's going to happen if he keeps doing Tuttnauer's business."

I turned back to Tommy. "If you ever so much as come within a mile of me, any of my family, or any of my friends and neighbors, I'm not only going to sue you for stalking, I'm going after your family's assets, including their restaurant."

"His eyes widened. "You can't do that!" He turned to Spader. "She can't do that, can she?"

"Son, you picked the wrong woman to mess with. Better listen to her. She'll make your life so miserable, you'll wish we locked you up and tossed the key in the Atlantic."

I placed my balled hands on my hips and stepped between Spader and Tommy. "Do I make myself clear, young man?"

Tommy nodded.

"I can't hear you."

"Yes, ma'am."

"Good. Now fix my car." I turned on my heels and marched back to Spader's vehicle.

A moment later the detective joined me. "Wow!" he said, plopping his butt into the driver's seat. "Remind me never to get on your bad side. You're tougher than the nuns I had back in elementary school."

I didn't bother to remind him he was already on my bad side if he continued insisting Shane had murdered Tammy. "I never thought my teaching degree would come in handy once I left the classroom."

"Maybe you should go back. No way any kid would dare mess with you."

"No thanks. I hated teaching."

"Too many Tommys?"

"Among other things." I sighed. "I have to tell you, though, now that I've confronted him, I don't think Tommy Gravino killed Tammy."

"Why is that?"

"He caved too quickly. That kid doesn't have the stomach for murder."

Spader nodded. "My feeling, as well. Hopefully between the two of us, we've scared him straight." He paused for a moment, then added, "Does this mean you're coming over to my camp?"

I shifted in my seat to face him. "If you're asking do I now believe Shane Lambert is a killer, absolutely not. I'm merely ruling Tommy Gravino out as a suspect." Lawrence was too devious. Chances are he hired someone else to do the real dirty work. Tommy was a sacrificial lamb used as a diversionary tactic.

~*~

By the time my new tire and I arrived home, Zack had returned from his dental appointment. I found him in the apartment in front of his computer. He was sorting through the photos he'd taken of the demise of Betty Bentworth's house, which was now a leveled, empty lot surrounded by dirty mounds of snow. Ralph watched with rapt attention from his perch on Zack's shoulder.

"Why is Ralph up here?"

"I thought he might like a change of scenery and some company."

"You realize he's got you wrapped around his beak, right?"

Zack fished a sunflower seed from his pocket and offered it to the bird. "I have no idea what you mean."

"Would you like to hear what happened after you went to the dentist?"

The mirth in his eyes morphed into worry. "What?"

I filled him in on my afternoon escapade.

"Makes me want to put out a hit on Lawrence," he muttered under his breath.

I gaped at him in disbelief. "You are joking, right?"

He rose from his chair and turned to face me. Placing his palms on either side of my face, he stared into my eyes. "Of course, I'm joking. You think I want to risk spending the rest of my life behind bars?" He paused for a moment before cocking his head and adding, "Although eliminating Lawrence would eliminate one big problem in your life."

"And create a bigger one. Besides, I don't think they allow

conjugal visits in prisons anymore, do they?"

"I wouldn't know."

"Let's not learn the answer from personal experience, okay?"

Zack chuckled before planting a peck on the tip of my nose. "I said I was joking, didn't I?"

"Next thing, you'll be suggesting we take out a contract on Lucille."

"Don't tell me you've never fantasized about *that* scenario."

I bit down on my lower lip and glanced away. "All I'll admit to is that I'm looking forward to her forced vacation at the taxpayers' expense."

"Ha! I thought so."

Since the boys had evening plans to go skating and out for pizza with a group of friends, Zack suggested we try one of the new restaurants that had recently opened in town.

"Just you and me?" I asked after we returned to the house. "You don't want to make it a threesome with Ralph?"

Zack removed the bird from under his coat and placed him in his cage. Ralph protested with a flap of his wings and an angry squawk. "Sorry, Ralph. The restaurant doesn't allow parrots. We'll bring you a doggie bag. I promise."

I raised an eyebrow. "A doggie bag?"

Zack bowed to the bird. "Pardon me, Ralph. I stand corrected. A parrot bag."

Ralph answered with a second squawk before adding, "*Then here's a man stands, that has brought his pardon. All's Well That Ends Well.* Act Two, Scene One."

"I hope that means he's accepted my apology," said Zack.

I eyed Ralph. He offered me a blank stare in return. "I'd say it depends on the contents of the parrot bag."

~*~

Thanks to a last minute cancellation, Zack secured us a reservation at Café Jacqueline, one of the newer restaurants on the Southside across the street from the train station. After handing over our coats, we followed the maître D' to a table in front of a large plate-glass window etched with the restaurant name in flowing script surrounded by filigree embellishments. A rope of white twinkle lights ran around the window's perimeter. Evergreens and holly, interspersed with crystal candlesticks and faux-lit candles, lined the windowsill.

"Our chef's special this evening is duck l'orange," said the maître D' as he handed us menus and the wine list.

I perused the menu as Zack studied the wine list. "Good grief!" I whispered.

Zack glanced up. "What?"

I continued to whisper, "I had no idea this place was so pricey. Good thing we're not going Dutch. I'd have to hand over my entire paycheck for the week." I'm not often prone to hyperbole, but the prices at Café Jacqueline rivaled the finest Manhattan restaurants.

Before Zack had a chance to answer, the sommelier approached our table. "Would you like to order a bottle of wine, sir?"

Zack looked over at me questioningly. "I finish the antibiotic tonight," I said. "I don't think it's an issue at this point."

He accepted the wine list from the sommelier, quickly glanced at it, then passed it back and said, "We'll have a bottle of Cristal."

I raised an eyebrow. At least one of us wasn't fazed by the enormous charge that would hit his AmEx this evening.

"Excellent choice, sir."

After the sommelier returned, uncorked the champagne, poured it, and departed, I asked, "Are we celebrating something?"

"Two somethings, actually."

"And what would they be?"

Zack lifted his flute. "First, Tommy Gravino didn't kill you today."

I lifted my flute and clinked it against his. "I'll definitely drink to that." It's always a good day when someone doesn't succeed in killing me. I took a sip of the champagne. "And the second something?"

"I sold the photos I took today for an obscene amount of money."

My jaw dropped open. I set my flute on the table and held it with both hands to keep from shaking. "How obscene?"

Zack grinned. His eyes twinkled along with the lights around the window as he continued to hold his flute in the air. "Obscene enough that this dinner won't put a dent in it."

"Even if I order dessert?"

"Even if we both order dessert."

I raised my flute again. "Congratulations! I'll drink to that, as well."

We had just clinked flutes for the second time when someone called out, "Celebrating?"

Zack and I turned to find Trey Krause hovering several feet from our table. He wore the same Burberry camel hair topcoat as when he dropped in at Shane Lambert's house. He crossed the short distance, pulled out one of the two empty chairs at the table, and joined us without waiting for an invitation.

"What a fortuitous coincidence," he said.

"And why is that?" asked Zack.

"I'm about to offer you another reason to celebrate." He paused, a look of anticipation on his face. I suppose he was waiting for one of us to ask him what that reason might be, but Zack and I simply continued to stare at him.

He concentrated his attention on Zack. When he didn't receive a response, he shifted his gaze to me, but I remained stone-faced and mum. The seconds ticked by.

Finally, as it became apparent neither of us had any plans to break the awkward silence, he cleared his throat and continued. "I'm about to offer you the opportunity of a lifetime. You have a chance to get in on the ground floor of a new IPO guaranteed to make you a bundle of money."

Finally Zack spoke. "No, thank you."

"What?" Krause's mouth dropped open. He stared dumbfounded at Zack. "How can you say no? You haven't even heard the deal yet."

"We don't need to hear it," I said. "We're not interested."

His face reddened. "That makes no sense," he said. "No one in his right mind would turn down a deal like this. It's a sure thing."

"Mr. Krause—" said Zack.

He turned to Zack and applied all the charm he could muster. "Call me Trey."

"Mr. Krause," continued Zack, "you and I both know there are no *sure things* in the stock market."

"Well, of course, nothing in life is one hundred percent guaranteed, but—"

"And," continued Zack, "any time a broker offers a *sure thing*, the only person who stands to make money on the deal is the broker."

"No, you've got this all wrong." Beads of sweat broke out on his upper lip. "I'm only approaching you because I know you're friends with Shane Lambert, and—"

"Has Shane invested with you?" I asked.

"That's privileged information."

The waiter arrived to take our order. "Will the gentleman be joining you this evening?"

"He was just leaving," said Zack. He turned to the interloper. "If you don't mind, Mr. Krause, you're interrupting our evening."

Krause stood so abruptly the chair tipped over backwards. The waiter's hand shot out, preventing the chair from crashing to the floor. "You'll be sorry," said Krause, his voice rising.

TWENTY

Diners at the nearby tables turned to stare at us. The waiter signaled the maître D' who rushed over to our table and asked, "What seems to be the problem?"

"This gentleman is annoying our dinner guests," said the waiter.

Surprise filled the maître D's face. "He's not dining with you?" he asked Zack.

"Absolutely not."

"My apologies, sir." The maître D' then took hold of Krause's arm. "I'm going to have to ask you to leave, sir."

Krause dug in his heels and shouted at us. "I was about to offer you the chance to make a fortune."

"I must insist," said the maître D' tugging on Krause's arm. "If you don't leave immediately, I'm going to have to call the police." He nodded to the waiter who grabbed Krause's other arm. The two men marched him from the restaurant, depositing him on the sidewalk.

Krause stepped in front of the window and pounded on the glass with his fist. "You had your chance," he shouted. Then he turned and stormed down the street.

The maître D' and the waiter returned to our table. "I'm terribly sorry about that," said the maître D'.

"It's not your fault," I said.

"But it is. When he walked in, he told me he was with you."

"Definitely not," I said.

"Please allow me to make it up to you," he continued. "Dinner is on us this evening."

"That's very generous," said Zack, "but it's not necessary."

"I insist," he said. "Please, order whatever you'd like. I do recommend the duck l'orange, though." He then signaled for the sommelier and said, "Bring this table another bottle of Cristal on the house."

After the maître D' left and we'd placed our order, going with his recommendation of duck l'orange for our entree, I asked Zack, "Do you think Trey Krause showing up here was a coincidence?"

Zack shook his head. "My guess is he was stopped at the traffic light in front of the restaurant and happened to notice us sitting inside. He saw an opportunity and grabbed it."

"I'm sure he wouldn't have accosted us had we been eating burgers at Five Guys."

"No, I'm guessing he figured anyone who can afford to dine here has money to invest. That was an act of desperation if ever I saw one."

"So you think he's in debt up to his designer haircut?"

"I'd bet on it."

"Hmm." I grew thoughtful as I sipped my champagne.

Zack smiled at me. "I sense something percolating in that brain of yours."

"You sense correctly. Trey Krause has access to quite a bit of money, both from his brokerage clients and as treasurer of a nonprofit."

"True."

The waiter arrived with our salads. I speared a piece of marinated asparagus but before placing it in my mouth, I continued my thought. "One thing life has taught me since Karl's death is that when it comes to money, desperate men often resort to desperate measures."

Zack nodded. "Our federal prisons are filled with white-collar criminals who embezzled funds from their clients and employers." He grew thoughtful for a moment as he chewed on a cherry tomato. Then he added, "I wonder when the food bank last had an independent audit of its books."

"Should we let Shane know of our suspicions?"

"Definitely. He handed Krause a sizeable check the other day."

"He didn't particularly care for Krause showing up for that check when he did. And he was certainly clear about not being interested in investing with him."

"Yes, but Shane strikes me as the sort of man who would put his personal feelings aside if his contribution would help a large number of people."

"The food bank certainly does that," I said.

Zack pulled out his phone. "I want to make sure that money goes were Shane intended it."

"You're calling him now?" Café Jacqueline struck me as the sort of restaurant that frowned upon cell phone use at their tables.

"Sending a quick text, asking if we can stop by later this evening."

After a few seconds, Zack's phone dinged, notifying him of an incoming text. He glanced at the screen, then nodded to me before returning the phone to his pocket.

~*~

An hour and a half later, having consumed one of the best meals either of us had ever eaten, Zack left a sizeable tip for both the waiter and the maître D' before we departed for Shane Lambert's home.

Much to my surprise, I discovered Alex's Jeep parked in the driveway. Half a dozen other cars I recognized as belonging to some of his friends were parked on either side of the street. As we approached the house, music and teenage laughter sounded from inside.

"Other Westfield parents must agree with us," I said.

"About?"

"Shane's innocence." I cocked my head toward all the cars. "Alex and Nick aren't the only high school kids here."

"And?"

Zack is such a natural with Alex and Nick that I sometimes forget he's never had kids of his own. I spelled it out for him. "If you thought the father of one of your kid's friends killed someone, would you allow your child in the same house as the accused?"

Zack rang the doorbell. "Definitely not."

"Shane should take some solace in knowing we're not the only people in town who believed he didn't kill Tammy."

The front door swung open. "You're not the pizza delivery guy," said Shane, stepping aside to allow us entry.

"Sorry to disappoint," said Zack.

"I'm not the one you're disappointing. I've already eaten, but I've got a dozen starving teens fading fast."

"Is that the pizza?" called Sophie from somewhere down the hall.

"Afraid not," Shane called back.

"I thought they were eating at the skating rink," I said.

Shane shrugged. "So did I, but apparently the pizza at the rink doesn't meet the high standards of their discerning palates. Sophie generously offered our house." He checked his watch. "They called in the order nearly an hour ago. Half of Westfield must be ordering take-out pizza tonight."

We handed over our coats, and as Shane hung them in the hall closet, the doorbell rang again. Zack opened the door to find a pizza deliveryman balancing eight large pies.

"Finally!" said Sophie, running down the hall with Alex on her heels.

"What are you guys doing here?" he asked, stopping short in front of me.

"Hello to you, too," I said.

My son had the decency to blush but tried to cover up his embarrassment by turning to the delivery guy and relieving him of his load. Since the telltale rosy flesh extended to his ears, he failed miserably. The pink had faded only slightly when he closed the door behind the deliveryman and turned around.

"Sorry, Mom," he mumbled, not looking directly at me. "I'm was just surprised to see you and Zack."

Sophie pulled on his arm. "Come on. Everyone's starving, and the pizzas are cooling off by the millisecond."

Alex glanced up, waiting for me to say something. I nodded toward the kitchen. "Go. Enjoy your pizza."

He offered me a sheepish grin. Then he and Sophie bolted for the kitchen.

"Should I grab you a few slices before they're all inhaled?" asked Shane.

"No thanks," said Zack. "We already ate."

"Something to drink, then? Wine? Beer?"

We declined that as well. After two bottles of champagne, the last thing either Zack or I needed was more alcohol.

Shane suggested we talk in his office, as far away as possible from the teenage cacophony in the kitchen and great room. Once inside, he closed the French doors behind him, not that it helped much to muffle the noise.

Shane led us to a burnt sienna leather sectional sofa off to the side of the room. The sofa wrapped around two sides of a live edge teak coffee table that held another bronze Remington, this one of a cowboy on a horse.

Once we were seated, Zack filled Shane in on our encounter with Trey Krause. He finished by adding, "His unsolicited—not to mention downright desperate—sales pitch raised suspicions in both of us."

Shane nodded. "He tried to hook me with a deal too good to pass up yesterday, refusing to take no for an answer. But at least he buttonholed me at home; he didn't ambush me at a restaurant. Still, I nearly had to drag him out the door to get rid of him."

"I thought I saw him on your street yesterday afternoon," I said.

Surprise crossed Shane's face. "You were here?"

I told him about stopping to see Ira's new house. "On the way home I caught a glimpse of a man who looked very much like Krause, but I couldn't be a hundred percent certain."

"What was he doing?" asked Shane.

"Standing across the street. He looked anything but happy."

Shane shook his head. "Something about that guy doesn't sit well with me."

"That makes three of us," I said.

"He could be running some sort of scam," said Zack.

"Or up to his eyeballs in debt and desperate for more clients," I added.

"Maybe both," said Shane. "I just hope that check I gave him buys food for the needy and not another Rolex."

"That's why we decided to stop by," said Zack. "You might want to contact the board president to alert him. I'm assuming the board knows of your initial offer to match whatever amount the kids raised?"

"Yes, but unless Krause told them, they don't know I doubled the amount when I wrote out the check. He may have pocketed the difference."

"Exactly our concern," said Zack.

"And if so," I said, "he might have to hock his Rolex to post his bail."

Before leaving, I poked my head into the great room to wave goodbye while Zack followed Shane to the foyer to retrieve our coats. The kids were camped out in front of the television, watching one of the Marvel superhero movies, while consuming copious amounts of pizza. Alex, Nick, and Sophie jumped up and ran over to me.

Alex spoke in a whisper, "Mom, do you have plans for tomorrow?"

"Why are you whispering?"

"It's a secret. We don't want Mr. Lambert to hear."

I nodded as I whispered back, "Other than chores? No, why?"

Sophie answered for him, also in a whisper, "Would you mind if I used your kitchen tomorrow morning, Mrs. Pollack? I want to surprise Dad by baking some of his favorite Christmas cookies."

"I can pick Sophie up before I go to work," whispered Alex. "We'll stop to buy the ingredients when I drop Nick off at work, then I'll drive her to the house."

I turned to Sophie. "You're not working tomorrow?"

"Not until three o'clock."

"Sure," I said, "I'll even help you if you'd like."

She threw her arms around me and whispered in my ear, "Thanks, Mrs. Pollack. You're the best!"

~*~

On the ride home I told Zack about my cookie baking date with Sophie. "I'll make myself scarce tomorrow," he said.

"Why?"

"I think Sophie would benefit from some pseudo-mother-daughter bonding, don't you?"

His comment startled me. I shifted in my seat to look at him. "You think that's what this is really about?" I had taken Sophie's request at face value. Shane was under house arrest. How could she surprise him if she baked the cookies at home?

"I think Sophie admires you, but more importantly, I think she needs a positive female role model in her life, especially now."

I mulled over his words. "Well, Dr. Freud, I suppose I can't disagree with your analysis."

"The bigger question, though," said Zack, "is how do you feel about stepping into that role?"

Did I have a choice? My son's relationship with Sophie had thrust me into the middle of the Lambert family drama, whether I wanted a part in it or not. "I like Sophie, even if she does come with baggage."

"So do I, but I think we both know that's not the point. What happens if she and Alex split up?"

"Which, given their age, is more likely than not."

If that happened, Sophie might feel abandoned all over again. Yet, how could I deny her a relationship she so desperately needs? I sighed. "Right now I think I'll pull a Scarlett O'Hara and think about that tomorrow." Or next week. Or next millennium.

We arrived home to find a voice message on the house phone. "Mrs. Pollack, this is Officer Harley. I wanted to let you know we found your mother-in-law and her cohorts. Give me a call. I'm at the station."

I punched in the non-emergency number for the Westfield Police. Harley picked up. "Good evening, Mrs. Pollack."

If only Caller ID worked as well for all the spam and scam calls I receive! I pushed the speaker button so Zack could listen. "Where did you find them?" I asked.

"Islamorada, Florida."

"In the Keys?"

"Kleinhample's old VW buggy broke down on one of the connector bridges. Tied up traffic for miles. When the local cops showed up, they ran the plates and realized they had a baker's dozen of felons on their hands."

"What happens now?"

"We haul them back to New Jersey to stand trial. I'll keep you posted."

After he hung up, I said to Zack, "Ira suggested they might make a run for Cuba."

"Looks like he may have been right."

"Too bad they didn't succeed. It would have been a fairy tale ending."

Zack raised an eyebrow. "For you, at least."

"For everyone."

"How so?"

"Think about it." I clicked off the reasons on my fingers. "First, Lucille and her revolutionary sisters would probably be treated like octogenarian rock stars in Cuba. Second, I'd be rid of her. Third, the boys would get their own rooms back. Fourth,

Mephisto would no longer have to put up with her *s'mothering*. And last but not least, New Jersey taxpayers would be spared the cost of extradition, a trial, and the incarceration of thirteen little old Bolshevik ladies."

"A win-win, huh?" He chuckled. "You do have a unique way of putting a positive spin on things."

I sighed. "I could have used a fairy tale ending."

~*~

Alex dropped Sophie and two bags of groceries off at eight-thirty the next morning. As she unpacked the cookie ingredients, Zack entered the kitchen. "I'm off," he said, wrapping an arm around my waist and planting a kiss on my lips. "I'll see you later this afternoon."

Was he headed to Macy's to buy underwear or on a secret spy mission for his alphabet agency of choice? He hadn't mentioned his itinerary for the day. I tamped down my curiosity. The mundane didn't matter; the extraordinary would, as usual, remain a secret. I told him to enjoy himself and turned my attention to Sophie and Christmas cookie baking.

I had mixed feelings about spending several hours alone with Sophie. For one thing, I was used to teenage boys, not girls, and the two sexes really do hail from completely different planets. With thoughts of my own teenage years uppermost in my mind, I'd hoped for sons during both my pregnancies. In hindsight, my mother deserved sainthood for surviving those years.

Add to that all the baggage Sophie carried around from Tammy's desertion and Shane's arrest, and I could have been in for one rollercoaster of a morning. However, much to my delight, Sophie checked all her baggage at the curb, and we spent a comfortable and surprisingly enjoyable few hours baking cookies. At times it felt like we'd known each other her entire life.

The experience had me reconsidering my dread of hormonal teenage girls. If I weren't on the cusp of my mid-forties, I might even consider trying for a daughter. Then again, I'm sure even Mama would admit I'd had a few good days every so often back in the day. I glanced over at Sophie as she packed up five tins of Christmas cookies. Having witnessed enough of her emotional highs and lows the last few days, it was a good thing I was in no position to contemplate another pregnancy.

~*~

My cell phone rang as I pulled into Shane's driveway later that afternoon. I placed the car in Park and engaged the handbrake, then checked the phone's display. Naomi. "I'd better answer this," I told Sophie. "It's work. I'll come inside to say hello to your father as soon as I'm through with the call."

"Okay." Sophie fished her house key from her coat pocket and opened the car door. Then with the five tins of cookies clutched against her chest and anchored with her chin, she hopped out of the car. Before closing the passenger door with her hip, she stuck her head back inside and said, "I'll leave the front door unlocked for you."

I nodded to her as I answered the phone. "Hello, Naomi."

"Anastasia, I wanted to let you know power has been restored to the office."

"So back to business as usual Monday?"

"Absolutely. I'm scheduling a staff meeting for first thing in the morning since we've all been working from home for several days. Do you have anything you want me to include on the agenda?"

"Yes, I have a few new layout ideas I'd like to propose and would also like some feedback on one of my upcoming projects." I rattled off a list of items. Naomi jotted notes, interspersing an occasional comment as I spoke. After a few minutes we hung up from each other. I cut the engine and exited the car.

As I entered the house, I heard Sophie's panicked screams coming from the kitchen. "No! Let me go!"

"Not a chance, kid."

My initial instinct was to race down the hall, but I froze when Sophie let loose a bloodcurdling shriek. "Oh my god! He's dead! You killed him!"

TWENTY-ONE

"He ain't dead," answered a muffled male voice.

"He's not moving," cried Sophie.

"And you'll wind up just like him if you don't quit struggling. We can do this the easy way or the hard way, your choice. Makes no difference to me."

Calling 911 at that moment wasn't an option. I couldn't make a sound for fear of giving myself away. How did I stop that guy from taking Sophie? What if he had a gun?

What if?

Of course he had a gun! Why wouldn't he? So how in the world was I supposed to disarm him without getting both Sophie and myself killed?

Sophie choked back a loud sob and asked, "What do you want?"

"What I'm owed."

"I don't understand."

"You're old lady promised me a huge payday if I helped her, and I aim to collect. You're my meal ticket."

"What are you going to do to me?"

"If you behave yourself? Nothing. We're just going for a ride. When your old man pays up, you get to go home. Not before. Now move it."

I ducked into Shane's den before either Sophie or her assailant saw me. Somehow I needed to incapacitate the guy, but gun or no gun, for all I knew, he stood seven feet tall and weighed four hundred pounds.

I scanned the office and caught sight of the bronze Remington statue on the coffee table. Working as quickly and quietly as possible, I dropped my purse on the sofa and removed my coat. I then slipped off my boots so my footsteps wouldn't give me away. With both hands I hoisted the statue, cradled it against my chest, and positioned myself inside the office entrance, hoping to remain hidden as Sophie and her captor headed toward the front door.

As I heard them drawing near, I hefted the horse and rider over my head. While I waited, I sent up a silent prayer to the ghost of Frederic Remington and every weightlifter who had ever lived. I had no idea how much the Remington weighed, but the spasms creeping into my arm muscles seriously hampered my attempted transformation into Wonder Woman.

"Oww! You're hurting me!" cried Sophie. "Stop twisting my arm. You're going to break it."

"You think this hurts? Pick up your feet and walk, or I'll break every bone in your body."

I heard Sophie's sobs grow louder as they approached. Then I watched as they passed the entrance to the den. He held Sophie from behind, one hand twisting her arm behind her back, the other gripping a gun pressed against her ribs. I took a deep breath, and silently crept out into the foyer.

"Open the door," he said.

As Sophie reached for the doorknob with her free hand, I slammed the statue against the back of his head.

A sickening crack echoed in the foyer followed by the assailant slumping onto the foyer area rug. Sophie turned, took one look at me, and threw her arms around me, sandwiching the Remington between us. We both stared at the body sprawled on the floor. A black ski mask covered his head and face. Blood soaked through the fabric and the rug.

"Is he dead?"

"I don't know." I kicked the gun away from his body. When it hit the hardwood, it skittered down the hall, landing halfway to the kitchen.

"I hope he is, but maybe you should hit him again just to be sure." She dropped her arms, stepped back, and pointed toward the gun. "Or shoot him."

The man didn't make a sound. No moans. No groans. I nudged his leg with the tip of my boot. He didn't move. "I don't think that's necessary. He's not going anywhere."

I placed the bloody Remington on the foyer table next to the other one. Then I hurried down the hall and stooped to retrieve the gun before Sophie took matters into her own hands.

"He hurt Dad." Sophie ran past me into the kitchen. I jogged behind her, trampling on broken cookies strewn across the floor once I entered the kitchen. Shane lay motionless alongside the island. Sophie had dropped to her knees beside him. Her body draped across his torso, she sobbed uncontrollably.

I placed the gun on the island and grabbed the kitchen phone to call 911. That's when I noticed an ominous typed note on the island.

As I waited for the call to go through, I crouched down to

check Shane's pulse and noted the huge goose egg on the side of his head.

Sophie raised her head. Her entire body trembled. "Is he going to be okay?"

I had no idea, but I didn't want to scare her. "He's breathing, and his pulse is strong. Those are good signs."

"911. State your emergency."

"I need the police and an ambulance." I gave Shane's address, my name, and told the operator two men had sustained head injuries. "Both are unconscious."

"We need to do something now," said Sophie. "We can't wait! Shouldn't we raise his head? Or is it his feet?" She shook her head from side to side and wailed, "I can't remember! I took First Aid, and I can't remember what to do!" She looked up at me, her eyes wide with fear. "Why can't I remember?"

The dispatcher heard Sophie and asked me to describe Shane's injuries. His color looked good. From what I could tell, he wasn't in shock, although I didn't know if someone could even be in shock while unconscious. But his skin wasn't gray. I didn't see blood anywhere.

"Wait for the paramedics," said the dispatcher.

I placed my hand on Sophie's shoulder in an attempt to calm her. "No, we shouldn't move him. We don't know what other injuries he has."

I returned to the dispatcher. "I also need Detective Spader here immediately."

"Why is that, ma'am?"

"One of the men is the killer he's looking for."

"Help is on the way, ma'am. Stay on the line."

Sophie raised her head again. Her jaw dropped open. "That's the man who killed my mother?"

I nodded. She eyed the gun. "No, Sophie. That won't help."

She sighed. "I know, but if Dad dies, I'm going to sue that detective."

I changed the subject. "Do you have any duct tape or rope in the house?"

"I think Dad has a roll of duct tape in his workshop."

"Get it for me."

"Why?"

"In case our killer wakes up before the police come."

She sprang to her feet, opened the door to the basement, and flew downstairs. A moment later she returned with a roll of gray tape.

I took the tape from her and before heading back to the foyer, grabbed the gun and stuck it in my waistband. Not that I didn't trust Sophie, but why take chances with a still maturing teenage brain? Kids didn't always make the best decisions. Besides, I might need the gun if the killer woke while I worked. I had just finished securing his hands when I heard the wail of sirens approaching.

I opened the front door. An ambulance and two squad cars pulled up to the curb. The paramedics rushed inside, stopping short when they saw the duct-taped killer.

"No!" cried Sophie as they bent over him. She pulled at the arm of the female paramedic. "Leave him."

Startled, both paramedics stared at Sophie and me.

"He's a killer," I said.

"You have to help my dad," sobbed Sophie.

"He's in the kitchen," I said.

"Hurry!" Sophie pleaded.

"Go with her," the paramedic said to her partner. "We'll need backup. I'll radio for a second ambulance."

Like Sophie, I wanted them both concentrating their attention on Shane, but I suppose that went against some sort of paramedic code of ethics. My callousness startled me at first, but I quickly rationalized my decision. What if they only had time to save one victim? Wasn't Shane's life more worthy than that of a killer?

Now wasn't the time to ponder existential philosophy and the worthiness of individual life. The police had followed on the heels of the paramedics, entered the house, and began to question me.

Detective Spader arrived before I got very far, and I started over. When I'd finished, he bent down, slipped a pen under the edge of the ski mask, and pulled it up to expose the man's face. "I don't believe it!"

"Who is he?" I asked.

"Our eyewitness."

"The guy who claimed he saw Shane with Tammy at the motel? I thought you checked his alibi."

Spader grimaced. "We did, but as you so recently reminded me, Mrs. Pollack, alibis can be bought. Looks like you were right all along."

Discretion being the better part of valor, I bit my tongue and refrained from saying, "I told you so."

But then again, I didn't have to. At that moment the paramedics headed toward us, wheeling Shane on a gurney. Sophie jogged alongside holding one of Shane's hands. "I told you my Dad didn't kill anyone," she screamed at Spader when she caught sight of him. "You should have listened to us. If my dad dies, it's your fault!"

Spader eyed me as he spoke. "Maybe I should have, but I had to follow the evidence. Cops can't rely solely on intuition." He turned to Sophie. "Or daughters who claim their father's are innocent. All daughters think their fathers are innocent."

I raised an eyebrow at Spader. Cynthia Tuttnauer Pollack died because she knew her father wasn't innocent and had threatened to expose him. However, once again I held my tongue. Sophie had fewer qualms. She stuck hers out at Spader as she passed us on her way out to the ambulance. At least she refrained from mentioning a lawsuit.

After Sophie exited the house I indicated the man at our feet and asked, "Do you think he'll survive?"

Spader studied the body and shrugged. "Hard to tell. The second ambulance is on the way." Then he turned to me. "You all right, Mrs. Pollack?"

"Not really. I already have his blood on my hands." I held them out to show him. "Literally. I don't want his death on my conscience."

"Taking a life is never easy, even when justified."

"Is that supposed to make me feel better?"

He shrugged. "I suppose not."

~*~

Sophie rode with Shane in the ambulance to the hospital. After Spader finished questioning me and allowed me to leave, I followed in my car, first sending a text to Alex, asking him to cover Sophie's shift.

"Y?" he texted back. "Everything OK?"

I replied with a thumbs-up emoji and "Will explain later." Then I started to send Zack a text, but struggled with exactly what to say. I deleted what I'd typed, deciding to call as soon as I arrived at the hospital.

Once I parked in the hospital garage, I placed the call to Zack. It went straight to voicemail. I sighed. Leaving a message was only slightly better than sending a text, but at least he'd hear my voice and know I was okay. "Hey, there's been an incident. Shane's in the hospital. Call me."

Sophie and I were forced to wait outside the room while the doctors worked on Shane. She paced up and down the hall, chewing on her thumbnail and jumping at every sound. With little else to do, I slumped against the wall and watched her.

All that pacing finally exhausted her, and she joined me. "He'll wake up soon, won't he?"

"He's a healthy man, Sophie. That counts for a lot."

But what if it didn't? What if Shane had sustained irreversible brain damage? Somewhere else in this hospital doctors worked on the man whose greed could very well make Sophie an orphan. I wrapped my arm around her shoulders and hoped for the best.

"How did you know that man was my mom's killer?"

"From what I heard him say to you."

Puzzlement clouded her face. "I don't remember what he said. All I could focus on was what he'd done to Dad, and that he was trying to drag me away from him."

"He said your mother was his accomplice. He called you his meal ticket. I think he and your mother planned to kidnap you and force your father to pay to get you back."

"Do you think he killed her because he didn't want to split the ransom money with her?"

"I don't know. We might learn more after Detective Spader questions him."

She pulled away and faced me. Rage filled her voice, but tears streaked her cheeks. "I'm glad I never knew her, and I'm glad she's dead. She was a monster. What kind of mother would do something like that?"

I drew her back into my arms. "I can't imagine."

One of the doctors exited the room and held the door open for us. "He's awake. We're going to keep him overnight for observation, but you can see him now."

Sophie pushed past him and flew toward her father, stopping short when she saw him hooked up to a myriad of machines. "Dad! Are you okay?"

Shane forced a smile. "I will be."

She grabbed his hand. "I was so scared. I thought you were dead."

"It's going to take a lot more than a knock to the head to get rid of me, Soph." He looked at me and said, "I hear I have you to thank for saving the day."

"She was awesome, Dad! Alex was right. His mom is Wonder Woman."

My son thinks I'm Wonder Woman? I filed that thought away for a later date. "I couldn't have done it without your dad's help, Sophie."

Confusion spread across both their faces. "Me?" said Shane. "I was knocked out. How did I help?"

"You collect Remington bronzes. Without the one sitting on your office coffee table, I wouldn't have been able to thwart Sophie's kidnapping."

"She clobbered him with it."

Shane chuckled, then winced.

"Dad?"

"Hurts to laugh. Along with a concussion, I have a few cracked ribs. He must have kicked me after I passed out."

Sophie's features clouded with concern. "But you're going to be okay, right?"

He offered her a weak grin. "Good as new in a few weeks, Sweetheart."

LOIS WINSTON

"Promise?"

"Cross my heart."

A knock sounded on the door. I stepped across the room and swung the door open. Detective Spader and an officer I didn't recognize stood in the hallway. "I'd like to speak to Mr. Lambert," he said, "but first I need a word with you, Mrs. Pollack."

I stepped into the hall, closing the door behind me.

"I thought you'd like to know you didn't kill the perp," he said.

"How badly did I injure him?"

"Not bad at all. He came to in the ambulance. Either you're not as strong as you think, or he's got an extremely thick skull."

"But I heard bone shatter, and there was so much blood."

"Head wounds tend to bleed a lot. The scalp has lots of blood vessels close to the surface of the skin. As for what you heard?" He shrugged. "Who knows? Chalk it up to all that fear and adrenaline coursing through your veins at the time. Good thing you had the presence of mind to bind him up, though. He could just as easily have come to before we got there."

A shudder skittered up my spine. "I don't want to think about that."

"You okay?"

I nodded. "Yes, thank you for telling me, Detective. I didn't relish the thought of living the remainder of my life knowing I'd killed someone."

"Even if he deserved it?"

"Even if he deserved it." I nodded toward the door. "You said you wanted to speak with Shane?"

"I do. I've got some good news for him."

The two of us, followed by the other officer, entered the room. Sophie narrowed her eyes at her nemesis. "Why are you here?"

"I came to remove the monitoring device from your father's ankle." He addressed Shane. "In light of today's events, the district attorney believes he indicted the wrong person. You'll be happy to know all charges against you have been dropped, Mr. Lambert."

"It's about time," said Sophie.

Spader ignored her comment. He nodded to the officer. "Go ahead, D'Amato."

The officer approached Shane's hospital bed and removed the device. After he left the room, Spader addressed Sophie. "I hope someday, young lady, you'll understand that this was never personal. I was only doing my job."

She glared at him, her fists on her hips. "That's what the Nazis said at Nuremberg." She affected a mimicking, singsong voice. "I was only following orders. I was only doing my job."

"Sophie!"

She spun around to face her father. "Well, it's true, Dad. We learned about it in history class."

"Apologize."

"For what? Telling the truth?"

"For your insolence."

"Sure." She cocked her head in Spader's direction. "When he apologizes for arresting you."

"Now, Sophie!"

"Whatever." She turned to Spader. "I'm sorry, Detective Spader."

Spader nodded his acceptance, even though we all knew Sophie didn't mean a word of her apology. He redirected his attention to Shane. "I have other news if you're interested."

"Of course," said Shane.

"The guy who assaulted you and tried to kidnap your daughter is Boone Calvin."

Shane's eyes widened. "Not Trey Krause?"

Spader's eyebrows knit together, his forehead wrinkling. "The stockbroker?"

"You know him?" asked Shane.

"Of course. His firm handles the county employees' pension fund. Why on earth would you think Trey Krause attacked you?"

Shane glanced in my direction. "After last night—"

Spader spun around to face me. "What happened last night?"

"I didn't realize you thought it might be Krause," I told Shane. "I was about to mention I didn't recognize the guy."

"I see," said Shane. He pinched the bridge of his nose. "Would you mind explaining everything to the detective? My brain is still scrambled. I don't want to leave anything out."

"Tell me what?" asked Spader, pivoting his head back and forth between Shane and me. "What's going on here?"

Spader was not going to like what I had to say, but given that he'd spent most of his career working in Essex County, maybe he didn't have too much invested in the Union County pension fund. Hopefully, Krause didn't also handle pensions for Essex County employees. "I may have some bad news for you, Detective."

I then proceeded to tell him how Krause accosted Zack and me. "Shane has also been the recipient of his extremely aggressive sales tactics on two separate occasions. Between those incidents and what happened last night at the restaurant, we suspect there's something fishy going on regarding his finances."

"Fishy in what way?" asked Spader. "I hope you're not suggesting what I think you're suggesting."

"Embezzlement? I am. The guy seems over-the-top desperate for money."

"I have a call into the food bank board president to alert him," said Shane, "but I haven't heard back from him yet."

"We could be completely wrong," I said, offering Spader a crumb of hope.

Spader ran his hands through what was left of his hair. "Damn, I sure as heck hope you are wrong." Then he locked eyes with me. "The trouble is, Mrs. Pollack, I'm beginning to realize you're rarely wrong."

"Told you so," muttered Sophie under her breath.

Spader grimaced. "I'll notify my captain of your suspicions." He turned back to Shane. "So Boone Calvin. Ring a bell?"

Shane shook his head. "Should it?"

"I thought maybe you knew him from back in the day. He was your ex-wife's partner-in-crime."

"They must have hooked up after Tammy walked out on us. I've never heard of the guy."

"The two of them were arrested numerous times for running scams but convicted only once."

"Why is that?" I asked.

"Some of Calvin's many talents are witness tampering, intimidation, and bribery. Witnesses would either refuse to testify or claim they couldn't remember. In a couple of cases evidence disappeared. His other major talent is hacking."

"Hacking?" I looked from Spader to Shane, then back to Spader. "The burglary?"

"We think so. That's also how he entered the house today and got a jump on Lambert."

"I changed the password," said Shane. "There's no way anyone could have guessed it."

"Passwords don't seem to be a problem for this guy," said Spader. "That's how good he is."

"Did he admit to killing Tammy?" I asked.

"Not in so many words, but we'll tie him to it."

"If he and Tammy were longtime partners," asked Sophie, dropping her confrontational attitude, "why did he kill her?"

"When your mother learned your father had won the lottery," said Spader, "she and Calvin hatched the plan to kidnap you and hold you for ransom. It appears once she saw you at the crafts fair and spoke to you, she got cold feet and refused to go ahead with the scheme."

Sophie turned to me. "So I guess she was only half a monster."

I had no response. Shane may have assumed they'd dealt with Sophie's anger issues years ago, but how could the kind of damage Tammy inflicted by abandoning her daughter ever completely disappear? In Sophie's case her rage had apparently laid dormant, sizzling just beneath the surface, only to return with a vengeance when Tammy reentered their lives. I feared the havoc Tammy had wreaked by her brief reappearance would require years of painstaking work to undo. I made a mental note to talk with Shane about getting more counseling for Sophie.

Spader continued with his take on the murder. "I suspect Calvin flipped out when she tried to call things off," he said. "Whether he killed her accidentally or intentionally, we don't know at this point. A crew is combing through his motel room as we speak. They've already discovered signs of a struggle and an attempted cover-up of evidence. The D.A. is confident the crime scene unit will uncover enough to get a conviction."

"But you said he's gotten away with all sorts of stuff before," said Sophie. "What makes you think he won't this time?"

"He's never killed anyone before," said Spader. "DNA doesn't lie."

My phone rang. I glanced at the screen, saw Zack was

returning my call, and stepped from the room. "What happened?" he asked, after I answered.

I filled him in. "The good news is Sophie wasn't harmed, Shane will be okay, and the D.A. dropped all charges against him."

"That is good news. I have some news, too."

"What's that?"

"I can explain Krause's aggressive behavior and why he's so desperate to sign new clients."

TWENTY-TWO

"Why?" I asked.

"He's got a drug habit."

"How did you discover that?"

"I witnessed a drug buy going down."

"What! Where were you? Irvington?" And if so, what was Zack doing in that crime-infested hellhole?

He chuckled. "You think I'm crazy enough to drive my Boxster into Irvington and risk a carjacking?"

"I hope not. So where were you?"

"I was sitting in a long line of traffic on Route 22 in North Plainfield and happened to glance to my right. I saw Trey Krause standing beside a car in the empty parking lot of a boarded up strip mall. At first I thought maybe he'd had car trouble and pulled off the road. I considered turning into the driveway to ask if he needed help when a black Escalade with tinted windows entered the parking lot from the side road entrance and parked next to him. I put two and two together, grabbed my trusty camera off the passenger seat, and captured the entire deal going down."

"Talk about coincidence."

"Yeah, nothing like being in the right place at the right time."

Or was it? A part of me wondered how much coincidence played in Zack witnessing that drug deal. Maybe he'd spent the day shadowing Krause. I decided against voicing my suspicions. Instead I asked, "What are you planning to do with the photos?"

"I've already presented them to the drug task force. They confirmed the two guys in the photos with Krause are known dealers. Both have outstanding warrants. The officer I spoke with ran the Escalade's plates while I was there. Turns out they were reported stolen off a Kia at the Linden train station yesterday."

"Detective Spader will be interested in seeing those photos."

"Why? He's homicide."

"He was homicide in Newark. Now he handles a variety of crimes. He told me Krause administers the county employees' pension fund."

Zack whistled under his breath. "Time to hire a forensic accountant."

"Maybe they can team up with the food bank and get a two-for-the-price-of-one deal."

I hung up from Zack and reentered Shane's hospital room. "The plot thickens," I said.

As I explained what I'd learned, I watched anger harden Detective Spader's features. His hands balled into fists, and muttering under his breath, he stormed out of Shane's hospital room.

A few minutes later I convinced Sophie we needed to leave to allow Shane some rest. She reluctantly agreed.

"Might I impose on you once again?" asked Shane before we exited the room.

I nodded, knowing he didn't want Sophie spending the night alone in their house. "Sophie's more than welcome to stay with us tonight."

"Thank you."

On the way home we stopped to pick up some clothes for Sophie, sweep up the broken cookies, and put the house back in order. The crime scene unit had taken the blood-soaked Navajo area rug from the foyer and the Remington bronze as evidence. At least I didn't have to deal with cleaning up Calvin's blood.

"All that work," said Sophie, frowning as she dumped pecan lace, shortbread, raspberry almond, and gingerbread cookies into the kitchen trashcan. She scanned the floor. "We're missing a tin."

I looked around and discovered a tin with its lid still secure under one of the bar stools. "Here it is." I retrieved the tin and pulled off the lid. "These survived." Only a few of the iced sugar cookies had sustained minor damage.

"But most didn't," said Sophie, frowning again at the accumulation of broken cookies we'd tossed into the trash.

"If you're up to it, I think I have enough ingredients in the pantry to bake several new batches after dinner."

She immediately brightened.

~*~

Zack's cell phone rang Sunday morning. "That's your father," he told Sophie as she helped clear the breakfast dishes.

She held out her hand. "Can I answer?"

Zack handed her the phone. "Hi, Dad! Are you coming home soon?"

"As soon as I sign the release forms. Let me speak with Zack, okay?"

She passed the phone back to Zack. "He wants to talk to you."

"I guess that's why he called me," said Zack.

Sophie blushed. "Guess so. Sorry."

Zack grinned at her and placed the phone on the counter. "You're on speaker, Shane."

Shane said, "Hey, Zack, you and Anastasia have been so kind to Sophie and me. I really hate to ask for another favor, but—"

"Need a ride?" asked Zack.

"I can call an Uber if you have plans."

"My plan was to pick you up."

Shane chuckled. "Man, do I ever owe you and your girlfriend big time."

"Not in the least," said Zack. "We've enjoyed getting to know you and Sophie."

"Even under these conditions?"

"That's all behind you now."

"And you have no idea what a relief that is."

"I'll see you in half an hour," said Zack before disconnecting the call.

"Can I come?" asked Sophie. She bounced up and down on the balls of her feet, her hands clasped in front of her. "Please?"

"As long as I can borrow a car," said Zack. "Mine only seats two."

Sophie cast pleading eyes first toward me, then Alex. We answered at the same time.

"Of course," I said.

"Take my Jeep," said Alex.

Zack opted for the Jeep. "Better traction," he said, noting the gathering clouds outside.

"Not for Mom," said Alex, deliberately ignoring the *Mom*

Look I leveled at him.

A few minutes later Zack and Sophie drove off in Alex's Jeep. We agreed that if Shane felt up to it, Zack would bring him back to the house where we could help care for him the remainder of the day.

Ninety minutes later the three of them returned as a light mix of icy rain and snow began to fall. "I hope this doesn't last," I said, frowning at the sky. Winter was still officially ten days away. Snows this early in the season were often a harbinger of wicked weather throughout the next few months. "I hate snow."

"So I've heard," said Zack, hanging coats in the hall closet.

"I take it you're not a skier?" asked Shane.

"She's more the stay-in-the-lodge-sipping-hot-cocoa-by-a-roaring-fire type," said Zack.

"While the crazy people risk frostbite and colliding into trees," I added. "I'm no dummy."

"Noted," said Shane, punctuating his comment with a chuckle.

For a man who'd suffered a concussion and was out cold less than twenty-four hours earlier, he showed no outward signs of his ordeal. If anything, he looked like a new man, robust even. The dismissal of a murder rap definitely trumped a whack on the head and a kick to the ribs. Even so, Sophie insisted her father camp out on the sofa and allow her to wait on him. Shane wisely didn't object.

After lunch Sophie suggested we all watch a Christmas movie.

"Now?" said Nick, his eyes widening with shock.

"Why not?" she asked, holding up several DVDs she'd pulled from the bookshelf next to the television. "How about *Elf*? Or maybe *The Grinch Who Stole Christmas* or *The Santa Clause*?"

"We're not watching a Christmas movie," said Nick.

"It's Sunday," said Alex.

"So?" asked Sophie. "Is there some law against watching Christmas movies on Sundays?"

"Heck, yeah," said Nick. "It's called the NFL Law."

Sophie turned to me for support. I shrugged. "Sorry, Sophie. Short of a power outage, nothing comes between my guys and football on Sunday afternoons during pigskin season." Or Sunday nights or Monday nights or Thursday nights, for that matter.

She huffed a resigned sigh. "Fine. We'll watch football." Then she plopped onto the sofa between her father and Alex.

Shortly after the Giants scored their first touchdown, we heard the nails-on-blackboard screeching of brakes, followed by a loud crash and the intermittent wail of a car alarm. Zack jumped up and hurried from the room. I followed. As he swung open the front door, he yelled back to me, "Call 911." Then he raced outside, without bothering to grab his coat and leaving the door wide open.

I pulled my phone from my jeans pocket as Zack sped toward a gold Audi that had jumped the curb and barreled into my oak tree. While I waited for the call to connect, an ominous creak filled the air in-between the alarm wails. I watched in horror as the tree dove in slow motion toward the car.

"Look out!" I screamed to Zack.

"911. State your emergency."

Zack's head jerked up. He jumped back from the car as the massive trunk landed with a loud thud across the car's roof, the skeletal branches swallowing up the vehicle.

"911. State your emergency," repeated the operator. "Ma'am?"

"Sorry," I said, heading toward Zack and the car. A dusting of snow covered the sidewalk and street, and I soon discovered—after my feet nearly slid out from under me—masked a thin coating of ice. I let loose an involuntary gasp, as I fought for purchase. The last thing I needed was to fall and reinjure my wrist.

"Ma'am? Are you there? What's your emergency?"

I apologized again. "A car plowed into a tree." I then gave the operator the location.

"Are there injuries?"

"Probably. I can't tell. The tree came down on the car. The roof is crushed, and the limbs are blocking access to the doors."

"Can you tell how many people are in the vehicle?"

"Any passengers?" I asked Zack.

"I won't know until we cut away some of these branches. I can't hear anyone, not even the driver."

I relayed the information to the operator.

"The police are on their way," she said. "Stay on the line."

Zack ran to the garage, returning with a saw and a tree pruner. He began hacking through the larger limbs surrounding the driver's side door while I used the pruner on the medium-sized branches. Sirens in the distance grew louder as the emergency vehicles approached.

Alex, Nick, Shane, and Sophie joined us. Shane reached for the pruner. "Are you kidding?" I said, refusing to release my grip on the tool. "You've got cracked ribs."

"I'll do it," said Alex, taking the pruner from me.

Two patrol cars turned onto the street and came to a stop behind the tree-covered Audi. Officers Harley and Fogarty stepped from one of them, two officers I recognized but didn't know by name stepped from the second squad car.

A fire truck followed, then an ambulance. The firemen and policemen immediately took over for Zack and Alex. In no time they'd exposed the driver's side door, but couldn't force it open. The firemen grabbed the Jaws of Life, prying open the vehicle to free the driver.

Two firefighters reached into the car and extricated the driver. He pushed their arms away and staggered to his feet. My jaw dropped to my toes when I saw the man's face.

TWENTY-THREE

"Well, look who it is," said Officer Harley. "We've been looking for you, Mr. Krause."

Trey Krause cast a glassy-eyed, loopy expression at the collection of people staring at him and grinned. "Is that so?"

"Yeah, there's a BOLO out on you."

"Guess I'm a popular guy."

"Not the word I'd use," said Harley.

"What's a BOLO?" asked Sophie.

"Be on the lookout," said Alex.

I zeroed in on my son. "How do you know that?"

"Really, Mom? With everything that's happened to us over the last year?"

He had a point.

Krause reached into his coat pocket, pulled out a zip-locked plastic sandwich bag, took one look at the contents and said, "Oops! Wrong pocket."

He quickly shoved the bag back and reached into his other

coat pocket, withdrawing a stack of crumpled business cards. "I guess my reputation precedes me," he said, attempting to press a card into the palm of each policeman, fireman, and paramedic.

Everyone glared at him, making no effort to accept the cards. No doubt Spader had spread the word about our suspicions, and they were all worried about the money in their pension funds.

When he got to Zack, Shane, and me, hope waved the cards in the air and said, "Any chance you've changed your minds?"

"You have to ask?" I said.

He shrugged. "You can't blame a guy for trying to make a living."

"He's definitely on something," said one of the paramedics.

"No duh," said Fogarty. He slipped his hand into Krause's coat pocket and removed the sandwich bag. "Is this what I think it is?" he asked one of the paramedics.

The paramedic took the bag and studied the contents. "Fentanyl," he said.

One of the other officers crawled into the car and opened the glove box. "Well, look what we have here," he said, holding a pad of blank prescription slips once he exited the vehicle.

Harley grabbed Krause's arms and cuffed him. "Trey Krause, you're under arrest for possession of a controlled substance and driving under the influence, and that's just for starters."

Fogarty then read Krause his rights before handing him off to the two other officers who placed him in the back of their squad car.

After they drove away, Officer Harley turned to us. "I'll need statements from all of you."

I hugged my torso, rubbing my hands up and down my arms. The icy rain and snow had tapered off, but the temperatures had plummeted. "As long as I can give mine in the house. I'm about to turn into a Popsicle.

Once inside, the boys and Sophie returned to their paused football game. Harley and Fogarty joined Zack, Shane, and me in the kitchen. Harley pulled out his spiral notepad and began questioning me while I made a fresh pot of coffee. "You have any idea why Krause showed up at your house, Mrs. Pollack?"

Startled by his question, I stopped scooping grounds into the filter and turned to face him. "You think he was headed here? Why?"

"From the position of the car it appears he was attempting to park. My guess is he hit the gas instead of the brake. The vehicle hopped the curb and slammed into the tree. Sound familiar?"

"Shades of Harriet Kleinfeld," said Zack.

"Exactly," said Harley. "I guess you don't have to worry about her doing battle with that tree any more, not that she'll have a chance any time soon."

I sighed. If it weren't for Harriet's repeated assaults, my oak tree might have survived today's attack. "I figured Krause was on his way somewhere else when he skidded on a patch of black ice and plowed into the tree."

Although, given the thousands of homes in Westfield, it did seem rather coincidental that he'd crash in front of mine. We didn't live on a main thoroughfare; we lived on a small side street.

Then I remembered the gun in his glove compartment. Every nerve in my body stood at attention, vigorously waving red warning flags. I turned to Zack. "Is it possible he discovered you're responsible for turning over evidence against him to the police?"

"What sort of evidence?" asked Harley.

Zack explained how he'd stumbled upon Krause and the dealers on Route 22, captured the drug buy, and turned the photos over to the police.

"That explains the BOLO," said Fogarty. "Good thing you were in the right place at the right time and happened to have your camera with you. No telling how long this has been going on."

"I suppose you'll find that out after an audit," said Zack.

"If that guy's pulled a Bernie Madoff with our pensions," said Harley, "every cop and firefighter in the county will want to string him up by his thumbs."

"It won't get our money back," Fogarty muttered under his breath.

~*~

Detective Spader showed up shortly after we'd gathered around the dining room table for dinner that night. "What now?" I asked when I opened the front door and reluctantly ushered him inside. The man had a habit of arriving with bad news, and I'd had more than my fill lately, as had our guests. I shot a quick glance into the dining room and noted the tension on Shane's face and the anger on Sophie's.

"No need to panic," said Spader, following my gaze. "I came to thank Mrs. Pollack and Mr. Barnes. I figured under the circumstances their efforts warranted more than a phone call."

"Thank us for what?" asked Zack. He pushed away from the table and joined us in the foyer.

Spader nodded toward me. "Once again Mrs. Pollack has helped crack a case, this time a crime we had no idea had even been committed. I thought you deserved to know what we've learned."

"About Krause?" I asked.

Spader scowled and mumbled something better left unrepeated under his breath. I offered him a smile and waved my arm in the direction of the dining room. "Why don't you join us, Detective?

Have you eaten?"

"I...well..."

I doubted the detective encountered many such offers in the course of his investigations, especially from residents friendly with a former suspect and particularly when that former suspect currently sat at our dinner table.

Noting Spader's hesitancy, Zack added, "Please, have a seat, Detective. We have more than enough to go around."

I doubted the amount of food had anything to do with Spader's hesitation. However, I knew Zack wanted him to feel welcome. Spader glanced in Shane's direction. When the former murder suspect nodded, Spader heaved an audible sigh and said, "In that case, thank you."

He settled into one of my dining room chairs. Zack headed to the kitchen, returning a moment later with a place setting for Spader.

Shane had insisted on ordering take-out to repay us for our hospitality. As we passed around platters of chicken scaloppini, spaghetti with meat sauce, fried eggplant, and salad, Spader documented Trey Krause's tailspin from successful stockbroker to opioid addict.

"About two year ago," he said, bypassing the salad and helping himself to a large serving of chicken, spaghetti, and fried eggplant, "Krause took a bad spill while skiing in Vail with his family. As a result, he needed back surgery. Like so many people these days, afterwards he got hooked on prescription pain meds."

"And when he couldn't obtain more pills through legal channels, he turned to drug dealers?" asked Zack.

"Precisely. And those dealers have a way of bleeding their customers dry. Krause started draining his savings. When his wife noticed the missing funds and discovered his addiction, she gave him an ultimatum: go into rehab or else."

Sophie's eyes widened. "He chose the 'or else'?"

Spader swallowed a mouthful of chicken before answering. "He tried rehab, but sometimes it takes more than one stint to get clean. These opioids are brutal, worse than heroin. Too often they kill. After three failed trips to rehab, his wife had had enough. A few months ago she cleaned out what was left of their savings, kicked him out, and filed for divorce. That's when he resorted to some creative bookkeeping at his brokerage firm and the food bank to feed his addiction."

"And no one suspected anything?" asked Shane.

"Addicts are very good at covering up their addictions," said Spader.

Of course, they are," I said. My kids and I can certainly attest to that.

"His wife didn't tell anyone?" asked Sophie.

"She probably kept quiet to protect herself and her children from hurtful gossip," I said.

Alex and Nick glanced my way, but neither said a word. Zack reached under the table and squeezed my hand. Been there, done that. Only, unlike Mrs. Krause, I'd never had the opportunity to issue Karl an ultimatum over his addiction.

"How much did he steal?" asked Shane.

"Luckily, not too much," said Spader, "thanks to these two." He waved his fork at Zack and me. "He'd only recently started dipping into the tills and cooking the books. Otherwise he'd be in much bigger trouble. My guess is the D.A. will offer him a plea deal."

"What sort of deal?" asked Alex.

"A light or suspended sentence in exchange for giving up his brokerage license and paying restitution."

"How will he pay back what he stole if he has no money?" asked Nick.

"I guess for starters he'll have to sell that fifty-thousand-dollar bauble he wears around his wrist," said Spader.

Shane leaned back in his chair, his expression growing thoughtful as he chewed a mouthful of food. Finally he asked Spader, "This was a first offense?"

Spader nodded. "The guy was well respected and as clean-cut as they come prior to getting hooked."

"So you'd agree he deserves a second chance?"

"If he can kick his habit. He's got a long road ahead of him, though. Why do you ask?"

"I'd like to help him get that chance," said Shane. "I'm assuming you can contact him?"

"I can."

"Tell him I'll pay for his rehab at a residential clinic, no strings attached."

Spader's eyes widened. "That's an incredibly generous offer, Mr. Lambert. Why would you do such a thing? You hardly know the guy."

"And now, Detective," said Sophie, "you know exactly the kind of man my dad is."

Spader stared at Sophie. "You're absolutely right, young lady."

"Told you so," said Sophie.

EPILOGUE

A week later life had returned to normal—or as normal as life ever gets at Casa Pollack. Mephisto had returned to the fold, his diagnosis the best I could have hoped for under the circumstances. All his tests came back negative. The vet attributed his piddle puddle to old age.

"Walk him as late as possible each night," he said, "and don't let him sleep in. As soon as you're awake, get him up and take him for his morning walk."

Of course, that resulted in a tug-a-war between the sleepy dog and whichever of my sons had morning Mephisto duty, but so far it had prevented any further piddle puddles.

Unfortunately, our Lucille reprieve was short-lived. She and her cohorts arrived back in New Jersey the day after the start of Judge Roland's annual winter vacation. The judge presiding in his stead was new to the bench and either unaware of Lucille's history or unwilling to take past transgressions into consideration. Perhaps she reminded him of a favorite eccentric elderly aunt.

Whatever the reason, the judge seemed more amused than appalled and let the entire Commie Cotillion off with a stern warning to respect the law and behave in the future.

Little did he realize the Sisters of the October Revolution were unwilling to follow advice, directives, or rulings handed down by the court or any law enforcement or government official. He'd soon learn. I had no doubt Lucille and her minions would wind up back in his courtroom before Judge Roland returned from his four-week vacation.

~*~

Alex, Nick, Zack, and I had spent Monday evening decorating the Christmas tree that now stood in all its glory in front of the living room bay window. Zack and I were sitting on the sofa, admiring our work, and the boys had retreated to their bedroom to finish homework, when Alex returned to the living room. "Mom, we need to talk."

Rarely does anything good come from a conversation that begins with *we need to talk*, and the solemn expression on Alex's face told me this conversation would be no exception.

Once again my Worrywart Gene jumped right to early-onset grandmotherhood. No matter how many times Alex had assured me he and Sophie hadn't taken that giant leap into adulthood, hormones will be hormones. Couple those teenage hormones with the emotional stress of the last two and a half weeks, and sex had probably entered the equation.

I fought to tamp down my dread and remain calm—at least until I learned the topic of this talk. After that, all bets were off. "Have a seat," I said, patting the cushion next to me. "Do you want Zack to leave?"

Alex shook his head. "Definitely not."

I swiveled my head between my son and Zack. Whatever was

up, I sensed I was the only one in the dark. I wasn't sure whether to be annoyed that Alex had confided in Zack first or grateful that he had a man in his life he could go to for advice.

"Does this concern Sophie?" I asked, hoping the Queen of Jumping to Conclusions was once again wrong.

"In a way," said Alex.

I threw my head back against the sofa cushions and closed my eyes. In as calm a voice as I could muster, I said, "Alex, you promised the two of you hadn't—"

"What? No, Mom! We haven't!"

My eyes sprang open. "Then what's going on?"

"I got into Harvard early decision."

Two emotions immediately took up battle inside me as I processed my son's words—pride over his accomplishment and sorrow that he wouldn't be able to attend the school of his dreams. At the same time I fought back tears of frustration. "You know I can't afford Harvard, not after what your father did. Why did you even apply?"

Then another question popped into my head. "*How* did you apply?" My son had neither a checking account nor a credit card. "How did you pay the application fee?"

"I wrote the check for him," said Zack.

I spun around and faced him. "Behind my back? Do you plan to pay his tuition and room and board as well? Because I certainly don't have that kind of money."

"It's all taken care of, Mom."

"What!" I swiveled to face Alex, then turned back to Zack once my son's words sank in. "Absolutely not! I can't permit you to do this. It's not right."

Zack held up his hands. "Hey, all I did was write the check for the application fee. And Alex gave me the money for that."

"Then where's the money coming from?" I asked Alex. "Did a money tree suddenly spring up in our back yard?"

Alex forced a laugh. "Wouldn't that be nice?"

There was only one other possible explanation. "It's Ira, isn't it? He offered to pay your tuition." I didn't know which disturbed me more, accepting such a huge sum of money from my lover or from my deceased husband's half-brother.

"It's not Uncle Ira," said Alex. He handed me a sheet of paper I hadn't noticed he'd been clutching in his hand. "I've been offered a full ride."

I scanned the email Alex had printed out from Harvard and sighed. I was about to burst my son's bubble. I handed the paper back to him and shook my head. "I'm afraid this is a scam. I've read about bogus emails like this being sent to students. You can tell because it doesn't even mention the name of the scholarship you were awarded."

"It's legit, Mom. I called the school earlier today to verify it. They said the scholarship came from an anonymous donor. I'm pretty sure I know who."

I glared at Zack. "Anonymous donor, huh?"

Once again he held up his hands. "Not me. I swear."

"Then who?" I asked Alex.

"Mr. Lambert."

"Shane? Why would Shane pay for your college education?"

"To thank us for all we did—believing in his innocence, protecting Sophie, finding the real killer. Mom, without you Mr. Lambert would have gone to prison for the rest of his life."

"But why would Shane do this without even telling us?" I asked.

"Because Sophie said that's what he does. He's like a multi-millionaire Secret Santa."

"He didn't keep his donation to the Food Bank a secret," I reminded him.

"That was different. He wanted to help Sophie make friends at school. It's hard being the new kid, especially arriving senior year. But most of the time he helps people anonymously because he doesn't want the publicity."

"That's understandable," said Zack, "when you consider how people reacted after word got out he'd won the lottery."

"But that's hardly the case with us," I said. "Alex, did you tell Sophie about your father gambling away your college fund?"

He nodded. "She's the one who convinced me to apply early decision. I told her there was no point, but she said I'd always regret not knowing whether or not I could get in. I bet she told her dad, and the scholarship came from Mr. Lambert's foundation."

"It makes sense," said Zack.

"Still, it would be nice to thank him," I said. "He doesn't have to worry about unwanted publicity from us."

I pulled my phone from my pocket and scrolled down to Shane's number. When he answered, I said, "I'm calling to thank you."

"For what?"

"You know for what," I said, choking back tears. "I'm overwhelmed by your generosity—to Alex and to me, for what you've done."

"Anastasia, I have no idea what you're talking about."

"Of course, you don't. Good night, Shane."

"Good night, Anastasia."

ANASTASIA'S
NO-CRAFTING-TALENT-REQUIRED
GLASS BALL CHRISTMAS ORNAMENTS

(Find more Christmas ornament designs on Anastasia's
Killer Crafts & Crafty Killers blog.)

With only a few basic craft supplies (available at craft stores, fabric stores, and online) and a minimal amount of time, even readers who claim they were born without a crafting gene will be able to create these decorative and sophisticated-looking Christmas ornaments.

Note: All the ornaments will require a piece of ribbon for hanging. You'll need approximately 9"-12" of 1/4"-1/2" wide satin or grosgrain ribbon in a complementary color. As an alternative to the ribbon, you can use yarn, twine, thin braid, or a thin strip of fabric.

Marbled Paint Ornament

Materials: clear glass ball ornament, 2-3 colors DecoArt Americana Crystal Gloss Enamel paint (or any glass paint in squeeze bottles), disposable plastic cup

Carefully remove the metal cap from the glass ball.

Squeeze a small amount of paint into the glass ornament. Rotate the ball to swirl the paint around the interior of the ornament. Repeat with the second color. Add a third color if desired.

Allow paint to dry. To keep paint from pooling at the bottom of the ornament, turn the ornament upside-down and set over the disposable plastic cup. Any excess paint will drain into the cup.

Reattach the metal cap. Tie ribbon through the loop for hanging.

Sequin and Glitter Ornament

Materials: clear glass ball ornament, decoupage medium (you can also use either liquid floor wax or thinned tacky glue), disposable plastic cup, assorted sequins, glitter

Carefully remove the metal cap from the glass ball.

Pour decoupage medium or thinned tacky glue into the glass ornament. Rotate the ornament to swirl the glue around the interior to coat the entire ornament.

Turn the ornament upside-down and set over the disposable plastic cup to drain excess glue.

Add sequins, rotating to distribute around inside of ornament.

Pour glitter into ornament. (You can make a funnel from a piece of rolled paper for easier pouring.) Place your finger over the opening and shake the ornament to distribute the glitter. Pour out excess.

Allow glue to dry with cap off until glue turns clear. This may take up to several days, depending on temperature, humidity, and the type of glue used.

Reattach the metal cap. Tie ribbon through the loop for hanging.

Melted Crayon Ornament

Materials: clear glass ball ornament, two crayons in the same color family or opposites (examples: pink and red, yellow and orange, blue and yellow, blue and pink, etc.), crayon sharpener or craft knife, hair dryer

Use the crayon sharpener or craft knife to shave pieces from the crayon.

Carefully remove the metal cap from the glass ball.

Place a small amount of the shavings into the glass ball. Hold the hair dryer close to the area of the ornament where the shavings are and heat the ornament to melt the crayons. Be careful you don't touch the ornament with the hair dryer. As the crayon begins to melt, turn the ornament to spread the color. Alternate colors, continuing until the desired look is achieved.

Reattach the metal cap. Tie ribbon through the loop for hanging.

Note: If the ornament becomes too hot as you're working, take a break to allow it to cool. You may also want to use an oven mitt or glove to protect your hand from the heat.

Metallic Braid Ornament

Materials: clear glass ball ornament, 5-yds. 5mm braided metallic cording (choose silver, gold, or 2-toned combination colors such as red/gold or black/silver)

Carefully remove the metal cap from the glass ball.
Feed metallic braid through opening into ornament.

Reattach the metal cap. Tie ribbon through the loop for hanging.

Basket Filler Ornament

Materials: clear glass ball ornament, crinkle-cut paper or excelsior (the kind used for gift basket filler) in your choice of color/colors

Carefully remove the metal cap from the glass ball.

Fill the ornament with the paper or excelsior.

Reattach the metal cap. Tie ribbon through the loop for hanging.

Other Ideas for Filling Ornaments

Scraps of yarn	Confetti glitter
Crumpled colored tissue paper	Tulle
Plastic beads	Netting
Small-scale potpourri	Ribbons
Small feathers	Rickrack
Tinsel	Mini pinecones
Faux Christmas greenery	Miniature gift packages
Mini jingle bells	LEGO pieces
Pompoms	Sand and small seashells
Twigs	Ribbon roses
Assorted silk florals	Cloves and/or cinnamon sticks
Family photos	Candy
Popcorn	Bottle brush trees & fake snow

Scraps of fabric cut into strips with pinking shears

ABOUT THE AUTHOR

USA Today bestselling and award-winning author Lois Winston writes mystery, romance, romantic suspense, chick lit, women's fiction, children's chapter books, and nonfiction under her own name and her Emma Carlyle pen name. *Kirkus Reviews* dubbed her critically acclaimed Anastasia Pollack Crafting Mystery series, "North Jersey's more mature answer to Stephanie Plum." In addition, Lois is an award-winning craft and needlework designer who often draws much of her source material for both her characters and plots from her experiences in the crafts industry.

Connect with Lois at the following sites:
Email: lois@loiswinston.com
Website: http://www.loiswinston.com
Killer Crafts & Crafty Killers Blog:
http://www.anastasiapollack.blogspot.com
Pinterest: http://www.pinterest.com/anasleuth
Twitter: https://twitter.com/Anasleuth
Bookbub: https://www.bookbub.com/authors/lois-winston

Sign up for Lois's newsletter at:
https://app.mailerlite.com/webforms/landing/z1z1u5